Praise for *The Faithful*

'A wonderfully evocative novel that slowly reveals its secrets'
Red

'Fans of well-crafted period fiction will gobble down this second novel from the author of *Before the Fall* . . . West has a sure sense of the era's sexual politics as well as its ideological ones as Hazel navigates a new life in London, while the rollicking plot becomes denser and ever more inexorable as it hurtles onwards to 1941'
Metro

'Superb . . . Juliet West writes incredibly moving and atmospheric war-era novels, full of strong women, secrets, conflict and desire'
Saga

'Spins a tale of family secrets against a backdrop of war and extremism'
Good Housekeeping

'Compelling, nuanced . . . suffused with historical detail. West weaves a subtle mystery, luring us towards truths so skilfully exposed that the effect is truly shocking'
Historia Magazine

'West's book takes us from the tranquility of the English countryside to the horrors of the Spanish Civil War with great effect . . . nail-biting'
The Lady

'West is a terrific character writer. The difficult relationship between young Hazel and her vibrant, borderline-alcoholic mum, Francine, feels pa . . . attention to detail is fla . . .

'Rich and multi-layered . . . At once heartbreaking and full of hope'　　　　　Isabel Ashdown, author of *Little Sister*

'Vibrant prose and characters'
　　　　　Vanessa Lafaye, author of *Summertime*

'Enthralling'　　　　　Jane Rusbridge, author of *Rook*

'Vivid and unforgettable . . . A must-read'
　　　　　Ann Weisgarber, author of
The Personal History of Rachel Dupree and *The Promise*

'Written in exquisite, economic prose . . . the story builds beautifully, the plot naturally quickening in pace to a gripping denouement'
　　　　　Martine Bailey, author of *An Appetite for Violets*

'Beautifully written . . . A clever, moving page-turner'
　　　　　Anne Cater, *Random Things Through My Letterbox*

'A poignant, heart-wrenching story that will leave you bereft when you finish it . . . A sure-fire summer bestseller'
　　　　　Mairead Hearne, *Swirl & Thread*

'Such a richly rewarding read that I'm now firmly in Juliet West's band of faithful readers'
　　　　　Kathryn Eastman, *Nut Press*

'Full of emotion, vivid characters and an absorbing plot, *The Faithful* is a superb read that I just loved'
　　　　　Emma's Bookish Corner

Praise for *Before the Fall*

'As poignant as it is powerful . . . Her characters – including London's East End itself – are unforgettable'
Alison MacLeod, author of *Unexploded*

'My favourite Great War novel . . . incredible writing'
Joanna Cannon, author of
The Trouble with Goats and Sheep

'An astonishing literary achievement'
Ann Weisgarber, author of
The Personal History of Rachel Dupree

'Arresting . . . poignant and confidently handled' *Daily Mail*

'A superb read . . . Intelligent, wise, and full of passion and courage'
Louise Douglas, author of
The Secrets Between Us

'A breathtaking portrayal of life and love in all its complexity'   Suzannah Dunn, author of *The Lady of Misrule*

'West paints an evocative picture of war-torn Britain that's both poignant and powerful'   *Good Housekeeping*

'A highly accomplished debut . . . It stands out for the quality of its writing, and for the way in which it depicts the moral spectrum of its period rather than ours'
Cornflower Books

THE FAITHFUL

Juliet West worked as a journalist before taking an MA in Creative Writing at Chichester University, where she won the Kate Betts Memorial Prize. *Before the Fall*, her debut novel, was shortlisted for the Myriad Editions novel-writing competition in 2012. Juliet also writes short stories and poetry, and won the H. E. Bates short story prize in 2009. *The Faithful* is her second novel. She lives in West Sussex with her husband and three children.

Discover more at julietwest.com
And @JulietWest14

Also by Juliet West

Before the Fall

THE FAITHFUL

JULIET WEST

PAN BOOKS

First published 2017 by Mantle

This paperback edition first published 2018 by Pan Books
an imprint of Pan Macmillan
20 New Wharf Road, London N1 9RR
Associated companies throughout the world
www.panmacmillan.com

ISBN 978-1-4472-5912-1

1 3 5 7 9 8 6 4 2

A CIP catalogue record for this book is available from the British Library.

Printed and bound by CPI Group (UK) Ltd, Croydon, CRO 4YY

Visit **www.panmacmillan.com** to read more about all our books
and to buy them. You will also find features, author interviews and
news of any author events, and you can sign up for e-newsletters
so that you're always first to hear about our new releases.

For Steve, with love

PART ONE

PART ONE

I

July 1935

Even as he queued to board the coach at Victoria, Tom thought about turning back. He would tell his mother that he was ill, a sudden stomach upset, and he'd be better off spending the week at home on his own. She'd cluck and fuss but she might just let him go.

A pigeon eyed him from its perch above a newspaper stand, its head cocked, the stump of one foot hovering over a sign for Pears Soap: PURITY ITSELF.

A week at home on his own. Imagine. He could invite Jillie round; a little more comfortable than their usual spot by the back doors of the Gaumont. Tom fought down a sudden stab of desire. He mustn't think those thoughts – he was with his mum and dad, for pity's sake. Anyway, did he really want Jillie at his place, picking up the family photographs, drinking tea from his mum's best cups? Jillie was getting a bit too attached as it was.

The coach doors opened and a cheer rippled through the queue. In a neighbouring bay, a bus moved off to the shouts of 'Stand clear!' Petrol fumes billowed into the still morning air.

'Should leave on time after all,' said Tom's dad, looking up at the clock. The minute hand jerked forward. Five to nine.

His mum turned and flapped a hurry-up hand. 'Come on, Tom,' she said. 'Chop chop.'

This was the moment, thought Tom. He would clutch his guts, retch a few times – it was the weather for stomach upsets, after all – and groan something about a ham roll bought from a milk bar on the Strand. Could he get away with it? He'd never been much good at lying. And now the thought of putting on such a performance began to make him feel genuinely queasy. Everyone would stare, and his mother would fret, and in all likelihood she'd miss the coach too, escort him back to Lewisham and dose him with Milk of Magnesia. He'd end up spoiling the holiday for her and that would be plain cruel because she'd been looking forward to Bognor ever since they'd paid their half-crown deposits before Christmas.

'Just a bit tired,' said Tom, stepping forward to close the gap between them. 'I woke up at five.'

'It'll be the excitement,' she said. 'You were always the same before Scout camps.'

They had reached the coach door. Bea grabbed the handle and hauled herself up onto the boarding step. 'There are still a few seats at the front, Harold. You have got the sand-wiches, haven't you?' Tom's dad raised his eyebrows and lifted his old khaki tote bag.

Tom climbed the steps and inhaled the smell of motor oil and disinfectant. Too late now – he was here and there was no chance of escape. Beggsy and Jim called to him from the very back of the coach, loud and larky. Tom gave a short wave but took a seat across the aisle from his mum and dad: Beggsy was a pain in the arse at the best of times.

As the coach moved off into the sunshine of Belgravia, Tom's mood began to shift. The seat beside him was empty; he wouldn't have to make small talk or listen to some droning bore from HQ. The whiff of disinfectant gave way to something different, to peeled oranges and chip paper, towels made stiff by saltwater and sun. Yes, the coach smelt different now. It smelt of promise.

They crawled through Clapham and Wandsworth until finally the roads cleared, and the coach picked up speed as it motored into the open countryside. Skylarks rose above fields and the verges shimmered with bees and butterflies.

At Dorking, Mrs Winters began to stalk down the aisle handing out information leaflets about the camp. And then – in case they couldn't read, Tom supposed – she stood swaying at the front, reciting every line of the leaflet. Most of the coach passengers were travelling in civvies, but Mrs Winters wore her uniform, the skirt a little too tight, coarse black hairs poking through her tan stockings.

'There will be four good meals daily,' she called out. 'The camp is complete with a shop, shower baths and a mess marquee.'

Tom's mum turned wide-eyed towards his father. 'A marquee, Harold!' Harold blinked his heavy lids, gave the faintest nod in response. Bea fanned herself with the leaflet as Mrs Winters continued.

'Cricket matches, rounders, quoits and badminton,' she said, grabbing on to the back of a seat as the coach swerved around a sharp bend. 'Punchballs for those who want to hit something, and boxing matches when two people want to hit each other.'

This caused a great laugh, and Beggsy at the back cheered. Tom's insides crumpled at the mention of boxing matches and punchballs. Boxing, fencing, ju-jitsu – all manner of sports would be laid on, and he wasn't interested in any of them. He didn't want to punch anyone, or prance around with a daft sword. The enforced exercise was just the start, though: there'd be meetings too – speeches, lectures, patriotic songs. Damn it. He should have trusted his instincts, should have bailed out while there was still time.

2

If Charles did that thing with his jaw once more she would have to leave the table. It was bad enough that her mother had invited him to stay yet again, but at least generally they got up late and she didn't have to breakfast with them. Now here they both were, strangely energetic for this time of day – zestful, even – and every time he chewed there was a vile sound, like small bones cracking.

Her mother dropped a fig stalk carelessly onto the tablecloth, took a sip of tea and turned to Hazel. 'I've decided to go up to town,' she said. 'Charles needs to get back for . . . urgent business. And I'd rather like a change of scene. You won't mind, will you, darling?'

Hazel swallowed her mouthful too quickly and the dry toast scraped her throat. 'When are you leaving?'

'We thought midday,' said Francine.

'But what about this afternoon?'

Francine narrowed her eyes and raised a questioning shoulder. Her jade silk dressing gown clung to her skin, sinking into the dip of her collarbone. 'This afternoon?'

'The shopping trip. You were going to buy me some more summer things. Last year's dresses are –' she paused, feeling her cheeks colour – 'you know.'

'Oh, darling.' Francine laughed and gestured towards Hazel's bust. 'Don't be bashful, of course I know. It's just rather hard for me to accept. My little girl growing into a woman.' She turned to Charles and put a hand on his arm. 'Honestly, Charles, if you'd seen her this time last year, she was flat as a board. Then *whoosh* came the monthlies, and now look!'

Hazel could only stare down at the toast crumbs on her plate. At Rosewood House, amongst the other girls, conversations about monthlies were had in whispers, if they were had at all. What was wrong with her mother, broadcasting the subject at breakfast? Oh God, he was probably looking at her, just as Mother had suggested. Hazel hunched her shoulders and curled her spine, hoping that the evidence would somehow disappear.

'She's going to be a great beauty,' said Charles, 'just like her mother.'

The mantel clock struck nine. Francine gave a high laugh that clashed with the chime. A major seventh, thought Hazel. Horrible.

'Flatterer,' said Francine. She traced a painted fingernail down Charles's forearm. 'Don't sulk, Hazel, for heaven's sake. How about this for an idea? I'll buy you some dresses in Selfridges while I'm in town. There'll be more choice.'

'But *I* wanted to choose.'

'Plenty of time for shopping once I'm home. I won't be gone long. Just a few days. Perhaps a week. And in the meantime Mrs Waite might be able to let out some seams.'

Francine put another fig into her mouth and began to chew. The seeds cracked like miniature bullets firing, and Hazel knew that it was pointless arguing, pointless feeling surprised. This was how things were now. Mother wanted Charles more than she wanted her.

The horizon was starting to fuzz and shimmer and that meant the day would be hot and the sea would be warm enough for bathing. Later she would change into her turquoise costume (that, at least, still fitted), walk down to the end of the garden and climb over the wall onto the beach. If the sea stayed calm she might even swim out towards Pagham.

She opened her bedroom window and leaned forward on the sill, listening to the layers of sound – the outgoing tide pulling away from the shore, the scream of a young gull, the blind dog from next door snuffling in the box hedge. And then another layer, growing louder until it eclipsed all other sounds; heavier, mechanical: the hazy drone of aircraft. The planes appeared in the sky to the west, flying over the sea in formation.

Hawker Furies.

Hazel watched them rise and fall, their polished cowlings glinting. The Hawkers flew out every morning now. Sometimes Hazel cycled past the base at Tangmere, and from the farm track you could see the planes, shadowy in their hangars, the pilots and the airmen scurrying around them, their laughter echoing across flat clay fields.

'Ha-zel!'

Francine's voice called up from the bottom of the stairs. Hazel hadn't spoken to her mother or Charles since breakfast, as a punishment for the London trip. Most likely the punishment had gone unnoticed. Charles had been in the hall, making calls on the telephone in a hushed voice, and Francine had been in her room, banging wardrobe doors. What on earth would she be packing? Francine didn't dress like normal mothers; neat summer suits with matching shoes and handbags. She threw things together higgledy-piggledy: peppermint trousers with a striped orange blouse, which might have been passable if she didn't then tie a floral cambric scarf around her neck. Yet she was forever receiving compliments on her style – 'Bravo, Francine, quite the Bohemian,' her London friends would say, or 'So wonderfully daring, Francine.' But London was one thing. In Aldwick Bay, her clothes caused nothing but backwards glances, amused stares.

'Darling, our car is here!'

Hazel slunk from the bedroom and peered over the banister into the hall below. Francine was standing at the wide-open front door, a cigarette burning in the black onyx holder. She was wearing the white sundress with a plunging neckline, pink glass beads and an orange belt that matched the marmalade shade of her hair. Charles leaned against the timber pillar of the porch, his face shaded by the brim of his panama.

'Darling, I won't leave without a kiss. Now stop sulking and come here.'

Hazel walked barefoot down the staircase, kissed her mother on the cheek and muttered, '*Bon voyage.*' Francine smiled and stroked the top of her daughter's head.

'I'll try to call but Charles's telephone can be horribly temperamental. Your father will ring, I expect.'

'There's no need, Mother.' She hung her head and pressed one finger onto the spoke of an umbrella in the stand.

'Oh, do liven up, Hazel. Aren't you pleased that I trust you enough to leave you? When I was sixteen, I was desperate for a little freedom.' She drew on her cigarette and her green eyes seemed to darken and mist, like pieces of frosted sea glass. 'You and Bronwen go out and have some fun. Here –' she reached for her purse and took out two ten-shilling notes – 'walk into Bognor one afternoon. Take tea at the Royal Norfolk. Or go to the cinema, why don't you? I'll be back in a week or so.' She lowered her voice so that it would not be heard beyond the hallway. 'And be nice to Mrs Waite.'

From the kitchen came the sound of a wooden spoon battering the side of a mixing bowl. Mrs Waite would be making some kind of sauce for tonight's dinner. Hazel took the money and thanked her mother. She gave a half-hearted wave as the taxi swept out of the cul-de-sac and onto Tamarisk Drive.

Might as well go to Sweaty Arnold's for a packet of Pall Malls, thought Hazel. She was getting rather good at inhaling. Last time she barely coughed.

Hazel waited until after lunch when Mrs Waite was in her room, resting. She shut the front door quietly and walked down the path, pushing her hair behind her ears and trying to smooth it flat against her head. Hopeless. Muggy days like this always turned it frizzy.

The estate was quiet but for the sound of a hand-mower wheezing up and down a neighbouring lawn. She reached the flint piers which marked the boundary of the estate, where the footway changed from grass-verged pavestones to the rough, gravelled tracks of Aldwick village. The little row of shops was just across the road, shaded by a line of lime trees. Coastguards' Parade, the shops were called, though Hazel had never seen any evidence of any coastguards; there was only the skinny butcher and the bespectacled grocer and

Mr Arnold, the newsagent, whose round face shone perpetually with tiny beads of perspiration.

The day was getting hotter. Cats lazed under shady bushes and Hazel wished she had worn a hat. A small black fly landed on her bare leg, just below the hem of her dress. She bent to brush it away and as she straightened up, she sensed a vibration in the ground, a light thumping. She looked up – Furies again? – but the skies were clear. Drumming, was it? Yes, drumbeats, growing nearer. Then the sound of a bugle piercing the hot air, boots hitting the ground. Marching.

Hazel stepped back from the kerb and retreated a few yards to the entrance of the estate. She leaned against one of the piers, and the knapped flint edges pressed into her shoulder blades. A column of drummers came into view. She had been expecting a British Legion parade, ex-soldiers wearing blazers and medals, a procession of eye patches and missing limbs. But these marchers were healthy men, three abreast, side drums low on their hips. Their uniforms were black, and oversize buckles shone on their belts – great square hunks of steel that flashed in the sun.

Behind the first column were rows of younger men, their marching less precise. Finally, the women and girls, scores of them, each wearing a black beret, shirt and tie, with a grey skirt close-fitted around the hips. One of the girls turned towards Hazel – a young woman, eighteen perhaps. She looked beautiful, Hazel thought, even before she smiled. Hazel smiled back, and the girl reached into a black leather pouch that hung from her belt. She took out a wad of papers, marched over and gave Hazel a handbill. Hazel blushed and mumbled a thank-you as the girl turned and strode back to the column, keeping step all the time with the beat of the drums.

Blackshirts. Hazel had seen them before, small bands dotted around Bognor selling their weekly newspaper, a penny per copy. She'd asked her mother about them. 'Political cranks,' Francine had said, hurrying past with a look of distaste. 'Don't flatter them with your attention.'

How strange to see them here, en masse, marching past Coastguards' Parade towards the beach. The butcher, Mr Gibbons, came out of his shop. He lifted his spectacles and smiled at the sight, but the grocer stayed inside, and through the plate-glass window it looked as though he was shaking his head.

Crank? What did that mean? It was the same as eccentric, wasn't it, a word for people who'd gone a little cuckoo and couldn't get on in society? There didn't seem to be anything cuckoo about these people, thought Hazel. They were full of purpose, so well turned out, so . . . organized.

When the parade had passed, she looked down at the handbill. BRITISH UNION OF FASCISTS. MOSLEY SPEAKS! THEATRE ROYAL, BOGNOR REGIS, 7 P.M. She folded the paper into a small square and slid it into the pocket of her dress.

She could follow the marchers down to the beach but it would be better, she decided, to go home and spy on them from the garden. If she stood on the table in the summer house, there would be a prime view over the garden wall, straight out to the bay.

Cigarettes. She crossed the road and pushed open the door into the newsagent's, trying not to breathe in too deeply. The smell was more pungent than ever.

Mr Arnold got up from his stool and wiped a hand on his trousers. 'How do, miss?'

'A packet of Pall Malls for my mother, please,' said Hazel, 'and a quarter of mint imperials.'

He sniffed and turned to take the cigarettes from the display behind the counter.

'Did you see the march?' asked Hazel.

'Cudn't miss it.'

'I wonder what they're doing here?'

'They've set up a holiday camp by all accounts, over at Pryor's Farm. On the fields behind your estate, miss.' He opened the jar of mint imperials and rattled the sweets into the bowl on the scales. 'Down from London, I s'pose.' He peered at the dial on the scales. 'Dozzle over?' Hazel nodded and he tipped the mints into a white paper bag. 'Ol' Gibbons is going to their meeting in Bognor tonight, but you shan't catch me there. I leave politics to them what's paid to know better.'

Hazel smiled and gave him a ten-shilling note. He sighed, rang open the cash drawer and scraped about for the change.

Walking back, she sucked on a mint imperial and thought about the blackshirt meeting. Perhaps they would march into Bognor, drums beating all the way. It was something different, it might be fun to watch, and that's what her mother wanted, wasn't it, for her to have a little fun, a little adventure? She'd have to persuade Bronny, of course, but that shouldn't be too difficult. They could go to the cinema afterwards. *It Happened One Night* was showing at the Odeon. Clark Gable was Bronny's favourite.

3

At last the parade was dismissed. Tom stood to one side as his column jostled and whooped through the narrow wooden gate leading from the lane to the beach. Finally he stepped through and headed left, away from the crush of excited cadets streaming down the shingle bank.

Tom had been to the seaside once before, on an outing to Margate organized by the social committee at his dad's old factory. He must have been nine or ten. Soggy oysters were what he remembered, thick rough shells that looked as though they were filled with globs of phlegm. He had shaken on plenty of vinegar and the fumes made his eyes water. There was a photograph of that day slotted into the wooden frame on the parlour mantelpiece. It was a picture of him on the promenade, holding his parents' hands, blinking against the wind, the sea a stormy smudge behind them. The following year his dad was laid off, and after that there were no more seaside trips. For a Saturday outing they would take the bus to Hyde Park and follow the crowds to Lansbury's Lido. There was a man called Mr Reeves who was teaching his two sons to swim, and he let Tom join in the lessons. But Tom's own dad refused to go in the water – his scars had never properly healed, and he claimed he would frighten people away if he showed himself in a bathing costume. 'Go on, Dad,' Tom would wheedle. 'If you scare everyone off we can have the place to ourselves.' His dad would smile from the deckchair and shake his head, knock his empty pipe against his thigh.

Now Tom stood and looked to the east, towards the pier at Bognor, and he thought he had never seen a sight so bloody marvellous. Here was a blue sea, not Margate grey, and the sky was cloudless, hazing down so that it merged with the shifting colours of the water. There were plants and grasses sprouting from the shingle, some with yellow flowers, others that looked like flattened cabbages. Everything was unspoilt and natural. It couldn't have been more different from Margate.

'Tom!' His mum waved as she made her way up the bank. Her face was red under her black woollen beret and a single trickle of sweat dripped from her temple. 'Come down to the shore, love. O.M. is going to bathe and there's a photographer.'

Tom shrugged. He hated the way everyone called him O.M., or the 'Old Man', as if they had a kind of intimacy or friendship with him. He wasn't even *that* old in any case. Bea often remarked on how far Sir Oswald had come, for a man not yet forty. 'Such determination,' she would say, with a sideward glance at his dad. 'Such drive.'

'I'm not being in any photographs,' said Tom.

She sighed. 'But love, it would be a shame to miss out. You can change behind the huts. You've got your trunks on, haven't you, under your uniform?'

Tom looked over to a row of five or six white-painted beach huts. Beggsy was there, along with Jim Dove and Fred Tester. They were unbuttoning their black shirts, stepping out of trousers. Fred pulled his shirt over his head to reveal a saggy knitted bathing suit that looked as if it must have belonged to his dead granddad, and Tom knew the other two would rag him something rotten.

'All right. Don't think I'm smarming up to Mosley, though.'

'Smarming up? I didn't say anything about smarming.' She took a handkerchief from her sleeve and wiped her brow. 'You used to be potty about Sir Oswald. That little scrap-book of yours . . .'

'*Your* scrapbook. You let me mix the paste.'

'Now you're just being silly, twisting things. Come along, get that uniform off and enjoy the weather. Mind you, this is a bit *too* hot for comfort.' She fluttered the handkerchief around her face in an effort to stir up the air.

'I wanted a swim anyway. But I'm not posing for any photographs.'

The tide was out and it was a fair walk to the sea. Tom stepped across the shingle, trying not to wince as the pebbles dug into his bare feet. Beggsy and the others were just ahead, Fred hugging himself with both arms to stop the lads from twanging the straps of his suit.

It was a relief to step from the shingle onto the sand. Ahead of him, Beggsy started to run, a wild sprint, wheeling his arms, head thrust down as if he was charging towards the finishing line in a running race. Tom smiled and started to jog. The sand became wet and clammy, grabbing each foot-print and sucking it down.

Mosley was already in the water, a fixed grin on his face. Beggsy and Jim stepped through the waves towards Mosley and his hangers-on, letting out short cries of surprise every time a wave lapped higher, over their thighs, their stomachs. They were freezing their bollocks off, thought Tom, but they didn't want to let on.

Tom turned to Fred. His fists were clutched to his chest and he stared down at the water, as if by concentrating hard enough he could make the English Channel warmer.

'Only one thing for it,' said Tom. 'On the count of three.'

Fred grinned. 'You're on,' he said, unfurling his fists and trailing his fingers into the water.

'One, two, three . . .' Tom plunged in and swam underwater, away from the Mosley crowd, the low rumble of the ocean pressing against his ears. He pushed his body on, strands of seaweed collecting between his fingers, his breath running short now, but still he kept swimming.

When he finally surfaced he couldn't see Fred. And then . . . there he was, a distant figure standing in the waist-high waves, one arm raised apologetically. Tom smiled to himself, turned onto his back and swam farther out. Somehow the sea felt warmer here, luxurious. He trod water and gazed back towards the beach. Mosley must have had enough; he was getting out already. Two women offered him towels and he took them both with an exaggerated bow.

From this distance Tom had a clear view of the buildings that backed on to the beach. Big as mansions they were, detached jobs, some with thatched roofs and exposed wooden beams, others built of red brick with slate tiles. They looked fairly new – one of those exclusive estates you saw advertised in railway station waiting rooms. He allowed himself to imagine the possibility, the thrill, of waking every day in one of those houses, wandering down a long leafy garden, climbing the back wall and dropping down to this beautiful beach on the other side. What a life.

A conifer stood in one of the gardens, its golden branches pointing towards the sky. In the shade of the tree was a summer house, white-painted timber with a green-tiled roof. The summer house was probably bigger than his bedroom at home, he thought, now that he'd moved into the box room to make way for Mr Frowse.

A small bird flew into the lower part of the conifer, quickly followed by another. Something in the shape, the squat muscular body, made him think of a bullfinch. Bullfinches, nesting? Would they nest next to the sea like this? Egg-collecting was a young lad's hobby, he told himself, time he grew out of it, but he couldn't suppress the twist of excitement that always came with the prospect of a new find. He'd like to get up into that tree and have a look.

Another movement caught his eye. Someone – a girl – was standing in the summer house, peering out across the beach. Either she was very tall, or she was standing on a chair. She brought her hand to her face and held it there for a second. She might have been laughing, or smoking – it was impossible to tell from this distance – but he fancied that she was watching him, and suddenly he felt foolish to have been staring at this house and garden so intently, to have imagined himself living there.

Tom heard his mother's voice calling from the beach. There she was, waving one arm above her head. He gave a reluctant wave, to reassure her that he wasn't drowning, and swam a slow crawl back towards the shore.

4

'No use knocking.'

The voice came from behind the topiary yew, which was clipped to resemble a peacock. Hazel lowered her hand from the door knocker, and the old gardener emerged from behind the peacock's fanned tail. He was holding a pair of pruning shears.

'Nobody home?' Hazel asked.

Adams smiled, and the dry skin cracked on his lips. 'Gone up to the grandmother's. She's taken ill.'

'The grandmother in Wales?'

'That's right.'

Hazel looked down at the honey bees droning around the lavender bushes. So much for the walk into Bognor, the cinema and Clark Gable. It was a shame about the grandmother, but still, Bronny might've called by, just to warn her that she was planning to disappear.

'Did they say when they'd be home?'

'No idea. Depends whether or not the ol' girl rallies. They think she might, you know . . .' He widened his eyes and drew the blunt side of the shears across his throat.

*

There was nothing to do but wander around the estate, hoping she might bump into someone, but she knew that Patricia was away in the south of France, and Lottie – poor thing – was fell-walking in the Lakes with an earnest god-mother. Hazel passed the social club and the tennis courts, where four women were playing a game of doubles. One of the women called, 'Thirty-fifteen,' and Hazel recognized Miss Bell's voice. She kept her head down. She hadn't practised the piano for days. If Miss Bell saw her she'd only ask how she was getting on with the Scarlatti or the Bartók. God, the Bartók. Just the thought of that piece made Hazel's stomach tighten. The jarring rhythms and the clashing notes. It made no sense whatsoever.

She could still taste the cigarettes, though she'd eaten half the bag of mint imperials. She'd smoked two Pall Malls in the summer house, standing on the wicker table so that she could see over the wall and onto the beach. It was odd watching the blackshirts. For one thing, they were incredibly *white*. Their ribs stuck out and there were shadows under their shoulder blades, especially on the younger lads, scrawny boys who acted as if they'd never seen the seaside before. Most of them couldn't swim, by the look of it, just fooled around in the shallow waves before shivering up the shingle, shaking themselves like dogs.

At home, Hazel told Mrs Waite she'd like her supper early. 'I'm going to Bognor with Bronny to watch a film,' she said. She scratched her nose and turned her face to the kitchen window, fixing her eyes on the pear tree where a blue tit pecked at a half-grown fruit.

'You're to be home before dark,' said Mrs Waite, dolloping

a lump of fish pie onto a plate. 'No later than nine. Did you want me to warm up the tart for pudding?'

'Just the pie, thank you, Mrs Waite. We'll get some sweets at the Odeon.'

The heat had dulled her appetite, but she did her best to force down the fish. The dining-room windows were open, and a slice of sunlight angled in, illuminating one of Francine's paintings that hung above the sideboard. It was an oil landscape painted somewhere on the Downs, greens and browns, with black brushstrokes (birds or bats?) swooping around what might have been a plough or a tumbledown barn. Hazel used to enjoy watching her mother paint – she always seemed to be happy as she took out her brushes and mixed colours on a palette. But Francine rarely set up the easel now; it was in one of the attic rooms, abandoned along with Father's violin and Hazel's packed-away toys.

She pushed the remains of the fish pie to one side of the plate and lay her knife and fork across the food in an attempt to mask the leftovers. Mrs Waite took the plate, tutted, and walked back to the kitchen. A year ago she would have chided Hazel, encouraged her to eat up, but her tactics seemed to have changed. There had been a power shift, and it felt almost as if Mrs Waite had given up on her. 'When I was your age I'd been out to work two years,' Mrs Waite had said recently. Hazel had been unsure how to respond. Should she apologize? But it wasn't her fault; she hadn't wanted to stay on another year at school. And in any case she didn't mind the idea of work, was looking forward to it, if she was ever given the chance. Anything was better than another term at Rosewood House, cooped up with scatty Miss Lytton and her obsession with ancient Rome. Hazel imagined herself escaping Rosewood and finding a job in London. She wasn't sure what kind of job yet. She'd long ago given up on the idea of concert pianist, because to achieve that she'd have to practise for hours and hours a day and she just couldn't be fagged. A piano teacher – that was possible, then again she'd be expected to teach the modern stuff, Schoenberg and the rest, all those discords that actually hurt her ears. Nursing? There was nursing, she supposed. She thought about Charles. Apparently he did some kind of medical work, although he was vague when Hazel once asked which field he practised in. 'Medical and social,' he'd said with an enigmatic air, and her mother had stifled a laugh.

Through the open windows came the distant sound of a bugle. Hazel gulped a mouthful of water and rushed upstairs to get ready. On her mother's dressing table she found a pot of rouge and rubbed a little into her cheeks. She dabbed her finger in the pot again to redden her lips. The rouge tasted like damp flannel. Disgusting. She flattened down her hair, looked in the mirror and smiled. Her smile would have been perfect but for the small chip in one front tooth. It had been Nanny Felix's fault, pushing her too fast on the bicycle so that she toppled over and hit the London pavement. Hazel smiled again, this time with her mouth shut. Her eyes looked more green-blue than blue-green, and her face had lost its chubbiness around the cheekbones. She looked older than sixteen, she thought. With her mother's white hat and the slip-on mules, she might even pass for twenty.

The parade was already halfway along Barrack Lane. Hazel walked as fast as she could without running. Once she had caught up, she carried along the pavement beside the drummers, her hat brim tipped low in case anyone she knew should be passing. It was a warm evening. The sun was still bright, its heat pulsing from the south-facing walls of the red-brick terraces and guest houses that lined the streets leading into Bognor. Families stood in their front gardens and stared, and when the parade reached Marine Drive the crowd of onlookers grew: bemused holidaymakers trailing buckets and spades; old women in headscarves; a group of young lads who mimicked the marchers, then sloped off when the standard bearer turned to glare.

Past the pier and on to the Theatre Royal. A blackshirt with a long neck and a loudhailer paced up and down the promenade opposite the theatre. 'Mosley speaks!' he called. 'Seven o'clock start, free admission!'

Hazel followed the swarm into the foyer and found herself shoulder to shoulder with a crush of uniformed blackshirts and others in ordinary clothes – men in pressed suits, women wearing fashionable hats and colourful summer wraps. The air crackled. Gone was the familiar theatre mustiness, the stuffy politeness. Even the flocked wallpaper and faded velvet drapes seemed shot through with anticipation. Hazel had watched Bronny's dreaded ballet shows here, she'd played piano in the music festival. How odd to find the theatre transformed like this, into somewhere thoroughly grown-up, somewhere almost glamorous. She stood to one side, near the doors, debating whether she might actually dare to go into the auditorium. A small man in a flat cap appeared next to her. As he pulled a wad of handbills from a canvas bag, his elbow jabbed into her arm. 'Sorry, miss,' he said, touching his cap. Hazel nodded in reply, trying to edge away, but still watching him as he stepped forward to press the leaflets into people's hands. She could just see the heading at the top: 'Stop the Fascist Lies', it said, and underneath was stamped a blood-red star. Most people glanced at the handbills in disgust and screwed them into pockets or dropped them onto the carpet. A few seconds later, two blackshirts approached the man and steered him away. He struggled but they held down his arms and forced him into the street, shoving him hard so that he stumbled into the gutter. 'Shame on you!' the man hissed. And then he lifted a clenched fist and yelled: 'Don't listen to the fascists! Evil lies!' He began to sing; a wavering tenor threading across the seaside street. '*So comrades, come rally, and the last fight let us face . . .*'

It was too hot in the foyer, difficult to breathe. A prickling sensation began at the back of Hazel's throat but when she coughed, the prickles intensified, as if there were insects crawling up her windpipe. She coughed louder and her eyes began to water. What was she doing here? She should leave now, walk over to the promenade and buy a lemonade or an ice to cool her throat. She looked at the entrance, but the crowds were still streaming in and it would be awkward to push her way out.

She noticed a sign for the ladies' lavatories. Yes, that was the answer. She could lock herself in a cubicle until the meeting started, then creep away unnoticed.

There was a queue for the lavatories, with three women waiting ahead of her. A blackshirt girl stood at the sinks. She was leaning in towards the mirror, poking tentatively at her eye as if there was a grain of sand stuck in there. On her hand she wore a gold ring with a tawny-coloured gemstone that caught the light from the bulb above the mirror. It was the girl from the parade earlier in the day: the one who'd given Hazel the leaflet. She recognized her sharp jaw, her large dark eyes. Now the girl blinked, looked at Hazel's reflection in the mirror and smiled again, raising her pencilled-in brows.

Hazel half-smiled back, just as the cough started again. She felt light-headed and reached a steadying hand towards the sink.

'Are you all right?' asked the girl. 'You look fearfully pale.'

'Yes, it's just . . .' Hazel trailed off.

'You're here for the meeting?'

'Oh, not really. I'm only passing.' She took a deep breath and felt her head clear a little.

The blackshirt girl rinsed her hands under the tap, then straightened up, turning away from the mirror. Her waved ebony hair shone under the ceiling light. 'Shame to miss Mosley,' she said. 'Quite a *tour de force* once he gets going.'

Hazel thought for a moment. She couldn't go home just yet, and the film would have started by now. Perhaps she would stay after all, buy a drink at the theatre kiosk to settle her throat. 'How long will the meeting last?' she asked.

'An hour or so, I should think. Then questions from the floor. That's when it gets interesting. Are you with your people?'

'No. I was coming with a friend but . . . she's not here after all.'

'Sit with us, why don't you? I'm Lucia Knight.' She spoke her name with a flourish. *Lu-chee-a* – the Italian pronunciation, Hazel supposed. 'And here's Edith now.'

Edith emerged from a cubicle and nodded as she turned on the tap. She was shorter than Lucia, with a thin expressionless mouth and the beginnings of sweat patches at her armpits. 'And your name is?'

'Sorry. It's Hazel.'

'We'll wait for you outside, shall we?' said Lucia. 'When you've finished?'

'Yes . . . yes, all right,' said Hazel, only now realizing that a cubicle was free, and that the woman behind her in the queue was shuffling with impatience.

Hazel let herself in through the kitchen door to find Mrs Waite bent over the gas ring, stirring a pan of milk. Her white hair was plaited and pinned into a loose bun which had begun to sag.

'Your father telephoned twenty minutes ago,' said Mrs Waite, not troubling to look up from the pan. 'All the way from France and you weren't here.'

Hazel made a show of checking her watch, though she knew perfectly well it was almost ten. She apologized, said the film had run on, and that she'd lost a brooch and had to search under the seats.

'You'd better wait in the hall. He'll be calling back presently.'

The milk sizzled to the boil just as the telephone rang. Her father was calling from a hotel telephone and he sounded harassed. He was having dinner with an important client. How long had her mother been in London, he asked, and why was she, Hazel, out so late?

If you care so much, why don't you come back? Hazel wanted to say, but didn't. She told him that her mother had left only that afternoon. The film was very long, that was all, and there was the fuss over the brooch.

'How's Paris?' she asked.

'Hot and dirty.'

'When can I visit?'

'Not just yet, Hazel. The project isn't quite going to plan.

I'm dreadfully busy. Look, I really must go. Take care. I'll try to telephone later in the week.'

Hazel replaced the receiver on the cradle and stood for a moment, tracing her finger along the bevelled edge of the telephone table. Her father had been in Paris for five months now, and it was getting harder to remember him as he was: a whole, breathing person who would come down to breakfast every morning humming a tune, tapping out the rhythm with a spoon as he broke the top of his soft-boiled egg. Now all the music seemed to have gone from him: he hadn't even taken his violin to France. Hazel found that when she thought of her father, she pictured only the lower half of his face, a mouth speaking into the telephone and the dark stubble of his beard, which was always visible, however close his shave.

She walked up to the landing and stood against the door of the linen cupboard, listening to the sounds from downstairs. Mrs Waite rinsed the milk pan, clattering it onto the draining board, then switched on the kitchen wireless. She'd be down there for a while now, sipping her cocoa and listening to the news.

Radio voices drifted up the stairs. Hazel longed to talk to someone, anyone, about the meeting. She put her hand to her chest. Yes, her heart was still pounding, and it wasn't just the run back along Barrack Lane. It had been pounding before she left the theatre.

She wandered into her mother's room. Talcum powder bloomed on the rug like bursts of white pollen, and the air was still heavy with a musky scent. The room was large and square, with an enormous black-varnished bed pushed against the wall facing the window. To the left was Francine's dressing table, strewn with jewellery and make-up, postcards propped against the mirror. A man's gold wristwatch lay next to a string of glass beads. Hazel lifted the watch and looked at the time on the ghost-pale face. Charles's watch, she supposed, stopped at ten past seven. Ridiculous, the little pantomime they acted out whenever Charles stayed. He would go up to the guest room, but Hazel knew that once all the bedroom doors were closed, he crept out to join Francine in the double bed. This was where he undressed. Where he unfastened his watch.

Hazel opened the bottom drawer of the dressing table and felt around for the photograph that was buried under a tangle of stockings. She slid the frame out and clutched it to her chest, then sat on the bed and switched on the side light.

Her father was dressed in army uniform, his shoulders angled slightly but his eyes gazing straight at the lens. Even in the dulled photograph she could see that everything was polished to a high shine: his cap badge, his medals, the leather strap across his tunic. Hazel had no idea what the medals were for. No idea, in fact, where her father had been or what he had done during the war. She simply assumed that he hadn't had too bad a time of it. He always appeared to be perfectly healthy, and cheerful enough. Until last year, of course.

The photograph must have been taken when he was in his twenties. She supposed he was handsome in an understated way: heavy brow and sensible moustache; small dark eyes; well-defined jaw. She stood up from the bed and pushed the photograph back into the stocking drawer. It was odd because Father couldn't be more different from Charles, with his tousled brown hair and his jangly limbs. Charles was . . . sort of *loose*; he would lounge on a sofa or a beach chair, the top button of his shirt undone. Her father wasn't like that at all. She couldn't imagine him lying down in anything but a bed, at night, when it was time to go to sleep.

How serious was it between her mother and Charles, she wondered? He seemed keen, and there was an easiness between them that Hazel found disconcerting. Perhaps it was because they had known each other for so many years. For ever. Apparently they had holidayed together as children – the families were friends – but when Hazel had once asked about that time Francine had snapped shut her cigarette case and told her to stop being so tiresome.

Charles couldn't be after their money, that was certain. From what Hazel could gather, they were getting poorer by the day. Her father was an architect, but he couldn't be a very good one, because his projects so often seemed to fall through. In any case, Charles seemed to have plenty of his own money. Just yesterday he'd been full of the new car he was planning to buy. A Brough Superior, motto 'Ninety in silence'. Her mother had looked through the brochure with gleaming eyes.

Hazel crossed the bedroom to the low bookcase that stood under the windowsill. The shelves were filled with romances and mysteries – Agatha Christies and Georgette Heyers. Tucked amongst them was something far more interesting: a pale yellow, cloth-bound book by someone called T. H. van de Velde. *Ideal Marriage* was the title, which was odd, because the book had appeared just at the time when her parents' marriage was quite the opposite of ideal. Still, Hazel preferred not to dwell on the possibility that her mother or father had actually *read* the book. It was too awful to think of them reading, let alone acting on, Mr van de Velde's words. Words that, even now, she barely understood but knew instinctively to be salacious. Erogenous, effleurage, secretions.

No, the book was meant for younger people, girls like her, who needed the mysteries of sex explained. She had reached Part III: 'Sexual Intercourse, Its Physiology and Technique'.

It was almost midnight when she put the book down and switched off the light. She had found Part III confusing. The section began by discussing the importance of the 'Prelude' to lovemaking, the differing arts of coquetry and flirtation. Coquetry was a little like teasing, van de Velde explained, and must not be used excessively. *Lovers – beware!* So was it better to be direct, to flirt and fawn, the way she'd seen her mother behave after a couple of cocktails? That seemed to be van de Velde's conclusion. *Flirtation may beautifully refresh and renew erotic feeling. For, if conducted to the rules of this oldest human art, through purely psychic stimuli, it produces an unmistakeable physical symptom in both man and woman. This symptom is the lubrication of the genitals which physically expresses the desire for closer contact.* Ugh. Lubrication. Why did it all have to sound so repellent?

Hazel tried to sleep but she couldn't have felt less tired. When she shut her eyes it was Lucia's face she saw, the smile around her lips as she watched Mosley deliver his address. Hazel had felt oddly detached at the start of the meeting, self-conscious, as if she was watching herself from a seat in the upper tier. She couldn't claim to belong with the black-shirts, couldn't even claim any knowledge of their ideas. Politics was rarely discussed at home or at Rosewood House, unless you counted the Senate of Ancient Rome.

The first speaker at the Theatre Royal had been a man called Beckett. He wore small round spectacles and spoke in a quiet voice. His words were measured, with over-long pauses as he let the audience absorb each point. He talked about the dangers of Britain trying to compete with Oriental labour and the threat of cheap Eastern imports. It was the 'roast beef' standard versus the 'handful of rice' standard. The Tories wouldn't be happy until all working men had been brought down to coolie level, whereas Labour would prefer every worker to join the Communist Party and starve to death. Fascism was a third way, he said, the roast-beef way. People cheered and clapped at that. Lucia touched her on the shoulder and whispered, 'He's terrific once he's warmed up. You watch, he'll take off his spectacles.'

Beckett began to outline the third way – a corporate state in which business would be run jointly by management, workers and consumers. And he did take off his spectacles, flung them onto the lectern and stared out into the darkness of the theatre. International bankers, private finance – these crooks were ruining the world's economy, shouted Beckett. The time had come to act in *Britain's* interests.

Hazel joined in the applause when Beckett stepped down and took his seat on the stage. Mosley now marched towards the podium and the audience began to rise, right arms outstretched in a fascist salute. 'Hail, Mosley!' they chanted. 'Hail, Mosley!' Lucia and Edith jumped to their feet, but Hazel stayed seated. She felt embarrassed, out of place. She wasn't truly part of this, she shouldn't be here. Leaning forwards, she glanced towards the aisle but she'd have to push past several people to get out, and that would only draw attention to herself. No choice but to stay put, she thought. In for a penny . . .

Mosley listened to the chants for a minute or more, nodding in approval, his nostrils flared, his chin jutting forward. Finally, he motioned for the audience to sit.

They were several rows back, but Hazel had a clear view

of Mosley. He began to speak, and there was something extraordinary about the way his dark eyes seemed to glint and entice; widening one moment, narrowing the next, casting out into the audience like a thousand invisible fishing lines, hooking every single one of them. He had a wonderful voice, she thought. Commanding but somehow gentle and utterly in control. She did her best to follow every word, but really she knew nothing about economics. 'International finance' was the phrase that kept cropping up. It was the root of all the country's problems, said Mosley. It was time to make a choice between the man who invests his money abroad and the man who invests not only his money, but his *life*, in British land.

'National socialism' was what Mosley advocated. Hazel seemed to remember her father calling himself a socialist, during a dinner-party argument she'd overheard from the top of the stairs. She had asked him afterwards what socialism meant, and he said that it was a way of making life fairer for everyone. National socialism. Yes, that made sense. A fairer Britain. How could any decent person disagree?

But now, lying awake, she remembered the man with the handbills in the foyer. *Lies*, he had shouted. The anthem he'd sung began to play again in her head. *The internationale unites the human race* . . . Hazel found it hard to untangle her thoughts. Was it possible to package up lies and pass them off as fact?

Whatever the truth, she was sure of one thing. The blackshirts weren't cranks. Her mother was wrong about that.

5

Each time Tom began to doze, Beggsy would snore: a sudden, violent snort that left his nerves jangling. And then Fred let one off in his sleep, and that made Tom smile, despite himself. He wondered if the other lads had heard it too, but . . . No. Just the heavy breathing, the tooth-grinding, the sound of everyone else having a lovely bit of shut-eye, snoring and farting and doing whatever else came naturally, never mind how he was wide awake in the airless gloom and sick of the bloody lot of them.

It was too dark to check the time on his wristwatch, but he reckoned it must be after midnight. The camp was silent. Rules were clear on that point: NO CAROUSING AFTER 11 P.M. Mosley hadn't come back to the camp after the meeting: he had climbed into a Bentley, saluting the crowds through the open window as the chauffeur pulled away from the theatre at top speed. No camp bed in a bell tent for Mosley. Doubtless he was staying in some swish country hotel, or with one of his aristocratic friends, carousing to his heart's content. They were a nobby bunch, the blackshirt high-ups. Tom had become more aware of this fact recently, and it made him suspicious. Winchester College, Sandhurst. They looked after their own, that sort. However much Mosley claimed to be for the people, however much he courted the working classes – the labourers, the unemployed, the street-fighters – surely he didn't really care for them? This corporate state he was so intent on setting up, there'd be fat cats just the same, wouldn't there? And Mosley would be the fattest of the lot, cream dripping from his well-groomed moustache, while the rest of them would still be scrabbling around to keep a decent pair of boots on their feet.

Sleep seemed impossible now. Foolish to even try. He had to get outside, clear his head.

He crept from the tent, unpegged his trunks and towel from the guy rope and draped them over his bare shoulder. It was only a five-minute walk to the beach, ten at the most. There was nothing in camp rules about bathing after eleven, was there?

The moon was rising, and a few shreds of pale cloud hung in the sky. When he looked up he felt dizzy, unanchored. Somehow the stars had multiplied a thousandfold between London and Sussex; there were no street lights to mask them, no drifts of factory smoke or plumes of blackened steam from the railway engines that converged at the Lewisham depot.

Silently he picked his way between the tents to the far side of the campsite, and then on through the gap in the hedge and down the bramble-edged lane that led towards the sea. The air was sharp and clean in his lungs and he knew, with absolute certainty, that if he'd grown up here he would be at least one inch taller, his shoulders a shade broader. He patted the fresh-burned skin that was taut and tender across his chest. He was tall and broad enough, and strong as any lad who spent his working hours racing up and down office stairs, lugging boxes round greasy Fleet Street pavements.

At the end of the lane he turned right, past the row of shops and on through the gate that led to the beach. He'd forgotten how loud the shingle would sound, the slide and crunch of pebbles and tiny white shells as he made his way towards the sea. Perhaps there would be less noise if he walked barefoot.

He sat on the stones and took off his loosely laced boots. The tide was out. Dotted along the shore were cuttlefish corpses, brittle white bodies like tiny ghosts. He looked at the sea, so vast, so black, and then up again at the endless sky, and he wondered whether bathing was a good idea after all. The expanse of the Channel unnerved him. Perhaps it was enough simply to have left the tent. He felt cooler now, at least.

Behind him, a little to the west, was the garden with the summer house and the golden conifer that overhung the wall. He remembered the birds he'd seen flying in and out earlier in the day. It wouldn't harm just to take a look, easy enough to climb the flint wall, and then up into the lower branches. If the moon stayed bright, he should be able to spot the nest. The birds themselves usually gave the game away. Rubbish parents, birds. If you approached a nest after dark, they would fly quietly off, abandoning eggs or chicks, watching from a higher branch or a nearby tree until it was safe to return.

Tom put his boots back on, tying the laces tight for climbing. When he reached the wall he found a foothold where the cement had crumbled between the flints. He wedged his boot in and grasped the top of the wall, but as he hauled himself up he felt a sharp pain in the palm of his left hand. Dropping back onto the shingle, he angled his hand towards the moonlight to get a look at the damage. A plump bead of blood swelled from a cut and slid down his wrist. He took a step backwards, gazed up at the wall and the silhouettes of jagged flints which stood proud at three-inch intervals. He tried to shake the blood off, then pressed a corner of his towel to the cut, blotting the flow, wondering whether to give up, to walk back to the camp and forget about the eggs. Shame to have come all this way, though . . . He dropped the towel and found a foothold further along, placed his hands carefully between the flints and heaved himself up so that he was astride the five-foot-high wall, facing the conifer with his back to the summer house. He edged closer to the tree, tested the branches and gripped the one that seemed sturdiest.

A sound made him jump, the squeak of wood on wood. Branches creaking, he supposed. And then he smelt smoke. Tobacco smoke. Tom froze. Someone in the garden? He turned around, almost losing his balance, and there on the threshold of the shadowy summer house stood a girl. One arm was clenched around her waist, the other was held away from her body, wrist bent and a cigarette between her fingers.

He looked down to the shingle on the beach side of the wall: he would jump down and scarper before she had the chance to raise the alarm. But just as he was about to leap, she spoke.

'Are you one of the blackshirt crowd?' Her voice was hushed, a little shaky, but there was a sharpness, a determination. She had some nerve, he'd give her that. Most girls would have screamed by now.

He stopped, heart racing, muscles still tensed for the jump. 'I was looking for a nest, miss,' he whispered.

'What nest?'

'Er . . . bullfinches?' And at that moment two small bodies flapped up from the branches, disappearing into the garden next door. Thank you, he thought. 'I collect the eggs.' He coughed and deepened his voice. 'At least I used to, when I was younger. Old habits, you know.'

She came out of the summer house, shut the door, and took a step backwards on the path, widening the distance between them. She would run up the garden now, thought Tom, tattle to her parents or whoever it was she lived with. How old was she anyway? Older than she looked? She took a drag on the cigarette and a momentary glow lit up her face. Old enough to be married? She might have a husband in the house. At the very least an angry father with a service revolver, a war memento stashed in a bedside cabinet.

But the girl didn't run away. She dropped the cigarette and trod on it with the sole of her sandal. He felt self-conscious standing on the wall, poised to jump as though he had something to hide. Slowly, he bent his knees and attempted to crouch so that he was closer to her level.

'Don't look so worried,' she said. 'I do believe you. About the birds.' She glanced down to his pyjama bottoms. Of course she wasn't scared of him. Who'd be scared of an intruder who came dressed in his pyjamas?

'All right . . . Thanks.' He turned away, thinking that their conversation was at an end, that he was free to leave. But again the girl spoke, and it seemed for all the world as if she actually wanted to keep him there a moment longer, to chat quite normally as if they'd just met at the Saturday dance.

'I was at your meeting this evening,' she said.

She tilted her head up towards him, and the moon was bright enough for him to get a good look at her face. She was about his age, he reckoned, maybe a little younger. Her fair hair was cut quite short, just below her ears, and it was very curly. Not the carefully styled curls that the girls all wore in town. This was more of a corkscrew frizz, no style to speak of. She had a very wide, friendly mouth. He liked how she looked. If you ignored the hair, you could say there was a touch of Ginger Rogers.

'At the theatre?'

Damn it, why did he mention the theatre? Now he'd good as admitted that he was a blackshirt. She could report him yet, and the police would come calling at the camp, first light tomorrow.

'Yes. I sat with Lucia and Edith. They've invited me to visit your camp.'

'Can't say I know them. We've come from all over.'

In fact the names did ring a bell. Lucia and Edith. Bossy posh girls. They'd been in charge of rallying the greyshirts for the tug-o'-war tournament that afternoon, and Lucia had drafted him in as referee.

'Where are you from?' she asked.

'Lewisham. That's in London.'

'Yes, I do know. I used to live in Bloomsbury.'

Bloomsbury. Blackshirts had a thing about Bloomsbury types. Loose morals. *Bohemicus Bloomsburyus*, he'd heard them called. *Bloomsbury Bacilli*. 'I work near there,' he said. 'Fleet Street. The *News Chronicle*.'

'A reporter?'

He hesitated. 'Yes. Cub reporter. They don't let me cover the big stories yet. Magistrates' Court, mainly. Drunk and disorderly.'

She smiled and patted the pocket of her cardigan. He wondered if she kept her cigarettes in there. Usually he could take or leave them, but right now he could just fancy a smoke.

'What about the eggs, then?'

For a moment he was baffled. Then she nodded towards the tree, and he remembered why he was here.

'Only, I'm going in now.' She smiled and he noticed a small chip in her front tooth. 'I won't tell anyone about our meeting. My friend's brother is an egger too. You'd better take them before he does. Go on, promise I won't say.'

'N-no. It's too dark really.' He couldn't climb up there now, couldn't be sure she wouldn't squeal in the end. Maybe it was a tactic to keep him on the property while she fetched her father. 'I ought to get back. It's very late. Just that I couldn't sleep.'

'Me neither. I've been tossing and turning, reading . . . but I just couldn't drop off. It was such an exciting meeting, don't you think?'

He shrugged. 'Not particularly. I've heard it all before.'

'Oh. Aren't you a . . . supporter?' She looked disappointed. If she expected him to start swanking about the movement, she'd picked the wrong person.

'It's my mother really. She's the Mosleyite.'

'*My* mother says blackshirts are cranks.'

Tom bridled. Did she think he was a crank? 'I wouldn't go that far. Membership reached forty thousand last year. It's a serious party. You thinking of joining?'

'Perhaps.' There was a distant tap and creak, like the sound of a window being opened. The girl looked over her shoulder towards the dim outline of the house.

'I'd better go,' she said.

'Might see you at the camp, then?'

'Yes. And if you change your mind, you can come back

for the eggs. I like to wander down here, you know, when I can't sleep. You can't imagine how dull this summer has been.'

Tom wasn't sure how to reply. For a moment he dared to picture himself returning tomorrow night, to picture the girl undressing in the summer house, beckoning him in with her wide smile, no, *dragging* him in by the string of his pyjamas, whether he liked it or not. He felt his cheeks flush. Thank God the clouds had blotted out the moon.

As he dropped back onto the beach he felt a throb in his left hand and remembered the cut. Shit. Blood had dripped onto his pyjama bottoms. He picked up the towel and pressed it hard to the wound.

6

Francine sat in the lukewarm bath water, eyeing Charles's toiletries. They were laid out neatly on a glass shelf above the sink: toothbrush and paste; cologne; the silver rectangular box that contained his razor. A few of Carolyn's things were there too: a bottle of skin tonic and some vanishing cream. No sign of any make-up. Carolyn must have taken her cosmetics case (if she possessed such a thing – her style was rather country) when she decamped to Gloucestershire. Shame, thought Francine, because the red lipstick she'd brought on the journey had melted in the heat, and the coral was down to the last scrapings.

He had disappeared at eight that morning, kissing her as she lay dozing in bed, and apologizing again for the unexpected appointment. She didn't mind terribly – he would be gone only a few hours. They had arranged to meet in Soho at one, at a new bistro that had become quite the rage.

She pulled the bath plug and let the water drain around her, enjoying the feeling of rushing emptiness, as if she might be swallowed, too. Her head was fuzzy from yesterday's champagne, and then of course there were the nightcaps they'd drunk back at Bruton Street. Yes, she probably had been a little tight when she went to bed. Still, lunch would clear that. She would have an iced tonic water, with just a dash of gin. Gripping the sides of the bathtub, she eased herself up and stepped onto the carpeted floor. The towel smelt of Charles, lemon soap and cologne, but it was musty too, in need of a wash. This housemaid he employed, Jean. She was hopeless. Couldn't bring up a pot of tea without tripping on the stairs and cracking a saucer.

Casting the towel onto the rail, Francine looked down at her body, pulled in her stomach and ran warm hands over her skin. Her breasts seemed as full and as firm as they had when she was twenty, and her waist was still trim. The figure was holding up for now: it was the face that suffered, once one reached forty. Thank Christ for the marvel of Max Factor.

Francine found a tin of primrose-scented talc in the mirrored cabinet above the lavatory. She patted the powder under her arms and between her legs, then sat on the bed and rubbed talc around her toes. It was so hot again. She would wear her cerise dress today, with the Oriental wrap that Charles had so admired. Assuming Jean had managed to press her things without mishap.

Sunlight beamed through a gap in the curtains, and her eye was drawn to the chest of drawers where Charles's gold cufflinks winked from the little porcelain jewellery dish. He had worn pewter cufflinks this morning, with the cornflower-blue shirt and a light linen jacket. In his breast pocket he'd folded a matching blue spotted handkerchief, finest silk from Jermyn Street. Smart as hell, yet somehow still raffish.

This woman he was meeting today, what would she be like? Charles was given only the most basic details before an appointment. It was better that way, he'd explained, to guard against any form of attachment. Occasionally there would be an advance meeting, if the client was particularly jittery, but this wasn't advised.

Important not to dwell. Francine opened the drawer of the bedside cabinet (Carolyn's side), pulled out a leather-bound New Testament and opened a page at random. It was the Book of James. *He who doubts is like a wave of the sea, driven and tossed by the wind.* Oh, not the sea again. She'd only just managed to get away from all that: the salty Sussex air with its threat of seaweed; those ugly green-brown mounds that would clump, fly-infested, over the shingle come late summer. No, the city was what she craved. How had she ever let Paul persuade her to move away from London? He'd put up a good argument, claimed that Aldwick Bay was attracting all sorts of interesting characters: intellectuals and artists, pens and paintbrushes in hand ready to capture the beauty of the Sussex coast and the Downs, so hidden and unspoilt. It would be better for Hazel, he'd said, to grow up away from the city. The talk of war would not go away, and if the doom-mongers were right, who knew what hell Germany would unleash on London this time? 'And if we don't like Sussex,' Paul had said, 'we can think again. Nothing is permanent.'

Well, he'd been right about that last bit.

In the taxi, she spotted Charles walking down Wardour Street. It was his Gladstone bag she noticed first, though why he needed that lumbering thing she had no idea. There was never anything in it but a half-bottle of brandy. Perhaps he felt it lent him an official air, the look of a learned medical man.

'Pull up here, please.'

The driver huffed, stepping too sharply on the brakes, and

Francine almost slid off the seat. She had planned to ask Charles to join her in the taxi, but if the driver was going to be like that, she'd get out at this very spot and they could walk the rest of the way to the bistro. She paid without speaking, and didn't leave a tip.

'Charles!'

His face broke into a smile when he saw her and she felt her heart lift. He was just too handsome, with those ridiculously blue eyes and the light brown hair that was thick and shiny as a schoolboy's. But it wasn't just his looks, it was his manner, too. Such a change from the diffident boy he'd once been. Charles as an adult seemed surprisingly carefree, so different from Paul – different, in fact, from any other man of her acquaintance. Perhaps it was because Charles hadn't fought in the war. There was a lightness to that, and a sense of equality between them. Equality, yes, that was it. Hadn't they shared their own horror, long before the guns started firing in France?

'Frangipane, darling. How was your morning?' His face was a little red, she noticed. Was it because of the heat, or the exertion of his appointment? A snip of resentment caught her, but she kept her smile wide, tilted back her neck and lifted the brim of her sun hat so that he could kiss her on the cheek.

'Wonderful,' she said. 'Yours?'

'Satisfactory in every way.' He ran his finger down her arm, tracing the lotus-flower pattern on the silk wrap.

'*Every* way?'

'Naturally, I can't know for sure. But all the signs were . . . promising.'

When they reached the restaurant on Old Compton Street the waiter apologized and said their table wasn't quite ready. They were shown to a small, sloping anteroom with velvet-upholstered armchairs that listed on the crooked floorboards. The waiter offered cocktails on the house, and as they waited for their drinks they played the guessing game. There were five categories and she had never scored full marks.

'Auburn hair,' she said.

He raised an eyebrow. 'Correct.'

'Straight not shingled.'

'Correct.'

'Twenty-eight-inch waist.'

'Hmmm . . . close.'

'Blue eyes.'

'Wrong. Brown as mud.'

She laughed, leaned across to his armchair and prodded his shoulder. 'How do I know you're telling the truth, anyway? You could say what you liked and I'd never be any the wiser.'

'A matter of honour,' he smiled. 'And if you don't believe me, you could ask Dr Cutler to show you her files. She records everything in great detail.'

'I'll bet she does.'

Francine had met Dr Cutler only once – a diminutive woman with a severe bun and wire-framed pince-nez. Hard to believe that someone who looked so coiled and Victorian could be so avant garde in her thinking.

'Do excuse me,' said Charles. 'Nature calls.'

Francine crossed her legs and picked up a copy of *Punch* from the small table. Above the hubbub from the restaurant she heard a muted rustling sound. A smatter of soot fell from the chimney onto the screwed-up newspaper in the grate. Then came a frantic beating against brickwork and, with a light thump, a speckled bird tumbled into the hearth. It was a starling. The bird lay dazed for a fraction of a second, before flapping off towards the closed sash window, crashing into the glass with a horrible thud and landing on the windowsill. Francine sprang up from the chair. She would open the window and free the poor thing. But then the bird rose again and flew straight towards her. She screamed.

'Open the window!' Francine shouted as Charles shot through the door. The bird was on the carpet now, one wing tucked in, the other outstretched and held at a strange angle. Charles bent to lift the bird from the floorboards, cupping it in both hands, gently at first, then tightening his grip. There was a sharp, jerky movement and then a snapping sound: light, almost delicate, like an eggshell breaking. It took Francine a second to realize that Charles had wrung the bird's neck.

'But it might have flown away,' she said. 'You just . . . killed it.'

Charles smiled. 'Darling, it was injured.' He walked over to the window, lifted the lower sash and tossed the corpse down into the alleyway at the side of the restaurant.

'And how is Paul?' Charles asked. He cut a thin wedge of Camembert and placed it on a cracker.

Francine took a sip from her gin. Generally, they didn't speak about their spouses; it was an unwritten rule. 'There was a letter, a fortnight ago, I suppose. He'll be in Paris until October at the earliest. Apparently the clients are proving difficult.'

'So I have you to myself for at least three months.'

Francine flushed. 'I'm completely yours, darling. But once

he's home we'll have to be more careful.' She sighed and stabbed a grape with a dessert fork. 'Hypocritical goat.'

Charles put his hand over hers and stroked it. She drained her drink and let an ice cube slip onto her tongue.

'Is Paul serious about the divorce?'

'I'm not convinced he can afford it. And it would be unfair on Hazel. He feels that, I'm sure. He wants the best for her. I just wish he'd agree to a truce, and then we could jog along, make the best of it. If one or other of us has a dalliance, what's the harm? It's how most marriages survive, isn't it? Look how marvellously it's worked for you and Carolyn all these years.'

'This separation might make him see sense. When Paul comes home from Paris and sets eyes on your irresistible face, you can be sure he'll melt.'

Francine crunched the remains of the ice cube. 'And is that what you want?'

'*Want* doesn't come into it. It's about making the best of our situations. As you said yourself, Frangie.'

They sat in silence during the taxi journey back to Mayfair. Francine's thoughts returned to the starling, the blue-black shimmer of its speckled feathers. Odd that such a drab-seeming bird could be so beautiful at close quarters. There had been flocks of starlings in the hawthorns at Lostwithiel, she remembered. Always a mess of droppings on the ground underneath.

The taxi swayed through the streets of Bayswater, and she felt a little sleepy after the gin, could almost imagine herself back in Cornwall, lazing in the Lostwithiel garden, the hammock under the oak tree pitching gently back and forth, back and forth . . .

'Bruton Street,' the cabbie called. Francine fumbled for her handbag, but she needn't have worried. In no time Charles had paid the fare, and now he was holding the car door open, waiting for her to climb out.

Was it the echo of Lostwithiel that had made her feel suddenly desolate? She rarely allowed herself to think of those times, still less discuss them with Charles. This was another of their unwritten rules, and one she was happy to embrace. What was the use in talking about that summer? Unpicking the events would only reopen the wound. Really, she must not give in to memory.

7

Hazel had been awake for several minutes before she remembered the boy. She had dreamed of Lucia, and Edith too, the three of them diving in the water off the rocks at Pagham. The dream had migrated to a beach in France, and Edith disappeared, buried under a sand dune, a paper kite stuck atop the mound like a bizarre headstone. The boy didn't feature at all, and when she remembered the midnight conversation at the bottom of the garden, she couldn't help wondering whether the boy on the garden wall was actually a dream, and the swimming with Lucia and Edith was perfectly real.

She heard Mrs Waite's slow tread up the stairs, the three quick raps on the bedroom door.

'It's after nine,' called Mrs Waite. 'I've left your breakfast out.'

The mention of food made Hazel suddenly ravenous. She had eaten such an early supper yesterday, and then nothing whatsoever after the meeting. All she could taste now was the musty after-effect of the cigarettes that she'd smoked – without coughing – in the moonlit summer house. How fortunate that she'd been smoking when the boy appeared. The Pall Mall had lent her courage.

Hazel stayed in her room until she heard the click of the latch on the front gate. Mrs Waite would be walking to the shops to place the orders.

In the dining room, she found four triangles of cold toast propped in the rack and a pot of stewed tea. She ate quickly, not bothering to butter the toast. It would be better to go out now, she decided, before Mrs Waite arrived home. She raced up to her room, dressed in cycling shorts and a tennis shirt, and put her purse into her haversack. At the top of the stairs she paused, then ran into her mother's bedroom. *Ideal Marriage* was on the bookshelf, exactly where she had replaced it last night. She dropped it into the haversack. In the kitchen, she scribbled a note: *Gone bicycling with Bronny. Having a picnic lunch. Back this afternoon.* She cut some cheese and two slices of bread, wrapped the food in greaseproof paper, and took the garage key from the hook by the kitchen door.

The campsite at Pryor's Farm was only a two-minute cycle along Nyetimber Lane, but she couldn't turn up this early. Eleven, they had agreed, and it was still only ten.

Hazel pedalled up Pagham Lane and left her bicycle against a stile that led into a cornfield. Harvest mice scurried and rustled ahead as she brushed through the waist-high stalks. She and Bronny had often tried to catch a harvest mouse. Hazel had once caught hold of a tail, but her nerve failed her at the last moment – it seemed too cruel – and she let it slip from her grasp.

In the far corner of the field was a sycamore tree. She sat underneath it and opened the book. *Different Kinds of Kisses*, was the next heading. A man, during the Prelude, was at liberty to kiss any part of a woman's body, however intimate, and vice versa. Kisses could be delicate, fluttering, brief or lingering. Kisses could become violent; they could even take the form of a bite. *Women are conspicuously more addicted to love-bites than are men. It is not at all unusual for a woman of passionate nature to leave a memento of sexual union on the man's shoulder in the shape of a little slanting oval outline of tooth-marks.*

Did Charles and her mother bite each other? She remembered how she had watched Charles when he first came to stay last year. The weather had been heavenly, hot as high summer though it was early May, and he was sunbathing after a swim, wearing only a pair of navy trunks. She would have noticed any love bites, surely? She had been lying on a towel in her bathing costume, with a sun hat tipped over her face, but she had a perfect view of him through the tiny holes in the woven straw. The beauty of it was, he hadn't a clue she was looking at him. The pinholes were like so many microscopes, and she could examine his smooth tanned skin, the sand sprinkled in the fair chest hairs, the fleck of seaweed that lay below his navel. At one point Charles propped himself up on his elbows and waved to her mother, who was still in the sea floating idly on a raft they'd moored to a groyne. Then, unmistakably, he turned to look at her. Examined *her* body. She had closed her eyes, anxious, suddenly, that her face wasn't quite masked by the hat, and she felt her skin burn under his gaze.

A green sycamore seed twirled down and landed on the book. She brushed it away, and checked the time on her watch. Almost eleven o'clock. Lucia and Edith would be waiting.

By the flagpole, Lucia had said. A Union flag flying twenty feet high. Hazel found the flagpole easily enough, but she couldn't see anyone standing next to it. A few young boys were playing nearby, spelling out HAIL, MOSLEY on the rain-starved grass using buckets full of pebbles. Beyond them, a crowd of children queued to buy ice cream from a wagon, coins rattling in their hands. Opposite the flagpole was a large marquee, and scores of blackshirts were sitting at picnic tables and benches outside the tent. Hazel felt like a perfect idiot. Everyone would be staring at her. The boy might be there, too, watching, wondering what on earth she was up to. She could at least have worn a dark-coloured blouse, instead of this silly white tennis top that marked her as an outsider. She scanned the field but there was no sign of Lucia. It was ridiculous to have come here where she didn't belong, expecting to meet two girls she barely knew. She decided to run, run as fast as she could, back to the hedge where she'd hidden her bike. But just as she turned, there was a call from one of the tables.

'Hazel! Over here!'

Lucia was waving, her long arm swaying in a wide arc. Hazel made her way to the marquee, keeping close to the edge of the field, and Lucia raced up to meet her.

'There you are,' she said. 'I didn't think you'd come.' She was wearing a different uniform today: black slacks instead of the grey skirt, and a silver badge pinned to the breast pocket of her shirt. 'But I kept hoping. Join us, won't you?'

They walked over to the crowded tables. Edith was next to another girl who held a paper parasol above their heads. No one else seemed to be taking any notice of her; perhaps she wasn't such a spectacle after all.

The talk was of the meeting last night, of how well the speeches had been received, and not just by the blackshirts but by the people of Bognor Regis who had come along out of curiosity. 'People like you,' said Lucia.

A whistle sounded and Edith groaned.

'Back to babysitting duties,' she said, brushing biscuit crumbs from her hands.

'Babysitting?' asked Hazel.

'The little greyshirt boys. We're supposed to be keeping them amused. Obstacle courses, gymnastics practice, that kind of thing,' Edith sniffed. 'Most of them are here without their parents and they're prone to run wild, just as they do in the slums of Shoreditch or wherever it is they're from. Military discipline is what they need, according to Mrs Winters. Catch 'em young and all that.'

'But I'm let off the hook until after lunch,' announced Lucia, rising from the bench.

'Really?' asked Edith, her voice suddenly sharp. The other girl, Alexia, snapped shut the parasol and they both looked up at Lucia, their eyes narrowed against the sun.

'I told Mrs Winters that Hazel might be visiting. She said I should show her around the camp. Make her welcome.' She turned to Hazel. 'You can stay for an hour or so, can't you? We'll have a wander down to the woods.'

Hazel nodded and lifted her haversack from the grass. 'I've nothing to get back for,' she said. 'Nothing at all.'

As they walked towards the copse at the bottom of the campsite, Lucia linked her arm in Hazel's. Hazel knew the copse well; it belonged to old Pryor, and when they first moved to Aldwick she and Bronny had often trailed down there to play in the stream. Yet today it felt like Lucia's territory, the way she trod the path, somehow leading the way though they walked side by side.

A magpie landed on a low branch and Hazel thought of the blackshirt boy, his muscles flexed as he crouched on her garden wall.

'I met someone else from your camp yesterday,' said Hazel.

'Oh, yes? What's her name?'

'It was a chap, actually. From Lewisham, I think he said.'

'And how did you meet him?'

It was a mistake to mention the boy, Hazel realized. She couldn't talk about their meeting like that, the fact that he was hunting birds' eggs in her garden at midnight. She didn't want to get him into trouble.

'Oh, it was just a brief chat. After the meeting.'

Lucia laughed and waved her hand dismissively. 'Well, don't expect me to know him. There are hundreds of boys here, and they all look identical in their uniforms.' And then Lucia was in full flow, chatting breathlessly about camp life, how the food was jolly good considering, but the beds were like boards and she had a crick in her neck from the lumpy pillow.

Lucia began to talk about fascism, opening and closing her eyes in an exaggerated blink, her voice wavering with emotion. Her eyes were almond-shaped, glossy like a deer's. It was almost as if she was in a state of bliss. She told Hazel that this was just the beginning and that the British Union was a wonderful force for good. Just look at the national socialists in Germany, she said. Unemployment falling every day and the country positively bursting with patriotic pride.

'I expect you've heard all sorts of rubbish about the black-shirts, haven't you? The press are against us, even the *Daily Mail* now, and the *Mirror*. Yet only a few months ago we could do no wrong. What newspaper do your people take?'

Hazel frowned. 'My father used to take the *Guardian* but . . . he works in France now.'

'Oh? Never mind,' said Lucia.

Never mind *what*? wondered Hazel. Was it to do with the *Guardian*, or the working in France?

'Anyway, I'll give you a copy of our paper before you leave. I'm sure you'd enjoy it.'

Hazel hesitated for a moment and Lucia laughed. 'What a bore I must sound!' she said.

'I'm not bored,' said Hazel. And it was true. She wasn't bored in the least. The way Lucia spoke was so vivid, so interesting. She made politics sound thrilling, and Hazel felt foolish for allowing her world to be so narrow and ill-informed.

They had reached a shallow stream where a rope swing hung from a tall ash tree. Instead of crossing the stream, Lucia stopped abruptly. She turned to face Hazel and grasped both her hands.

'The thing is, Hazel, I can't help chattering on. It's just that when one feels strongly about something, well, all one wants to do is spread the word. I can't tell you how wonderful it is, being part of the Union. Everybody is so passionate, working together for a common purpose. And to know in one's heart that something is right . . . it's simply the most glorious feeling.' She laughed again, squeezed Hazel's hands tighter. 'I felt it when we met at the theatre yesterday, Hazel. I knew you would be the most terrific friend. And in fact it was *before* we met, do you remember? It *was* you yesterday, wasn't it, leaning against the pillar in the blue dress, watching the parade? I felt, somehow . . . a connection.'

Hazel swallowed drily. It was odd to feel Lucia's hands in hers, their warm palms pressed together.

'Yes, that was me. I was on my way to buy cigarettes.'

Lucia dropped Hazel's hands and took a step back. There was something scolding about her expression, but then it softened and her lips broke into a conspiratorial smile. 'Cigarettes? Do you have some now?'

'In here.' She patted her haversack.

'Let's share one, shall we? Edith and the others are dreadful prigs about smoking.'

Hazel began to unbuckle the haversack. 'So's my friend Bronny.'

'The one who couldn't come to the meeting?'

'Yes. Her grandmother's ill so she had to go to Wales. I'm at school with her.'

'Boarding?'

'No, day school.'

'Pity for you. I loved my boarding school. Miss it like hell.'

'What do you do now?'

'I work in town, at the B.U.F. headquarters. Voluntary, of course. My father would think it terribly vulgar if I were paid.'

'Is he a blackshirt?'

Lucia laughed. 'No. My mother was. She died last year.' For a moment the brightness of her voice dimmed.

'I'm very sorry . . .'

'Don't be.' She twirled the ring on her finger. 'I find it best not to think about it. What about these cigarettes, then? I've spied the perfect place to sit.' Lucia pointed to a fallen tree trunk on the other side of the stream. 'Wish me luck.' She laughed again and took a running jump at the dangling rope. Somehow she managed to look graceful as she swung

57

across and dropped down onto the dusty bank. 'Your turn!' she called, slinging the rope back over the stream.

Hazel swung off, but as she landed on the bank she tripped on a half-buried rock and flung her arms outwards to save herself. The haversack thumped to the ground, landing upside down so that everything tumbled out: the cigarettes, the uneaten slices of bread, the book.

She scrambled to her feet, her hands stinging. Lucia rushed to her side.

'I'm fine,' Hazel said, trying to laugh as she grabbed at the scattered contents. But Lucia had picked up the book before she could reach it.

Lucia looked at the title and smiled, her eyes alight. 'Isn't it enthralling?' she said. 'Have you reached chapter eight? Quite filthy.'

'You've read it?' Hazel couldn't stop herself blushing, but Lucia didn't seem in the least embarrassed.

'Esther Levine had a copy at school. Stole it from her parents' house. We had to pay Esther, of course. Two shillings for one week's loan. She bought gin with the proceeds and sold it by the double. Quite the entrepreneur. Typical of her race, one might say.' She paused. 'What's your opinion of the Jew, Hazel?'

'Which Jew?' asked Hazel absently. She could think only of the book, of wanting to cram it back into her haversack, into darkness.

Lucia screeched. '*Which Jew?* Oh, you're too adorable.' She shook her head and began to leaf through the pages. 'Now, where was it . . . Ah, yes. It's all very well *reading* this stuff, but don't you think one is left with more questions than answers?' She pointed at the text and read aloud. '*By sexual intercourse we refer exclusively to normal intercourse between opposite sexes. It is our intention to keep the Hell-gate of the Realm of Sexual Perversions firmly closed. Ideal Marriage permits normal activities the fullest scope, in all desirable and delectable ways. All that is morbid, all that is perverse, we banish: for this is Holy Ground.'*

Lucia shut the book and held it out towards Hazel. 'What can he mean, do you think? "The Hell-gate of the Realm of Sexual Perversions"? Now that's the book *I* want to read.'

Hazel found that she could not meet Lucia's gaze. She wanted to be with someone familiar, with Bronny in her bedroom, playing a game of Sorry, or with Miss Bell, practising piano. Notes played in Hazel's head, a chromatic scale ascending.

'I don't understand most of it, if I'm honest,' said Hazel, stuffing the book into her haversack. 'It's just . . . well, it's interesting, that's all, because we'll have to get married in the end and so . . . we might as well know what to expect.'

'I'm not getting married for ages,' said Lucia. 'Never, if I can help it. Mother wanted me to come out. Parade me around the debs' ball like a show pony. At least that's one fight I'm spared.' She shuddered and sat on the fallen trunk, patting the space next to her. A ray of sunlight fingered through the canopy, flashing on her silver badge. Hazel could see the emblem closely now. It was a curious design, she thought: a bundle of sticks and an axe, bound together with rope.

Hazel made a show of looking at her wristwatch. 'I promised our housekeeper I'd be home by now. Sorry, but . . . take a cigarette for later?' She edged one from the packet and held it out.

Lucia shook her head. 'No, you keep them. Another time. But we must pop back to the camp first. I was going to give you the newspaper. And if you'd like to leave your address, I can sign you up for our postal list? It doesn't commit you to membership or anything. Just an expression of interest.' She stood and flicked a fragment of moss from her slacks.

It would be quicker to cut through the bottom of the wood to the hedge where she had left her bicycle, thought Hazel. But to disappear now might look as if she was running away. She would take the newspaper and sign up for the list because it would be rude to leave suddenly when, after all, Lucia had been nothing but friendly. It was amusing about the book. There really was no need to feel embarrassed.

8

When he saw her walking back from the wood with Lucia, he dodged behind a water tank next to the cookhouse rather than walk up to say hello. Lucia was talking at the girl non-stop, lecturing no doubt, and he knew that he wouldn't be welcome if he interrupted. As they passed twenty yards ahead, he peered out to have a proper look, to see her face in daylight. Her hair was a little tamer than last night, and it shone a kind of reddish-gold. He supposed that was what they meant by strawberry blonde. Her shirt was tight and he could see the outline of her figure, her bust and the dent of her waist.

Tom wondered whether she'd really meant what she said, about going back for the eggs.

At night, when the others were fast asleep, he finally made his decision. Madness, that's what it would be, to go anywhere near that garden again. He'd allowed himself to dream a little, to conjure a kind of romance, the type of soppy tale his mother brought home from the Lewisham library. But real life wasn't like those novels. He worked for a newspaper, didn't he? Knew how messy and fucked-up real life was. Sometimes, for a half-hour skive, he would sit in the public gallery at the Old Bailey, listening to the trials. Mind-bending, what people were capable of. Carnage.

In real life, lads like him didn't get friendly with girls like her. There would be a catch. The most likely catch being that her father would be standing on the other side of the garden wall, cigarette in one hand, garden spade in the other. No, the father wouldn't hold the spade. He'd have some lackey standing by to do his dirty work, to chase him off and make sure he never came close to his precious daughter again. And all the while the girl would be watching from her bedroom window, enjoying the drama of it, the thrilling slice of scandal, something to giggle over with chums when she went back to her finishing school or her exclusive secretarial college or wherever she was bound after the hols.

He pictured her standing at the door of the summer house, one arm around her waist. *You can't imagine how dull this summer has been.*

Blood sang in his ears, and an insistent pain throbbed where the flint had pierced his skin.

There was always Jillie. Jillie with her devoted eyes and her tendency to titter at everything he said, whether or not he'd meant it as a joke. She was decent enough, pretty despite the spots. But the weekend before he left for Sussex she'd come over all serious as they canoodled behind the Gaumont; she said she loved him more than anything, would let him do whatever he wanted. He was grateful and couldn't believe his luck, and afterwards she seemed grateful too, wouldn't stop kissing him as they walked back through Manor Park, squeezing his hand and saying 'I love you' till he felt so sickly and smothered he might as well have had lilac blossom stuffed up his nose. If he stayed with Jillie, next thing she'd be expecting and he'd be married by eighteen, just like it'd turned out for Ted Field. Poor bugger was stuck in his mum's back bedroom with a wife and baby. That was his life now, no going back.

Perhaps it would be better to break it off with Jillie, to let her down as kindly as possible. He'd tell her he needed to concentrate on his studies. True enough: he wanted nothing more than to go to evening classes, to learn typing and shorthand, because then he might be in with a chance of becoming a reporter. It was another dream, he knew that, but it wasn't unheard of for lads like him. Archie Kent, the *Chronicle*'s chief court reporter, had been in the workhouse before starting as a tea boy on a local rag in Essex. Tom wondered whether he might even approach old Kent and ask for some advice. If he was polite enough and keen enough, Kent might let him into the press box at the Old Bailey. Tom had often watched the reporters from the public gallery. Eyes down, scribbling for their lives, the quick bow and the dash out of court when it was time to file their copy.

Yes, he'd give Jillie the heave-ho, and that wasn't the only thing he needed to break off. He'd been agonizing over it for a while now, ever since that first conversation with Bill Cork last year. Bolshie Bill everyone called him, big in the union, always trying to drum up new members. Tom had decided to join, and when he got chatting to Bill and told him that he belonged to the blackshirts, that he was doing his bit towards a fairer Britain – a corporate state that would hammer the greedy capitalists and the corrupt politicians – Bill almost had a choking fit. 'You're being taken for a ride,' he said. 'Fascism isn't socialism. It's for jingoists and anti-Semites. It's the gospel of hate.' Tom hadn't known how to respond, had felt humiliated, but the more he read and the more he thought, the more certain he became that Bill

Cork was right. Fascism wouldn't look after the working man: far from it.

He wondered how he would break the news to his mother. Well, she would just have to bear it. There were worse things than a communist for a son.

9

Bea hadn't told Harold it was her birthday, and she knew he was unlikely to remember without the trail of hints that she generally left in the preceding days. Still, it would dawn on him eventually, and then he would feel guilty. He could be quite sweet when he felt guilty. Chocolates and so on.

It was her fiftieth birthday. Half a century – amazing to think. That fortune teller on Blackheath had got it all wrong, hadn't she? Read Bea's palm when she was seventeen and assured her she'd be married by twenty and would travel abroad – most likely America. *Your lifeline is strong. I see success and money.* What a hoot. Bea was twenty-eight when she and Harold married, and this field in Sussex was probably the furthest they'd ever travelled. You had to laugh.

'Something amusing?' Harold was next to her, squinting through his spectacles at yesterday's paper.

'Not really. Just recollecting.'

'Right-o.' He eased himself from the bed. 'I'll have a shave before it gets busy.'

Bea watched him leave the tent. His leg must be bad this morning, because his gait was more uneven than usual; he swung one arm in a semicircle to help him balance. But he hadn't moaned too much about the camp bed, despite his reservations about coming on the holiday. Perhaps he was even enjoying himself a little.

Lying back on the mattress, Bea stared up at the grey-white canvas. Spiders had appeared overnight, tiny money spiders weaving their webs in the seams. Well then, she might as well make a wish for money. She shut her eyes and imagined the perfect windfall. Fifty pounds should do it: enough to keep them comfortable over the winter, a proper feast at Christmas, a little Whitsun holiday in Broadstairs or thereabouts, and a nice sum for Tom to kit him out with new boots and a warm overcoat for work. They had him trekking the streets in all weathers, that blessed newspaper.

A shame Tom had ended up in a tent with Samuel Beggs, thought Bea. That boy was a proper ruffian, however much his mother insisted he'd turned a corner thanks to the black-shirts. Fortunately Tom didn't seem particularly enamoured of Samuel Beggs. Then again, he didn't seem enamoured of anyone or anything – he'd been in a strange mood for weeks now. More than likely it was just a phase. Her little brother Jack had turned sulky at a similar age. He'd glare if you asked him something perfectly harmless like 'Pass the salt.'

Tom had certainly been busy. There were so many activities, she barely saw him except for mealtimes, just long enough to sneak a dab of Vaseline on his cheeks. He was looking quite suntanned already, ever so handsome in fact. Almost a man. When Tom was a small boy, people would remark how like Harold he was, and it was true, he did have the same gentle nose, the heart-shaped face. But when she looked at him, Bea could see only Jack. Tom's eyes weren't quite such a startling amber, but he had Jack's straight white teeth and the dimple in the centre of his chin that all the girls adored. She sat up with a lurch of dread. That's to come, she thought, and it probably won't be long now. Tom will bring a girl home, and Bea hoped to God it would be a decent girl, not one of these modern sorts, with lips smothered in Tangee and eyebrows plucked to non-existence. If she *was* a decent girl, perhaps it wouldn't be such a bad thing. After all, a girl with manners might be an asset to the family. She might remember people's birthdays.

The tent flaps opened and Harold stooped back inside, one arm behind his back. 'Happy birthday,' he said, swinging his arm forward with a flourish. He held out a bunch of flowers: buddleia and valerian, two stems of hollyhock. 'Tom has the card.'

'Thank you, love.' She took the offering and smiled. Wild flowers from the lane. Well, at least he hadn't forgotten. Dipping her head she inhaled deeply, and tried not to recoil at the strong smell of cats. 'Though what we'll do for a vase . . .'

'I thought we might go for a drink this evening? There's a pub in Aldwick. Or we could walk into Bognor.'

'Not tonight, Harold. It's the beetle drive.'

'Ah. Tomorrow then?'

'One night this week. I'm sure there'll be time.'

Mrs Hunter had very small feet, and she wore the most beautiful shoes: black heels, with a dainty velvet bow at the front. Bea's own feet had swollen in the heat, and they puffed over the sides of her worn black courts like bread dough in a small loaf tin. Bea crossed her ankles and stowed her feet under the chair where they would not be seen.

The title of the meeting was 'Why Women are the Backbone of the B.U.F.', and Mrs Hunter left them in no doubt that all the women present were utterly crucial to the cause.

As Mrs Hunter warmed to the theme, her audience listened in careful silence. Outside the marquee, there were distant shouts and cheers, the sound of a tractor engine sputtering. But it was easy to ignore all that, with Mrs Hunter speaking in her quiet and friendly way.

'Sir Oswald has made it very clear that women are of exceptional assistance in the attempt to build a fascist Britain. In our efforts to combat the Jew, who could be better placed than the ordinary housewife? It is a plain *fact* that our local traders are being driven out of existence by the Jew, crushed and exploited by their alien presence. You, of all people, must act by boycotting Jewry in your midst!' Mrs Hunter's lips, which had thinned and twisted as she spoke of the Jews, relaxed into a smile. 'We shall entertain no talk of violence or unpleasantness. The inflammatory lies you have heard about events in Germany have been put about by communists and degenerates. Herr Hitler is in essence a peaceful man.'

Bea shifted in her seat. She had never liked this Jew talk, and lately it was getting more insistent. What would Mrs Hunter say if she knew that she, Bea, worked for a Jewish man? If Bea boycotted Mr Perlman, she would be two pounds a week poorer, and then that would be it, they'd be on the bread line. Tom's wages were hardly adequate to put a decent meal on the table. The money from the lodger was a help, but it added extra pressure, knowing she had to cook for Mr Frowse. The one time she served up a cheap cut, he left half his meal on the plate, went out and came back smelling of fried fish.

Of course there'd always been muttering about the Jews, that was just part of everyday life. Housewives grumbled to neighbours across garden fences; husbands carped as they queued for their dole. But it was only grumbling, nothing more sinister. It was a jokey thing, Bea told herself, saying that Jews were on the make, the way people said that the Irish were dozy or the French smelt of onions. Doubtless foreigners had their own jibes about the English, and where was the harm in that? Muttering was one thing, but boycotting – *combating* the Jews – that was another.

Bea wondered whether to raise her hand, to challenge Mrs Hunter. Because she knew there had been violence in Germany; it wasn't all communist lies. She'd seen the photographs plain as anything in Mr Perlman's paper.

But when Mrs Hunter finished her speech everyone applauded with gusto, and Bea didn't have the nerve to raise her hand. Perhaps she was being over-sensitive. She pulled a hankie from the sleeve of her blouse, sneezed and wiped her eyes. The country air must be getting to her.

It was all so complicated, thought Bea, and that was the problem with politics. You had to throw in your lot with one party, but you couldn't all believe in exactly the same thing. That was acceptable, wasn't it? You focused on the policies you did support – in her case, it was the fact that Mosley was the leader least likely to start another war with Germany. Peace was all Bea wanted. Tom safe at home. She thought of Jack, how proud he'd been when he came home from the recruiting office, brandishing his papers. The twist of Indian toffee he'd bought to celebrate. She hadn't eaten a toffee, not a single one, since the day Jack left for France.

Elevenses was served after the meeting: fruit scones with jam and whipped cream from the local farm.

Bea sat at a table in the corner, on the edge of a conversation. Samuel Beggs's mother was sounding off about foreigners, spitting out scone crumbs as she spoke: 'I'd put 'em all out to sea in a big ship, and then I'd pull the plug.' A woman at her side cackled.

Bea thought of Ivy and felt a shiver of loss, though her friend was ten years dead. What would Ivy have made of the blackshirts? They'd have wanted her on their side, that was certain. Ivy was a magnificent speaker, wouldn't think twice about standing on an upturned fruit crate in Lewisham market to harangue passers-by on the issue of women's suffrage. She was forever getting up a march, and Bea was always at her side, wearing her knitted green-and-purple scarf, chanting 'Votes for Women!' till her throat was hoarse.

How straightforward life had seemed in those days before the war. Bea had marched, she had chanted and canvassed – and she had never once questioned the cause. Votes for women! Yes, that had been a noble campaign, each one of them united in a common purpose. Men, too. Harold believed in women's suffrage: that's how she'd met him, when she was selling buttonholes at a rally in Hyde Park. Afterwards he'd bought her tea and shortbread at a cafe near the Albert Hall.

'Penny for them, Mrs Smart?'

It was Mrs Beggs, looking at her with slanted eyes.

'Just reminiscing. Were you a suffragette before the war, Mrs Beggs?'

She threw her head back in horror. 'Not likely! How old d'you take me for?'

The other women laughed and Bea felt a flush creep up her neck.

'I was twelve when the war broke out,' Mrs Beggs went on, patting her hair. 'Seventeen when I had Samuel.'

'We've a fair number of ex-suffragettes in the movement,'

said Mrs Wright. 'Mrs Richardson for one – fearless woman. Marched right into the National Gallery and took a meat chopper to that nude painting, didn't she?'

Bea nodded. '*The Rokeby Venus*,' she said. 'How they repaired it I'll never know.'

Mrs Beggs looked unimpressed. 'Some of them suffragettists were off their nuts, if you ask me. Anyway, who needs Mrs Richardson when you can have O.M.?'

There was more laughter, and a long wolf whistle. The cackling woman sang the opening lines to 'You Made Me Love You', and the table chorused in reply, '*I didn't want to do it.*'

Bea dolloped a large spoonful of cream onto her scone and stared out of the marquee into the field beyond. She pictured Mosley on the beach at Aldwick Bay, his broad shoulders bare and tanned. Extraordinary that he should have stripped off like that. So informal, yet so *right*: a show of solidarity towards the whole lot of them, young and old, rich and poor. Ivy would have admired Mosley, all right. And she would have supported his crusade against war, of that Bea was certain.

10

Hidden in her diary were two postcards; they had arrived before lunch and by a stroke of good fortune she'd got to them before Mrs Waite.

The first was from Bronny, a picture of St David's Cathedral on the front, and on the back a long message in impossibly small handwriting, detailing the tedious journey, the smell of boiled plums in the hospital, and her grandmother's long-haired terrier, Oscar, who bared his teeth and snapped whenever she tried to pet him. *I'm praying we'll be home by Saturday*, she signed off. *Mummy says she can't miss the hospital fete.*

The second postcard was plain, the type one could buy in packs of two dozen from the stationer. Lucia had drawn the blackshirts' emblem on the front in thick black ink: the sticks and the axe bound together with rope. She must have posted the card yesterday, after their walk in the wood. On the reverse she'd written a message, diagonally, so that Hazel had to tip the card into a diamond shape to read the writing. *Absolutely gorgeous to see you this afternoon. Edith and I plan to bathe tomorrow at four. See you at the beach huts? Fondest regards, Lucia.*

Hazel chewed her lip and looked at the clock. Almost

three. Was it a mistake to have given Lucia her address? Mother would be vexed if letters and literature started arriving from the blackshirts. Hazel would have to claim that she'd been talked into it inadvertently, that she'd found herself chatting to one of the newspaper sellers in the town, given her address without realizing what she was signing up to.

Lucia seemed determined that they should be friends, yet Hazel wasn't sure what was behind it, whether Lucia really liked her, or whether she was simply trying to recruit new blood for the movement. Well, whatever the reason, Hazel didn't much care. Goodness knows it had been ages since she'd met anyone interesting, and now there were two interesting people in as many days. A pity the boy hadn't come back last night. She'd been so sure he would reappear.

She changed into her bathing costume, pulling her beach dress over the top. It was a plain dress of white poplin, and there was an oil stain on the hem, but it would have to do. On the landing, she took a towel from the airing cupboard. When the doorbell rang, she jumped.

Hazel opened the front door, expecting the grocer's boy, and wondering why he hadn't gone round the side as usual, but there stood Lucia on the doorstep, wearing dark glasses and a pair of scarlet beach pyjamas.

'Surprise! I know I'm a little early. Thought I'd call for you *en route*.'

'Lucia, I was just getting—'

'It's all right, isn't it? My card arrived?'

'Yes . . . but I'm not quite ready.'

'Are your people here?' Lucia lifted her sunglasses onto her head and peered beyond Hazel into the hallway. She had put some kind of pomade on her hair, so that it was sleek and almost flat to her head in the old flapper style.

'No. Everyone's out. Is Edith with you?'

'Attack of the monthlies.'

'Oh . . . I see. Well, come in. I was just finding a towel.'

Lucia stepped inside and glanced around the hallway. 'Adorable house,' she said. 'Do you come here every summer?'

'Actually, we live here all year. We moved down a while ago. From London.'

'How perfect. Although I think it would drive me a little demented, living somewhere so quiet. I'd miss town.'

'I miss it every day. I'd like to move back,' said Hazel.

'Oh yes, you must. Really! I'm longing to flat-share. It's beastly at home, just Father and me.'

They stood facing each other. Hazel felt unsure, suddenly, of what she should do next. If it had been Bronny calling round, they'd go straight up to her bedroom. But Lucia was different. A proper visitor.

'Would you like a drink?' Hazel asked. There was lemonade in the larder, and if pushed she could make a pot of tea.

'You're sweet, but shall we head to the beach? It's such a glorious afternoon, I don't want to waste a moment indoors.'

Lucia shaded her eyes and squinted towards the shore, where a dozen or so boys scampered around the waves. 'Damn,' she said. 'I'd forgotten about the swimming lessons. Let's walk further on, Hazel, or Mrs Winters will rope me in.'

The wind was getting up, and high stems of marram grass whipped at their legs as they picked their way along the beach. Lucia's halter-neck top had a faint gold print like the scales of a mermaid and her skin was bronzed and smooth. Hazel couldn't have felt less glamorous with her freckled arms and her old beach dress. Still, at least her bathing costume was passable. Turquoise was the perfect colour for fair-skinned blondes; she'd read that in *Miss Modern*.

They reached an empty stretch of beach between two low-growing clumps of kale.

'Now for the conjuring act,' said Lucia.

She shook her rolled-up towel and a black bathing costume dropped out. Hazel realized with alarm that Lucia was going to change into her costume right now, on the beach.

'Be a sport and screen me with the towel, would you?' asked Lucia.

She'd just have to go along with it. What choice was there? Lucia was older, of course, more confident, and if Hazel acted coy she would look like a baby. So she nodded and took the towel, held it out with arms stretched wide and her head twisted to one side.

'Oh, don't be bashful on my account,' laughed Lucia. 'We're all girls together.'

She took off her trousers and drawers first, then bent down to wriggle into the legs of her costume. Next she untied the halter knot of the pyjama suit and pulled it over her head, flinging the top in a crumpled pile with the trousers. Even with her eyes turned away, Hazel could see the pale curve of Lucia's breasts. How carefree she was, thought Hazel. Standing there, half-nude, casually looping her arms into the straps of her costume, now fastening the clasp of the little belt around her waist . . .

'Finished!' she said. 'Your turn.'

Hazel unbuttoned her dress and stepped out of it.

'Oh, bravo.' Lucia raised her sunglasses and gazed at Hazel. 'You came prepared . . . and what a sublime shade of blue.'

*

They swam against the incoming tide, cresting the waves, lazing on their backs in the deeper water with their eyes closed to the sun. The sea had seemed cold at first but now they felt miraculously warm – you could almost be in Cannes, Lucia said – and they began speaking to each other in French, giggling at their poor pronunciation. *J'adore la plage. La mer, c'est magnifique.*

Hazel soon ran out of French phrases, and Lucia became quiet, still drifting on her back with her eyes shut. Hazel looked up at the gulls that wheeled and squawked overhead. At first she mistook the high-pitched scream for a young gull, mewling for its mother. Then the cry came again, and she turned her head to see a small hand in the distance, disappearing under the water.

Instinctively she began to swim, to swim with all her strength towards the ripples where the hand had been. It wasn't too far, perhaps twenty yards, and she reached the spot just as a young boy's head surfaced and his arms raised again, thrashing in panic. He looked no older than seven or eight and the skin around his lips was a strange grey-blue. Hazel grabbed him around the waist and cried out herself in surprise as his weight pulled her under too. Water gushed into her mouth, closed over her head, a deafening rush of bubbles.

They sank fast, and her feet grazed against a limpet-covered rock on the seabed. She pushed up and they began to rise, but the boy clamped himself to her, his body cold and slippery with panic. They were sinking again.

It was as if he was trying to kill her and in that moment she despised him. You will not win, she thought. You will not win. Her breath bubbled away, up and up towards the light, but she could not follow it, and now she had none left, and a pain began to rasp in her chest and there was a strange singing in her ears.

Think. She must think.

Under the arms, that was it. Grab him under the arms. How many times had she watched the demonstrations, the lifesaving teams on the sands each summer? The boy's grip began to slacken and she manoeuvred herself underneath him, hooked one arm under his, then pushed up again from the rock. Their bodies surged to the surface. As she gasped fresh air she heard a woman shouting, and the *whoosh* of a laboured breaststroke.

Hazel turned onto her back, and tried to keep the boy's limp body above water, his head half-resting on her chest. Now that she had managed a few snatched breaths she was strong enough to swim again. She kicked on her back for several yards until she was sure she must be back in her depth. Yes, her foot now balanced on a slimy rock. She held the boy to her as he spluttered and shook.

'Is it Leonard? Is it Leonard?' The shouting woman was shrieking now, half-swimming, half-walking towards them. Hazel hadn't the energy to respond, even if she had known his name. She could think only of the pain in her lungs and the violent tremble that ran through her body.

'I think it is Leonard, Mrs Winters,' Lucia called. She had swum to Hazel's side, and she was reaching out towards the boy. 'We just got there in time. Here, I'll take him now, Hazel,' she said in a breathless whisper. 'You must be exhausted.'

'Bring him in,' said Mrs Winters. 'Quick, Lucia, quick. I can't imagine what he was thinking. Striking off on his own like that. Wait till I get him back to camp.'

They waded to the shore. Mrs Winters herded the other

boys into a group and told them all to get dressed. Leonard vomited onto the stones, then lay on his side with his knees up, shivering, as Hazel crouched beside him and rubbed his back.

Lucia walked off, reappearing with their towels. She had thrown her clothes on, and the scarlet silk clung to her wet costume like dark blood. Draping her towel over Leonard, she helped him to stand. 'I have to take him back,' she said to Hazel. 'Do you need anything? A doctor? There's one at the camp, I believe.'

'I'm fine, just getting my breath.'

'Little rascal would've drowned if it hadn't been for us. Here –' she placed Hazel's towel and dress next to her – 'your things. I'll come and see you this evening, shall I?'

'It's fine. Honestly no need. I think I'll go straight to bed.'

'Tomorrow, then. Take care.' Lucia blew her a kiss as she walked away.

Hazel wrapped the towel around her shoulders and lay back, using her beach dress as a pillow. The sun felt warm on her skin. Her breathing was easier now and she was desperate to sleep. She ought to go home, she thought, but she would stay here just a moment, close her eyes.

'Are you all right?'

Hazel sat up. Someone stood above her, his face eclipsing the sun. She recognized his voice. Hushed, deep. It was him, she was sure of it.

'I saw what you did,' he said.

'I should have got there sooner. I thought it was a gull crying out . . .' Her eyes were level with his knees. Shell fragments and sand grains clung to his skin.

'I wanted to help, but I was too far away. Couldn't reach you.'

She shivered, remembering the drowning boy's arms clamped around her neck, heaving her down. The towel fell from her shoulders and he crouched to drape it back around her. She felt his fingers on the top of her arm. There was a cut on his palm, she noticed, the edges whitened by seawater. Their faces were level now. The wind gusted and she could smell his skin, hot and salty.

'You saved his life, though I think your friend might take the credit.'

'Lucia?'

There was a call from the far end of the beach. 'Smart!' Mrs Winters was waving him over. Hazel could just see Lucia disappearing through the gate, clutching Leonard by the top of his arm, a gaggle of greyshirt boys following behind.

'Better go,' he said, standing up. 'Sure you're OK?'

'Yes. Perhaps I'll see you later?'

He paused and brushed sand from his arm. 'The garden?'

'I thought you might come last night. I . . . I waited.'

'You did?' He crouched again, splayed his fingers on the stones to steady himself. His knee pressed against her thigh and the contact sent a startling ache through her body.

'I'll come tonight,' he said. And then he reached for her hand and brought it to his mouth.

It seemed to Hazel as if all the air had been sucked from the summer sky, as if the waves had folded into themselves and fallen still. The boy kissed the skin close to her wrist, kept his lips there for a second or two, and it was only when Mrs Winters called again that he let her hand drop, stood and turned away, unspeaking.

She lay back and closed her eyes. The ache was still there, but it was a bearable pain, a pain that was somehow necessary. The seagulls' cries began to detach from her consciousness, the waves *shushed* her and she fell into a dream, a black dream in which she was underground, following a tiny beam of light. She did not hear the approaching whine of the aeroplane, but when it was overhead the engine's howl shook her from sleep and she blinked up at the underside of the fuselage. The Fury was polished to an impossible shine, the dazzle so bright it seemed to imprint on her eyes, and even when she squeezed them shut she could not blot out the glare.

11

Francine stood in front of the wardrobe mirror and held the yellow dress up to her body. It was pretty, rather girlish, with a bow in the centre of the high neckline. Hazel would be pleased with it, she felt sure. She hoped she'd guessed the size correctly. Alarming how Hazel had transformed over this past year. Not just her figure, but her manner, too. She wore a permanent sullen look that seemed to accuse her mother, silently, of goodness knows what. The days of idolatry were over, and in truth Francine couldn't help feeling relieved that Hazel no longer worshipped her as she once had. Sometimes it was sweet, but as the years went by it became irritating, that doe-eyed gaze of adoration, and the way Hazel would slip away from Nanny Felix and follow Francine around the house or the garden – even the bathroom, for heaven's sake – always wanting a song, or a game of snap, pestering her to listen to the latest tune she was attempting to learn on the piano. The girl had needed a brother or a sister, that was plain enough. But a brother or a sister simply hadn't come along. And now, of course, it was far too late for all that.

She folded the yellow dress back into the tissue paper and took out the crimson satin nightgown. She would wear it tonight; it would be a surprise for Charles when he came back from his appointment, if she was still awake. Such a bore that he had to go out this evening after all. They had arranged dinner at Veeraswamy, but at lunchtime wretched Dr Cutler had telephoned to say that the meeting with the Chislehurst client – cancelled last month – was now back on. The client was a ditherer, kept changing her mind, but Dr Cutler had said she was somebody important whom they couldn't possibly afford to turn down. So at six Charles had taken a taxi to Charing Cross, promising to be home by midnight, and once again Francine found herself alone, with no one but Jean scuttling around the basement kitchen, attempting to cook up a light meal. A simple soufflé, Francine had suggested, perhaps some asparagus.

She lay the nightgown on her pillow, stroked the satin and sighed. Footsteps passed on the street outside and Francine moved across to the window to look down onto the pavement. She watched a young woman in high-heeled sandals click-clacking on the arm of a dashingly tall man. Were they married, she wondered, or engaged? What fun they would have, this balmy evening in Mayfair. How wonderful to be young and in love.

Her stomach groaned and she realized she had not eaten since their late breakfast. She would have the soufflé . . . and then what? There were the friends from her dancing days, Harriett or Flick, or perhaps Deborah Leigh. She could tele-phone the old gang, whip up an impromptu gathering. But it had been months – over a year, probably – since they had been in touch. Harriett and Jeremy's wedding anniversary, wasn't it, a rainy garden party in Hampstead the previous summer? It was around the time of Paul's first trip to Paris. She had gone alone to the party, drunk too many brandy cocktails, and found herself staying overnight in Harriett's

guest room. Had she heard from Harriett since that weekend? She couldn't remember receiving a Christmas card.

Francine took an address book from her handbag and
went downstairs to the telephone. She'd try Flick first. Flick
was always game. But there was no answer at her flat, and
when she rang Deborah's house, a maid answered, inform-
ing her that the family would be in Hertfordshire until late
August. Was it worth trying Harriett? Francine remembered
Harry's cool eyes the morning after the garden party, some
upset over a broken decanter. No . . . she shut the address
book, picked up the phone and asked for the Bognor Regis
exchange.

The operator put her through, and in no time Mrs Waite
had picked up, her curious faux telephone voice bringing a
smile to Francine's lips though she had heard it a hundred
times. There was the unavoidable small talk – yes, it was still
hot in Aldwick though the wind had got up, no, still not a
drop of rain and the lawn was looking parched. Once the
pleasantries were dispensed with, Mrs Waite went to fetch
Hazel from her bedroom.

'Hello?'

'Darling. Are you having a good week?'

'The telephone works, then?' said Hazel. She sounded
cross, not a hint of pleasure or gratitude at hearing her
mother's voice.

'Oh, yes. All fixed. Are you having fun, darling? Have you
been into the town with Bronny?'

There was a hesitation, a crackle on the line, and Francine
wondered if they'd been cut off. 'Hazel?'

'Sorry, yes, everything is fine. It's still very hot. We went
bathing this afternoon.'

'Bathing? Lovely. Shall I ring again tomorrow?'

'There's no need, you know.'

'Perhaps you're right. The day after that, then. I'll ring on Friday. But I wanted to tell you about the summer dress I found you in Selfridges, and a super little hat . . .'

Hazel listened and muttered a grudging thank-you. She asked Francine when she would be home.

'Monday, I should think. I have engagements over the weekend.' Francine decided against mentioning the tickets Charles had bought for *Anything Goes* at the Palace. She'd come home sooner if it wasn't for that, but she did so love Cole Porter. 'You'll be all right, won't you, until Monday? You haven't fallen out with Bronny?'

'No. I'll be fine, Mother.' Hazel sounded brighter. 'I'm having a perfectly good time.'

'Well, that's marvellous. Goodbye, darling.' Francine blew a kiss into the receiver, but the line was already dead.

She sat heavily on the stool at the telephone table. There was a greasy smell drifting from the open door that led down to the kitchen. She picked up the address book and fanned herself with it, then flicked through the pages until she reached *X, Y, Z*, a single entry for Martha and Richard Yelland. The Yellands had moved to America, the last she heard. New York, or Boston.

At the very back of the address book was a pouch where Francine had stored a few Kodak prints. She took them out and looked at each one: Hazel with a crab net on the rocks at Pagham; her mother and father under the yacht-club awning, two or three years before they died; Hazel with Cocoa, the little cat who had disappeared over the back wall one day and never returned. Finally, there was the photograph taken in Siena, where she and Paul had spent a fortnight in 1920. She'd forgotten about this picture, and the sight of it unnerved her. How odd to see the two of them together, smiling. Their bodies touching. They both looked so happy.

A knot of regret tightened in her gut. A large gin would loosen that. Music on the gramophone. Never failed.

The clock in the drawing room struck seven.

She shoved the snapshots back into the pouch and shut the address book. Photographs could make one feel so maudlin. She must concentrate all her energies on the present. She had Charles, hadn't she? It didn't matter that they could never be married, that he was tied to Carolyn and her bountiful wealth. She and Charles loved each other, had always loved each other, even during the many years apart.

But if only Charles were here *now*. Loneliness began to creep, like a sharp fingernail sliding across her heart, and Francine couldn't bear it.

'Dinner is ready, Mrs Alexander.' Jean appeared in the hallway, anxiously shifting from one foot to the other. Such unfortunate large feet, lumped on the end of those sparrow ankles.

'Thank you, Jean. I'll take it in the drawing room on a tray. And bring me a glass with ice, would you?'

Francine opened the drinks cabinet, took out a bottle of gin and set it on the side. She pulled a record from the stack next to the gramophone. The first track happened to be Duke Ellington, 'Cocktails for Two'. Ah well, she thought – the least she could do was pour a double.

Francine spritzed her face with soda water and slumped into the armchair. Strangely enervating, dancing alone. How many records had she stepped on? Only one, wasn't it, the

Sophie Tucker? The cracked disc was over by the standard lamp. She'd have to hide that; Charles need never know.

The smell of soufflé lingered and suddenly a sharp taste of bile flooded Francine's mouth. It was so hot in the room; no wonder she felt seedy. Fresh air would help. She stood and swayed across the floor, almost tripping on the tasselled rug. As she forced up the top sash with the heels of her hands, a heavy scent drifted in: the neighbour's plants, roses and lavender, their perfumes mingling as they had in the Lostwithiel garden.

Francine stumbled back to the armchair and closed her eyes, praying for the strength to bat away the memories. It was no good. She was too weak; it was easier to give in, to find herself back in the four-wheeled trap, lurching along the rutted track, packed tightly between her brother and their parents, suitcases stowed beneath their feet. Each moment replayed with perfect clarity, a cinema reel unspooling. From the high lane she could see down the valley into Lostwithiel, the wooded hill and the church spire rising beyond the rows of slate-roofed cottages.

'Charming,' muttered Francine's mother, pressing a hand to her tight-corseted midriff. The muscles in her neck flexed in an effort not to grimace. 'So very rustic.'

The trap stopped at the end of the lane outside a large red-brick villa. Mrs Lassiter appeared smiling at the gate, waving with excitement to see her London friends after so many years. In the lee of the porch, half hidden by a brick pillar, Francine saw the shadowy figure of a boy.

The boy was Charles, the Lassiters' only child, and Francine had overheard her mother talking about him to her father, explaining how difficult Charles had become, tending towards melancholy when left alone. He was rude to his governess, and had once gone missing for the best part of a day, found at dusk playing jacks with two young girls in the squalid backyard of a local tanner.

Francine and Edward were to befriend Charles during their two-week stay. He needed playmates, they were told, and the three children were close in age – each a year apart, almost exactly, with Charles in the middle. Yet somehow, as they sat silently together on the first evening, this closeness in age made them wary. Francine was eleven and she hated being the youngest. She wished that Charles had been a few years younger, because then at least they might have made a pet of him, and perhaps he would look up to his visitors rather than treat them as intruders.

By the third day, however, Charles showed signs of acceptance. They began to go on outings with Miss Heath, the desiccated governess, to the ruined castle at Restormel or to St Austell. When it was too warm for outings they took fishing rods down to the River Fowey where it ran through the town. Miss Heath accompanied them with her sketchbook, sitting on a fold-up chair on the grassy bank of the river, dozing between pencil strokes so that her drawings always looked fragmented, incomplete. Sometimes Miss Heath let Francine draw in the sketchbook, and Francine was grateful for her praise – praise that was never forthcoming from her own governess at home in Highgate.

They were invited back the following year, and the next. Edward and Charles's friendship grew, became almost secretive, and Francine found herself excluded from the fishing trips and the tracking expeditions, left instead to sit and read in the shady garden, eavesdropping on the conversations between her mother and Mrs Lassiter. They spoke about West End plays, and new fashions, and complained good-naturedly about their husbands' shared obsession with the stock exchange.

One afternoon Mrs Lassiter seemed genuinely irked. 'I sometimes wonder whether I shouldn't chalk up the share prices on my forehead,' she'd said. 'Perhaps then he would take notice of me.'

Francine's mother had found the notion hilarious, and she spluttered into her teacup, composing herself when she remembered that her daughter was within earshot.

Francine carried on reading, pretending to concentrate. The wind blew a leaden cloud over the sun. Mrs Lassiter shivered, and they agreed it was time to go indoors. As the maid gathered up the tea table, Charles burst into the garden from the path that led to the bridleway. He clutched his fishing rod to his chest and his face looked red and damp as if he had been running.

'Dear, where is Edward?' frowned Mrs Lassiter.

'On his way, I expect,' said Charles. He cast his eyes down and stomped towards the house.

'Is everything all right?' Francine's mother called out. Charles stopped, his shoulders hunched, then he turned around with an effort of politeness that seemed to pain him.

'Yes, Mrs Ellis. It's just that I forgot my hat and I'm too hot. A touch of heatstroke, I think.'

'Then you must lie down in your room, dearest,' said Mrs Lassiter. 'Close the curtains and Flynn will bring you iced water.'

The maid bobbed and hurried away with the tray.

Edward returned in time for tea, a large trout sliding in the bottom of his bucket. He didn't ask after Charles, and he sulked through dinner. Later, when they were alone in the bedroom, Francine asked Edward whether he'd fallen out with Charles. 'Something and nothing,' said Edward airily. 'He's an awkward cove, we've always known that.'

The following summer Edward said he wouldn't go with them to Lostwithiel; he'd been invited to a school friend's in the Peak District. Edward didn't come the next year either, the year Charles was sixteen and seemed more disconsolate than ever, due to the fact that his mother had 'spawned' (he spat out the word to Francine at the dinner table, hand cupped over his mouth), producing a plump baby brother whom Mrs Lassiter worshipped even more than her prized roses.

A midnight breeze blew through the open window. There was the sound of a front door opening and closing. Francine swallowed down her nausea and sat up from the armchair. It was no use; she would have to shut out the sickly roses, sacrifice the fresh air. Unsteadily she crossed Charles's drawing room and slammed down the sash.

12

Her body was still a little shaky, the muscles tender and tight, but overlaying that was a coil of energy, ready to spring. There was a clarity to Hazel's vision now. She had a sense that everything was brighter; life was magnified and outlined in outrageous definition. She was alive, Leonard was alive, the Lewisham boy was alive. And now she wanted to live her life. Live it properly, not waste it.

She lifted the piano lid, disturbing the fine layer of dust on the glossy black wood. Miss Bell had told her to start practising the Bartók at the most difficult passage. Master that and everything else will come, she said. But somehow that seemed wrong to Hazel, illogical. She began at the beginning – the simple run of quavers, the octave leaps – and when she reached the devilish bars a kind of miracle happened. Hazel kept the tempo, struck every note with perfect, stylish precision. It was a portent: the gods were with her.

In her bedroom she did a headstand on the rug and held it for one minute. She looked at the clock upside down. Still only nine. Reading would help pass the time. She sat with her back against the bedroom door and turned to chapter nine: *Physiological and Technical Considerations*. It sounded dry, but it turned out to be riveting. Equal rights for women was van de Velde's theme. She read the passage twice, to make sure she had properly understood.

> A woman is not the purely passive instrument which she has been so long considered, and is still considered, far too often. And in any case, she *ought not* to be a purely passive instrument! For sexual union only takes place if and when both sexes fully participate and feel supreme sexual pleasure. If, anywhere and in any circumstances, the demand for equal rights for both sexes is *incontestable*, it is so in regard to equal consent and equal pleasure in sexual union, and in the interests of *both*.

Equal rights in sexual relations? The idea amazed her. Bronny had related the exact opposite: a married cousin had told Bronny (after several glasses of Christmas punch) that sex was a second curse, a wifely duty one had to endure. But if this book was to be believed, that needn't be the case at all. And why *shouldn't* it be believed? Van de Velde was a doctor, after all, distinguished in his field. There was every chance that he was right, and Bronny's married cousin was wrong.

She crossed the room, took her notebook from its hiding place over the curtain pelmet and felt around for a pencil in the drawer of her bedside cabinet. On a fresh page she copied out the passage.

At midnight, when she was certain Mrs Waite was finally asleep, she slipped on her dress and tiptoed down the stairs.

She saw his hands first. One hand firmly gripping the top of the wall, and the other more tentative, just the fingers curled to help him balance. Then the whole of him appeared, dressed in flannel trousers and a shirt, untucked on one side. She stepped out onto the path. The wind felt cool and she hugged her bare arms to her chest as she called a quiet hello. He sat in silence on the wall, his legs dangling down. She thought that he would look up into the tree, mention something about the bullfinch eggs, but he simply stared at her. The wind gusted and caught his hair, blowing it into his eyes.

'You've come,' she said.

'Couldn't sleep.'

His voice was a beautiful baritone. Could he sing, she wondered? She would like to hear him sing.

'You can climb down from there if you like.'

He peered past her, up the garden and towards the house. She was about to reassure him, to let him know that no one was watching, that only the old housekeeper was home and she'd be snoring like a drain by now. But then she decided it might be wiser to keep him guessing.

'I won't be trespassing?'

She laughed, a little louder than she had meant to, and the sound lifted on the breeze. 'I'm inviting you, aren't I? Do you smoke?'

'Sometimes.'

'They're in the summer house. I have wine, too, if you'd like a glass. It's Trebbiano. That's from Italy. Have you ever been?'

He shook his head and jumped down, followed her into the summer house. They stood facing each other, the wicker lounger between them.

'I went to Italy once, when I was twelve,' she said. 'Daddy has friends there, in Rome, except they're not friends any more.' She paused, wondering how much she should say, and then decided she should say whatever she liked. *A woman ought not to be a purely passive instrument.* She took her tumbler of wine from the table and gulped another mouthful. It was her second glass, and her limbs had begun to feel odd: dense and liquid at the same time. 'It was silly, all my fault, really. I overheard a conversation between my father and his friend's wife, Adriana. They didn't know I was in the larder. I was stealing strawberries, great fat strawberries, bigger than you could imagine. I kept quiet, of course, watched them through a grille in the larder door. He kissed her. I felt sorry for my mother, felt she ought to know, so I found her and told her what I'd seen and what I'd heard. She slapped me and then apologized, said it was for stealing the strawberries. Then she cried and asked me to tell her again. To remember every last detail. So I did as I was told, and that turned out to be the wrong thing, too.' She paused, took a deep breath and realized what an idiot she must sound. 'Sorry. I'm gushing on. You don't even have your wine yet. And I'm Hazel, by the way. Isn't that funny? We haven't been introduced.'

'Thomas Smart. Tom is what everyone calls me.'

Tom Smart. She thought it was perfect for him. A perfect name.

She handed him a tumbler from the picnic basket that lay open on the floor.

'Help yourself to a cigarette,' she said, pouring his wine almost to the brim. She nodded towards the packet on the arm of the seat. He picked up the Pall Malls, slid one out by an inch and offered it to her. This was it, she thought. The way lovers find each other in the pictures. The leading man offered the lady a cigarette. She wondered why it was always that way around. The man offering first. Her head rushed like the wind in the marram grass. Here they were, just as she had planned. The Prelude. She had made this happen, and it hadn't been difficult at all.

The first match he struck flared and died, and they both smiled, raised their eyebrows. The second match kept its flame, and he held it to the tip of her cigarette. She thanked him with her eyes, inhaled lightly and turned her head to blow the smoke in a thin stream towards the open door.

Now his cigarette was lighted too, and he was drinking the wine, and they looked at each other in silence. It was his turn to speak, she felt. She had chattered enough, carrying on about Italy and her parents like that. Why hadn't he responded? A dreadful thought struck her. What if he wasn't the charismatic young writer she'd taken him to be? What if he was actually a bore?

He dropped the matchstick into the ashtray and looked up. There was no moon, only the dim glow of their burning cigarettes.

Finally, he spoke.

'And did your mother . . . did she confront your father, about Adriana?'

It was a good question. Direct, worthy of a newspaper reporter.

'Oh, yes. There were all sorts of unpleasant scenes. It was patched up for a while but they're apart now. My father is in Paris. They call it a trial separation, but no one can say when the trial ends.'

'Is it just you and your mother, then? I mean – do you have any brothers or sisters?'

'No. You?'

'Neither.'

'And your parents?' she asked.

He smiled. 'One of each. They're not too bad, as parents go. We live in Lewisham.'

'Yes, I believe you said.' So he lived with his parents. That was a shame. She had pictured him in lodgings; a first-floor room with a high ceiling, sparse but clean. His landlady (decrepit, Victorian) would not allow guests, but he would smuggle her upstairs, and if they were discovered she would claim to be his sister, or a cousin, visiting for the weekend.

'Tell me about your job on the newspaper. Is it awfully exciting?'

He swallowed two mouthfuls of wine, rubbed at an eye. 'I may as well say . . . Look, I gave the wrong impression the other night. I don't know why I said it – well, I didn't at first, you just assumed, but the fact is . . . I'm not a reporter.'

'What are you then?'

'A messenger boy. A runner. But I do work for a newspaper. On Fleet Street. That bit was true.' He stubbed his cigarette into the ashtray. 'I expect you'll want me to leave now.'

She thought for a moment. The lie was unfortunate, but it was obvious why he had lied: to impress her. If he wanted to impress her, that had to be a good sign. And his confession was sweet. She liked him more for it.

'I'd rather you stayed.'

'Really? Right.' He cleared his throat. 'Good.'

'I felt sure you'd come last night,' she said. 'I was down here till one.'

'I'm sorry. I wanted to come but . . .'

'You're here now.'

'Yes.'

He put his wine on the table and leaned across the

lounger. She leaned across too, just a little, and she could feel the warmth of his breath. The touch of his lips made her gasp: the sweet wine taste of them, the heat from his skin. He brought one hand up to the side of her face, ran a finger lightly along her left cheekbone. Instinctively, she raised her hand to meet his, and a dusting of ash fell from her cigarette onto his arm. She pulled away, twisted the cigarette into the ashtray. Her heart lifted and crashed as if it were a giant buoy, rising up in a storm. What should she do now? She couldn't remember a word of Mr van de Velde's advice. They kissed again, properly this time, their mouths opening, tongues – astonishingly – touching, and he pulled her downwards, until they were on the lounger, pressed together between the wicker arms, stray spikes of willow scratching at the back of her thin dress.

She kissed his face and his neck. Small, light kisses that raised goose pimples on his skin. Tom's hands ran beneath her dress, his fingernails tracing a delicate path on her thigh. Now his shirt was unbuttoned and she kissed the breadth of his shoulder, the roughness of his chest. Her teeth grazed his skin, and she took an oval of flesh into her mouth, bit down hard. Tom cried out, but she did not stop.

13

Charles untied the blindfold and stepped to one side like a conjurer revealing his best trick. 'Open your eyes,' he said.

Francine blinked into the morning light – the sun was horribly glaring in her fragile state – and gazed up and down Bruton Street. She saw a telegram boy pass on his bike. Two parked cars. A clump of dirty straw blocking a drain cover. What could Charles possibly mean? What surprise?

'Well?' He twirled the blindfold – one of his silk cravats – in an impatient manner that only left her feeling more befuddled.

'I'm sorry, darling. You'll have to give me a clue.'

'Ninety in silence?'

She looked at the mint paintwork of the car parked to her right. It was a Brough. A Brough Superior.

'The car? You've actually bought it?'

'Promised I'd make last night up to you, didn't I? Couldn't bear to think of my Frangie abandoned last night. I thought we could motor down to the coast after lunch. Give the beast a decent run out.'

'How marvellous! Brighton?'

'Aldwick, if you don't mind, Frangie. I could pick up my

watch from the house. I'm absolutely lost without it. I would have caught that train last night, you know, had I—'

'Yes, all right,' said Francine. 'But I'm not missing the Cole Porter.'

'We'll be back for the weekend, of course. Back in style.' He stroked the bonnet. 'And I know a perfect little stopping place *en route*. Very secluded.'

Why did it have to be Aldwick? she thought gloomily, as she went inside to dress for the journey. Brighton would have been so much more fun. It was a tawdry town, of course, but that was part of the charm. It made no pretence at gentility, unlike Bognor and its risible 'Regis'. Still, it would be an adventure to drive to Aldwick in the Brough. Hazel would have quite a surprise.

14

The rounders tournament dragged on, and by some fluke his team was in the final. Tom stood at his outfield post, a position he'd picked because from here he could see the edge of the copse. Every few seconds he looked towards the trees, then upwards to the murky clouds that were gathering from the south.

It was impossible to concentrate on the game, to ignore the raw energy coursing through his body. Every sinew and every nerve was stretched tight with yearning. He thought of her face in the moonlight. Her kiss. The shock of the bite.

He kicked a heel against the yellowing grass, replaying last night's conversation in his mind – awkward at first, and then her story about Italy; the wine they had drunk; the cigarettes; their bodies pressed together in the sunlounger. His hand brushing against her breast, her thigh. The bite. It wasn't the usual kind of love bite: Jillie had given him a couple of those, and he'd inflicted one in return. All spit and suction. Horrible. No, Hazel's bite was something completely different. Proper passion.

She had pulled back from the embrace, though, as if it had surprised or troubled her, then she'd straightened her dress and topped up their wine. They smoked another cigarette, spoke quickly in low whispers, making plans, plotting. They would meet again today, at five, in the copse at the bottom of the campsite, next to a rope swing that hung by the stream. From there they could walk through Aldwick to a cornfield she knew, somewhere they could be alone. She would have to be home for supper at seven, but later he could come to the summer house again. She'd wait for him.

'When do you go back to London?' she had asked. They were sitting on the floor, their backs against the side of the lounger.

'Saturday.'

'And after the camp. Will you write to me?'

'Every day. And I'll come down to Bognor, often as I can. I'll save all my money for the train.'

As he buttoned his shirt, she gave Tom a sly look. 'Will there be another march before you go home? I haven't seen you in your uniform.'

Tom shrugged his shoulders. 'If there is, I'm not sure I'll be marching.'

'Why ever not?' Hazel tilted her head to one side. She looked disappointed and he hesitated for a moment, wondering how much he should explain. He had to be honest, he decided. It had worked last time, when he told her he wasn't actually a reporter. If they were going to be together – and they *were* going to be together – they needed to be completely honest about every single thing.

And so he'd explained his doubts about fascism, how it had all started after the conversation with Bill Cork, and how he was reading about politics for himself, scouring every paper in the staff canteen from *The Times* to the *Sketch*. He stopped and apologized: 'Am I droning on?'

She put her hand over his. 'Not for one second. Tell me everything.'

'It's just . . . if you only like me because of the blackshirts, the uniform or whatever, well, that isn't really me. After this camp I'm going to leave. I've made up my mind. I just haven't had the guts to tell the old girl yet.' She squeezed his hand. He felt a jab of pain but did not flinch. 'Because I want to do something decent with my life, Hazel. My mates at home, it's like their lives are mapped out. They get their girlfriends in the family way, find themselves stuck in dead-end jobs . . . cooped up in a poky room with a wife and a screaming baby.'

She chewed the inside of her cheek so that her mouth looked all lopsided. 'But wouldn't the blackshirts help with all that? Open up better opportunities? The corporate state . . .'

'It's persuasive, I know,' he said. 'It all sounds perfect. But I think it's a kind of trap. The corporate state is just another con to keep poor people in their place.'

'It makes *sense*, though.'

'That's the point. Any argument can make sense if you don't question it, if you're blind to everything else. All these years I've been listening to my mother, accepting her pronouncements. I know she's a good person at heart, a kind person, but she's got this thing, you see, about Mosley. She's indoctrinated, and it's made *her* blind. She'll overlook the bad bits, because she only wants to see the good.'

He told Hazel it was because of his uncle Jack, killed in France at the age of eighteen. Jack had been dead longer than he'd been alive, but still his mum grieved. She came at politics from one angle and one angle only. War. Mosley could get along with the German fascists and the Italians for that matter, would never pick a fight with them. Only Mosley could keep the country from another war.

'So your mother is frightened for you? She doesn't want you to be a soldier.'

'That's about it.'

'She sounds perfectly dear.'

'Hmmm. You can decide when you meet her.'

'And what about your father?'

'Oh, he likes to humour her. I'm not convinced Dad really believes it any more than I do.'

He stopped speaking, regretting the turn that the conversation was taking. Hazel would ask him about his parents' jobs now. He didn't want to tell her that his dad used to be foreman of a biscuit factory, that he was laid off and now the only work he could get was the odd day unloading crates at his mate's market stall, and that his mum kept them afloat with her cleaning job at the jeweller's in Blackheath. If he spouted all that it would open Hazel's eyes to the gulf that lay between them. There might be only so much truth she could take.

But Hazel didn't ask any more about his family. She smiled and kissed his cheek. 'I expect you think we're very rich,' she said.

He didn't reply, just looked out of the summer-house window into the expanse of the garden beyond.

'We're almost broke, according to my mother. I don't suppose we'll be able to live here much longer. What Mother wants is to sell up and move to our London flat. It's a wonderful flat, by the British Museum. It's let at the moment, so they'd have to get the tenants out. I heard her telling Charles. She hates Aldwick, says she always has. Father persuaded her to move here.'

'Charles?'

Hazel paused for a moment. She let go of Tom's hand and reached for the cigarette packet. 'Mother's lover.'

'What's he like?'

Hazel frowned. 'I hardly know.'

They had walked out onto the path together. He put his arms around her and drew her close, so that the curls on top of her head nestled below his nose. She smelt of geranium petals, velvety and clean. For several minutes they embraced, unspeaking, her body soft against his. It felt somehow as if her body *was* his, and that his own heart had swollen outside of itself, melded with her heart, and he knew that this was what was meant by love.

'Catch!' The scream of his teammates came just in time. He threw his head back to see the rounders ball dropping from the sky. It thumped into his hands and he lobbed it to the fielder on last base, ignoring the pain where the ball had thwacked the scabbed-over cut. Lucia gave a shriek of frustration at being caught out.

Clouds rolled darkly overhead. He prayed the rain would hold off and they'd be able to walk to the cornfield as planned. She'd told him about the sycamore tree in the centre, the mice that scurried around the crops, the larks and lapwings and buntings that nested all around.

It was almost six. She wasn't coming. Why wasn't she coming?

The wood was alive with creaks and snaps, and the stream plashed over green-slimed rocks, stagnating in a pool of frothy scum where the water had collected behind a fallen bough. Crouching against the smooth trunk of a young ash, he picked up a stick and drew patterns in the dust.

It had never occurred to him that she might not come.

His mouth was dry and he wondered whether the water in the stream was safe to drink. He didn't like the look of it. The scum was a peculiar shade, as if the stream was an oozing wet wound.

He touched his shoulder beneath his shirt and felt the mark where her teeth had broken his skin.

Hands drilled into pockets, he wandered into Aldwick village and decided to meet his mum and dad at the pub after all. Tom went into the lounge bar and there they both were, sitting at a table next to the unlit fire. A buddleia flower was pinned to his mum's cardigan, drooping on the shelf of her bosom.

He bent and gave her a kiss on her cheek. Her skin was loose and pillowy, fuzzy with down. She smelt of aniseed and carbolic but there was something else he hadn't noticed before. An image of his dead great-aunt came to mind. That was it. She smelt of old ladies.

'This *is* nice,' she beamed. 'The three of us together.'

'A pint?' asked his dad, delving into his trouser pocket for his wallet.

'Thanks, Dad.'

'Sit yourself down, then.' Bea patted the space next to her on the upholstered bench. 'How did you get on with Fred?'

'What?'

'Your birdwatching.'

'Oh, all right. Saw some magpies in the woods.'

Her face clouded. 'It wasn't just the one?'

'No, two.'

'Smashing. Two for joy!'

Tom ran his fingers through his windblown hair.

'What's this?' she cried, reaching for his left hand. 'What have you been up to?'

'Caught it on a branch.'

'You're too old for climbing trees, Tom. Remember what I told you about the Dixons' lad?'

'All right, Mum. I'm not a baby.'

'Stop fussing, Bea.' His dad handed the pint to Tom. 'There you go, son. Your good health.'

By the third sherry Bea's face had reddened to the shade of an autumn apple. She started to reminisce, and his dad joined in too, and the pair of them were jollier than he'd ever known them to be. 'Do you remember, Harold,' she said, 'when Tom was two and we took him to the zoo at Regent's Park? He wasn't a blind bit interested in the animals. Elephants, zebras, lions – he couldn't give a monkey's. And then we were walking to the toilets and he saw a sparrow hopping around by a bin. The excitement! "Birdie," he yelled.'

Tom did his best to laugh along with them. It was nice, sitting here – the pint had helped calm him – but a tangled feeling still swirled in his stomach, the fear that Hazel had played him for a fool.

The pub door banged open and his mum stared for a moment at whoever it was. Colour ebbed from her cheeks. She picked up her schooner and put it to her mouth, holding it there for too long, as if her arm was stuck in that position. His dad didn't seem to notice; he was drawing on his pipe, sucking to get it going, and the smoke trailed around his head in a bluish mist. Tom turned to look at the newcomers. A tall man wearing a panama hat leaned with one elbow on the bar. Next to him stood a woman in flared trousers and a strange belt of dangling pom-poms. She had red hair and painted lips. He supposed she was the kind of person that people described as striking, but Tom felt a kind of pity for her because she was getting old – forty at least – and her get-up was faintly ridiculous. Perhaps that's why his mother had stared.

Bea put down the glass and now she was fiddling in her bag.

'You all right, Mum?' Tom asked.

'Let's get going,' she said, pulling out a handkerchief. 'Shouldn't have had that last drink. I've come over woozy.'

As they left, Tom heard the pom-pom woman talking in a loud voice. 'Perfectly marvellous,' she said as she walked towards the table under the window. 'Warm gin and no ice.' The man laughed and pulled out a chair for her. She winced as the legs scraped across the flagstone floor. 'Just a quick one,' he said. 'Here's how!' They clinked glasses.

Outside, his mum pulled her cardigan tighter, stretching it over her curves. The wind had an edge to it now, choppy and damp. She shivered.

Harold gave Bea a pat on the back. 'Happy birthday, Mother.'

'Yes . . . thank you,' she muttered, and hurried along the pavement.

The lads were playing poker in the tent. Tom joined in for a while, but he couldn't keep his mind on the game. He put his cards down and reached for his towel.

'Going for a shower,' he said.

Fred looked disgusted. 'Again? You had a shower yesterday, didn't you?'

Tom threw his towel at Fred. 'Some of us have standards

to keep,' he said. 'Clean living, that's what the movement's all about, isn't it?'

With a snigger Jim leaped to his feet and did the black-shirt salute. 'Hail, Mosley!' he said, bringing his heels together so that his bare ankles cracked.

When Tom got back from the shower block, Beggsy was lying on the groundsheet, rolling something between his thumb and forefinger.

'All right, pansy?' he said to Tom. He flicked his fingers and a hard green acorn struck Tom on the side of his head. 'Soaped yourself up nice and clean, have you?'

'Fuck off, Beggs.'

'Ooooh!' Beggsy propped himself up on his elbows. 'The pansy bites back.' He stood, took off his trousers, patted his chest and belched loudly. 'Now if you'll excuse me, I'm ready for some shut-eye.' Beggsy flopped onto his mattress, feet hanging off the end of the creaking steel frame.

'Wouldn't mind turning in either,' said Jim. They put out the candles and Tom lay in the darkness, watching a brown speckled moth crawl and flutter around the canvas, trying to escape towards a light which burned in a neighbouring tent. When the light died the moth opened its wings, spread them against the canvas and grew still. Tom waited another half-hour, slid his haversack from under the camp bed and stepped out into the night.

He jogged along Stoney Stile Lane and then slowed to a walk when he reached the parade of shops. Hazel wouldn't be impressed if he turned up sweaty, especially after he'd gone to the bother of a shower.

There would be a good reason why she hadn't met him in

the woods. She'd be waiting for him now, ready to explain. And if she wasn't there in the summer house, she would have found some way to let him know. A note stuffed into a crevice in the flint wall, perhaps. A coded sign on the summer-house door.

On the beach he opened his haversack and took out the uniform. It was creased after being stuffed into such a small bag, but Hazel wouldn't notice in the blackness of this night. Muffled booms of thunder sounded across the Channel, and a cold wind sliced his hair. On the horizon, a bank of light flared. At last, the storm was coming. His pulse quickened at the prospect.

Swiftly he dressed in the black shirt and trousers, threaded the wide leather belt through the loops and fastened the steel buckle. He traced his fingers over the ridges of the emblem embossed in the centre. The *fasces* of imperial Rome; a symbol of strength through unity. Strength through unity – it was a good motto, he had to admit. He'd be strong with Hazel, that was for sure.

When the lightning flashed again the buckle shone, and the *fasces* seemed to rise up from the shadow. He bowed his head for a moment. This was the last time he would wear the uniform. He'd never march again, not as a fascist. He'd tell his mother next week, once they were back in Lewisham. And after work one day he'd find Bill Cork and they'd have a proper debate. He was ready, now, to make up his own mind.

But this last time was for Hazel. It would amuse her, he thought. And then she would peel the uniform away, and she would see him as he truly was.

His hair was still damp from the shower and he ran his fingers through it, pushing the long strands back from his forehead. The wind dropped and the clammy air seemed to smother him, to cling to his face. It began to rain. He licked his lips and tasted salt.

15

The weather was wild tonight. At the window the curtains swayed, and every now and then a whirling leaf flung itself against the pane. Between gusts Hazel could hear strong waves breaking, the suck of pebbles in the undertow. She opened the window and leaned out, her elbows grazing the salt-specked ledge. On the horizon the lights of a ship winked and she imagined the world beyond the horizon; a house on the other side of the Channel where some other girl might be standing, staring north. Hazel felt suddenly insignificant, a pinprick in the world, no more important than this grain of sand digging into her elbow.

'Hazel?'

She turned to see her mother standing at the door.

'Why aren't you in bed?'

'I'm not tired.'

'Well, I am. This headache simply won't budge.' Francine stepped further into the room and shut the door, leaning back on the handle as if it were a crutch keeping her upright. 'Darling, please don't sulk. I thought you'd enjoy the surprise.'

'I was about to go out, that was all.'

'To meet Bronny, you said. And she could very easily have

come along with us for the drive. Why you wouldn't call round for her I can't imagine.'

'She gets motor sick.'

Francine sighed. 'You can see Bronny tomorrow. We're heading back to London first thing. I must say it's a rum affair when you're not welcome in your own home . . .' Her voice trailed away as she slipped from the room.

Later, when Hazel went to the bathroom, she saw Charles on the landing. He wore a towel around his midriff and his chest was bare. Charles nodded and said goodnight. She half smiled, hugging her arms around the too-tight nightie and wishing she'd worn her dressing gown.

The storm would not matter. The gods would be with her once more and Tom would appear. Downstairs, her heart began to hammer as she slid open the bolts at the back door. She stepped onto the terrace, the wind lashing her face and snatching at her hair. A black shape slid from the bushes and she almost cried out. Only a cat. It ran across the lawn, then sprang up over the neighbour's wall.

As she opened the summer-house door a flash of lightning froze the night, and she blinked at the shapes made strange by the storm. She stepped inside and knelt at the tea chest, pulled the book and her cigarettes from their hiding place under the pile of old newspapers and magazines. Rain began to strike the windows. She'd wait as long as she had to. Thunder did not scare her.

Another lightning flash blazed as she lit a cigarette. She stared hard at the garden wall but he was not there and when the lightning died the night seemed black as hell. She drew on the cigarette, hungry for its glow. At last there was a shift in the darkness, a thud on the ground. The door opened.

'Hazel,' he said, but her breath came too fast and she could not reply. She dropped the cigarette in the ashtray and let the book fall to the floor. A half-remembered instruction called from its pages: she must not throw herself at him – *Lovers, beware!* – and yet it was impossible not to step closer, to reach out for him, to press her mouth against his.

He was wearing his uniform. The steel edge of the belt buckle was sharp and cold. Underneath, his skin was warm.

PART TWO

16

She was not in the mood for drumming. It was a warm evening and there was no air in the hall. The red curtains were closed against the setting September sun, filling the room with a rich drowsy light. Hazel looked down at the parquet flooring. There were damp patches where the bugle players had cleared their instruments of spit, and little dents where Mrs Dunn sometimes banged down her standard in frustration at their mistakes. Mrs Dunn was hard on them but she was a good leader and her pride was infectious. When a rehearsal went well, she brought out a tin of humbugs and told them to take two.

They played through the march again and this time they were perfect – even Winnie with her overenthusiastic cymbals – and Mrs Dunn beamed. 'Wonderful, ladies,' she said. 'You'll be the talk of next month's parade. Let's make O.M. proud!' She looked towards the portrait that hung at the far end of the hall above a trestle table. Hazel half expected Mrs Dunn to genuflect before the image, to bless herself with – what? – the sign of the circle and flash?

Next to Sir Oswald's portrait hung a picture of the old

king. So solid and real: hard to believe he was gone. But Edward would be a good king, they all agreed on that. Very modern in his thinking, and he seemed to have some sympathy with the movement. Lucia had been to a cocktail party at his mistress's home in Cumberland Terrace. Mrs Simpson had complimented Lucia on her beaded peach dress and they had chatted for a short while on the merits of Schiaparelli over Chanel. Lucia told Hazel that Mrs Simpson had remarkably thin wrists, which was a sign of good breeding, whatever your thoughts on divorce.

Hazel lifted the strap of the side drum from her shoulder and rubbed at her skin where the leather had dug in.

'Coming for a drink?' asked Winnie.

It was decent of her to ask, and Hazel was tempted. Winnie was good fun. For one thing she was a great mimic, and had Mrs Dunn to a tee: the Yorkshire accent, the thrust of her chin and her habit of repeating, *Put some oomph into it, lass. Ooomph!* But Lucia didn't like Winnie, called her the 'shop girl' on account of her job at the Army & Navy.

'Well then, fancy coming?'

'Not tonight,' said Hazel.

'Going back to your flat?'

'Yes. I could do with an early night.'

'Bugger that,' said Winnie. 'Life's too short for cocoa.'

Hazel laughed and put the drum into its case. Mrs Dunn appeared, shaking the tin of sweets.

'Bravo, Winnie! You might just have cracked it,' said Mrs Dunn. 'Why don't you take two?'

It was busy outside HQ. The Westminster traffic inched along – roadworks on Victoria Street – and the fumes made Hazel cough. She'd eaten the humbugs already and now she wished she'd saved one; a sweet would have helped her throat. Her brogues pinched with every step. The wretched leather refused to soften, however much she wore the shoes or marched in them or rubbed inside the heel with soap.

At first Hazel had been reluctant to join the drum corps but Lucia was very persuasive. 'It's only one rehearsal a week,' Lucia had said. 'It ought to be jolly exhilarating but I don't have a rhythmical bone in my body. Take my place, won't you, Hazel?'

Hazel had never played a drum before, but she supposed she might be able to manage. Perhaps all those years of piano lessons would help. At the very least, she knew how to keep time. And, after all, it was important to show willing. That was only fair in the circumstances.

Mrs Dunn had been delighted with the proposal. 'It simply hasn't clicked for you, Lucia, has it?' she'd said. 'Hazel sounds ideal.'

Now, almost two months after that first practice, Hazel found she looked forward to Thursday nights. She was good at drumming; the uniform no longer felt so uncomfortable. If only she could wear in these wretched shoes.

At Westminster station, Hazel took the stairs down to the Tube platform, holding tight to the handrail and concentrating on each step. There were a dozen or more people on the westbound platform including, at the far end, a woman from the drum corps, one of the intense types who loved to lecture. She ought to join her – Mrs Forbes, was it? – but instead Hazel headed the other way, sat on the narrow wooden bench and lit a cigarette. After a couple of minutes a train arrived and she got into the first carriage. To her surprise it was empty, save for an unshaven man who was wearing dirty canvas shoes and no socks. She chose a seat well away from him and looked down into her lap. A quick march thumped in her head, and her fingers tingled from the vibrations of the drum.

Beyond Gloucester Road station the train came to an unexpected halt in the tunnel. She tried not to panic, took deep breaths between drags of the cigarette. The lights in the train flickered and then died: the carriage fell dark as a cave. Prickles began to scratch her throat, spiky as ants' legs scuttling up and down her windpipe. This ridiculous asthma, or whatever it was; it was so unpredictable, and when an attack came she had no idea how to control it. At the beginning of the year, when she was still living in Aldwick, her mother had taken her to the doctor. He had listened to her chest, asked her to blow into a brown-paper bag and said she had a good deal of puff. At the end of the appointment he pronounced her perfectly fit and asthma-free. 'Drink plenty of water,' was his advice, but Hazel found that sweets and cigarettes were far more soothing. She took another drag, glad of the momentary light from the glowing tip, and glanced over at the man. He appeared to be dozing, thank goodness, his ludicrous tatty bowler slanted over one ear. He clearly wasn't worried at all that they were trapped in a tunnel – the darkness had only sent him to sleep. She coughed to clear her throat, but of course that only made things worse. The cough turned to spasms and gasps; her throat was actually closing up, it was disappearing, and in her panic she began to see flashes of light in the blackness behind her eyelids. Impossible to breathe. Perhaps this was it, she thought. She'd keel over here, on the District and Metropolitan line, because it was too dark and there was no air, and she realized that she had no letters or papers in her bag, not a single name or address, which meant they wouldn't even be able to identify her when she was found at the next stop.

She became aware of a hand on her back.

A voice, musical.

Dare, the voice was saying. *Dare.*

Irish, was it?

There, there. Take a deep breath now. Calm yerself.

The down-and-out was patting her back and soothing her. She should feel frightened that he had approached her, that he had the impertinence to touch her, but any fear was somehow cancelled out by the relief that she would not die alone. She found a breath, and then another, and miraculously she felt her shoulders loosen, just as the lights came back on and the train accelerated hard, sending the man reeling across the carriage. He staggered into a seat opposite and prised a small metal flask from his trouser pocket.

'Are you better now, miss?' he asked.

Hazel was not sure she could speak. She stood as the train slowed into High Street Ken. 'Thank you,' she whispered, nodding in his direction. He smiled, stretched his arm to offer the flask. She shook her head and he took a long swig.

'You've buried it deep,' he said, screwing the flask lid back into place. 'Sure, it'll find a way out.'

She opened the train door and hurried onto the platform. The gall of the fellow! He meant well, she supposed, but already she was horrified at the thought of their odd encounter, his alcohol-sour breath near her ear. A ghost-hand made her shiver, the sensation of his palm on her back. Thank goodness she would never see him again. London was useful like that.

Anyway, she felt better now the cough was easing. Take the steps carefully, dangerous to rush. All she needed was to get into the open air. A cold drink would help. No doubt it was the heat and the engine fumes at Westminster that had set off the attack. Perhaps the doctor was right. A glass of water was all she needed – yes, she'd have a glass of water as soon as she got back to the flat. Lucia had promised to cook dinner. Doubtless it would be something simple but extravagant. Caviar with toast. Belgian chocolates for dessert.

The day of the great parade had come. It was disappointing not to have been chosen for the march proper, but their position at the Salmon Lane meeting was a vital one, said Mrs Dunn. There would be thousands of sympathizers waiting to hear Sir Oswald as he passed through the East End. Salmon Lane was the first of his four planned stops *en route*, and the women's drum corps would form up at the front of the platform where O.M. was to speak. They would drum him in, and when he had finished his address they would strike up again. It was sure to be intoxicating, said Mrs Dunn.

Of course there was going to be trouble – Hazel had learned to expect that. Wherever they went the Reds heckled and yelled obscenities. The journey here had been bad enough. The Tube was packed with communists, red handkerchiefs and scarves tied around their necks. She and Winnie were squashed at the far end of a carriage, trying to ignore the taunts and the jeers. Every so often you'd hear a few lines of the 'Internationale', and then the fists would go up in the air. Clenched fists, threatening. Not like the fascist salute – the hand outstretched in a sign of respect and peace. True, Hazel had felt silly when she first tried it out, self-conscious, but it had become almost natural now, and it was hard to deny the buzz of energy that travelled all the way to your fingertips as you chanted, 'Hail, Mosley!'

Hazel and Winnie had left the Tube at Stepney Green and walked south to Salmon Lane. Quite an eye-opener. Hazel had never been to East London before. Lucia had described it as an alien zone, overrun by Yids. 'Sub-men', she called them, and certainly it looked like a kind of underworld, everything squat and blackened, mean tenement blocks that appeared derelict until you looked up and saw babies' nappies hanging from rusted balconies. Was this how Jewish people lived? It made no sense to Hazel. According to Lucia, these sub-men were secretly filthy rich, siphoning off Britain's wealth.

Everywhere the pavements and the walls were chalked up and whitewashed with Red slogans: NO PASARAN, THEY SHALL NOT PASS!, DOWN WITH MOSLEY. She spotted one of their own slogans – a HAIL MOSLEY on a cinema wall – but someone had rubbed out HAIL and replaced it with KILL. Typical of the Reds, said Winnie. It always came down to violence in the end.

At Salmon Lane, they unpacked their drums from the waiting van and formed up as directed, four rows of four, with Mrs Dunn at the front carrying the standard. To the sides of them stood groups of black-shirted guards. They were strong boys from HQ, they wouldn't stand for any trouble. 'We don't start fights, but we know how to finish them,' Ken had said to her with a wink. He was over there now, leaning against the van door, arms crossed. Hazel thought he'd tried to catch her eye once or twice, but she'd done her best to ignore him.

'Not exactly a crowd of thousands, is it?' said Winnie.

Hazel looked out across the wide pavement. There were a

hundred or so spectators waiting on one side of the street, chatting away or looking at leaflets and newspapers. Some were sitting on the kerb, eating sandwiches and sausage rolls in the October sunshine. Against a row of iron railings lurked a gang of Reds. Young men, mainly, but women too – even a few children who were making a racket by dragging their sticks along the railings.

'It's early yet. The march isn't due for an hour.'

'It's going to be interesting,' said Winnie.

Hazel coughed and patted her blouse pocket. 'Do you think there's time for a ciggie?'

Winnie sucked in her breath. 'You're joking, aren't you? Smoking's not allowed in uniform.' She thrust out her chin and did her Mrs Dunn. '*Put out that fag, lass!*' Hazel smiled and Winnie stuck her hand in the leather pouch on her belt. 'Here, have a fruit gum.'

The advance speaker, a man from Limehouse branch, climbed up on the platform. He was good, thought Hazel, passionate enough to hold the pitch and keep the attention of the waiting crowds. More people began to gather, many listening carefully and hear-hearing, others jeering from the sidelines. The Red gang on the edge of the street swelled. They shuffled closer and a cabbage heart was thrown at the speaker. He dodged to the left and it missed his head, flopping instead against the baker's-shop window behind him. He shrugged his shoulders and looked towards the police who were pretending not to notice, eyes straight ahead. Cabbages were gentle fare, they knew, along with rotten eggs and flour. It was the rocks and broken milk bottles you had to watch out for.

Mrs Forbes leaned towards Hazel and spoke in a low voice. 'The Reds have come from all over the country,' she said. 'They've bussed them down from Glasgow, Leeds, Manchester. It's not the locals, you know. Locals here love us. Look how the crowd's grown.'

The street was certainly filling up – hundreds now, perhaps a thousand supporters – and people were starting to clap and cheer the speaker. 'It's time to mind *Britain*'s business,' he shouted. 'Britain for the British!'

Another yellowed cabbage flew towards him, and a woman in a smeared apron leaned from the third-floor window above the baker's. She sloshed a bucket of dirty water towards the platform, managing to drench the speaker's right arm just as the cabbage hit him on the thigh. There were whoops of delight from the Reds, and the blackshirt boys moved forward. Hazel was relieved to hear a policeman's whistle. Five or more officers stepped in, batons at the ready, and the two sides were kept apart.

Another Limehouse member got up to speak. The crowd hushed for a moment, the air thin and tense in the weakening sunlight. Beyond Salmon Lane came a constant drone of noise: chants and screams, whistles being blown, police bells ringing. The officers tested their batons in the palms of their hands.

The second speaker began, yelling about high finance and usury, and the pavement became more and more crushed until in the end Mrs Dunn was right – there must have been thousands of people waiting for Sir Oswald to appear and take the platform. Then, at the end of the road, came a shout from a young Red who'd shinned up a lamp post. 'Barricades are up at Cable Street. Mosley's turning back!' There was an ear-splitting chorus of cheers, and then a woman cried out. She had somehow clambered onto the roof of a street urinal. 'They did not pass!' she called, stomping one foot on the metal roof. '*No pasaran.* They did not pass!' The Reds cheered and began to chant, 'They did not pass! They did not pass!'

A dishevelled blackshirt shouldered his way towards the platform and spoke urgently to the speaker. Sweat and blood dripped from his forehead, pooling around his eye.

Word went round in seconds. The march had been turned back from Royal Mint Street. The blackshirts were marching west instead of east, back to HQ in Westminster. Mosley would not be coming to Salmon Lane after all.

There were countless scuffles now, Reds shouting, 'Fascist scum!' The sound of bottles smashing and women's screams.

'Stand firm, ladies,' said Mrs Dunn. She slammed her standard into the ground. 'Take position.' Hazel raised her drumsticks. Her hands were trembling but somehow she felt strong and her breath was steady.

'One, two,' called Mrs Dunn.

They began to drum but the police blew their whistles and motioned at them to stop. A sergeant produced a loudhailer. 'Meeting closed,' he called. 'Go home peacefully. Meeting closed.'

Winnie grabbed Hazel by the arm. 'I'm going to my aunt's in Bow,' she said. 'Georgie's coming too. Why don't you join us? We'll be safer together.'

Hazel glanced at her watch. 'Thanks, but I ought to get back. I don't want to be stranded out here if it really flares up.'

'Suit yourself.' Winnie looked around. 'You take care. They've got their blood up.'

Hazel began to walk away, then felt a hand on her shoulder. Ken's eyes shone with excitement. 'I'll see you home,' he said. He took out a handkerchief and wiped his forehead.

'Kensington, isn't it? We'll need a drink first, though.' He pointed to a pub on the opposite side of the road. 'My treat.'

Hazel was tempted to say yes. She was thirsty and she needed the lavatory, but when she looked up at Ken he winked and gave a sideways smile that was almost a leer.

'It's kind of you but I'll be fine. Plenty of police around.'

Ken looked towards the end of the street, still teeming as people streamed away, but there was no sign of any fighting. He shrugged, his face hardening at her refusal. 'I'd take that off if I were you.' He nodded down at her armband. It showed the new party emblem – the white lightning flash encircled in red – stark against her black sleeve.

'Yes. Yes, thank you.' She rolled the band down her arm and put it in her skirt pocket, then turned away from Ken and set off towards Stepney Green.

The sun was low and there was a chill in the autumn breeze. She shivered and hugged her arms around her chest, wondering where Lucia was now. She'd been in one of the marching columns at Royal Mint Street. If the march had been turned back as everyone said, Lucia would probably be at Westminster by now. She would be fuming.

'Mosley's whore.'

It was a woman's voice. Hazel jerked her head to look behind. There were three people, two men and a woman. Close behind. The woman took a large stride, moving to Hazel's side so that their shoulders clashed. Hazel looked again. She was a little older than her, twenty perhaps, tall and angular, wearing a thin sweater and a necklace of red paste beads. Hazel quickened her pace but they kept close, the woman next to her, the men behind. Was that a hand on her back, or the blade of a knife? When she reached a junction she stood on the kerb and looked around for a policeman or anyone who might help. 'Excuse me,' she blurted to a man wheeling a bicycle, but he looked at her, at her black shirt, and he shook his head and carried along the road.

The woman with the red beads stepped in front of Hazel and pushed her back from the kerb into a narrow shop doorway. 'Blackshirt bitch,' she said. 'You dare to come here?'

'We've a right to march,' said Hazel. 'It would have been a peaceful march.'

The woman stood on Hazel's toes and thrust her face forward so that it was less than an inch away. Hazel angled her head back against the cold glass of the shop door.

'Peace? You goad us, insult us—'

Hazel closed her eyes. A fleck of the woman's spit had landed on her lips. Her stomach heaved. She was about to be hit or stabbed, or sliced with a razor, and there was nothing she could do to protect herself. The other two had the doorway covered: escape was impossible.

'Leave her.'

Hazel opened her eyes. A fourth person had arrived. His cap was pulled low so that she couldn't see his face, but when he spoke again there was something familiar about the voice, the richness of it.

'Leave her. We're not thugs like them. Let her alone.'

'She's scum,' said the woman.

'She might be scum, but let her alone. Did you read the party guidelines? Non-violent protest, remember? We need to be bigger than them.'

'All right, comrade,' said the woman, her voice spiked with sarcasm. She rolled her eyes and stepped back. 'Come on,' she said to the others. They put their hands in their pockets and sauntered away.

Hazel slumped against the doorway, weak with fear and

hope. It was him, wasn't it? He had found her – found her and saved her.

'Tom?'

The man pushed up his cap brim, and now she could see his face clearly: small, wide-spaced eyes, grey hollows for cheeks. He was an older man, thirty-five at least. A stranger.

'You got me mistaken,' he frowned. 'And now I'd say it was high time you fucked off home.'

17

He'd been in the thick of it all afternoon. There were splinters and cuts in his hands where he'd helped haul pallets and old doors and rusting prams up to Cable Street, and a rat had bitten him on the ankle when he'd disturbed a nest in the dump behind Back Church Lane – but apart from that he was not injured. Bloody miracle, considering the way the police had charged at them, horses' hooves rearing and batons thwacking from all directions.

Now Tom walked down the Commercial Road, on his way to Bill Cork's place in Limehouse where Petra would be waiting for news. Tom had become separated from Bill at some point, hardly surprising in the chaos around the barricades. Perhaps Bill was home already, and by Christ they'd have some stories to share with Petra over lemon tea and slices of seed cake. He imagined Petra's face, her brown eyes aglow, her little gasps of alarm as they told her what had gone on.

At the junction of Commercial Road and Salmon Lane a huge crowd roiled around the pavements. Tom stopped, remembering that Mosley had planned to speak at Salmon Lane during the parade. It amused him to think of the blackshirts stuck waiting all that time, only to find that their dear leader hadn't managed a single step of his promised march through the East End. Those fascists would be looking for trouble now, Tom was sure of that. He could hear his lot chanting – 'They did not pass!' – the sound of drums and the blare of a loudhailer. It was tempting to join the celebrations. He stopped at the street corner, then thought again of Petra and her poppy-seed cake. He ought to get back to Bill's, no point taking risks. They might be worrying about him, and that couldn't be good for Petra in her condition.

Bill had a shiner swelling around his right eye. 'Walloped with a baton,' he said, flinching as Petra dabbed wet cotton wool on the bruise.

'Just a little witch hazel,' said Petra. 'You have any battle wounds, Tom?'

Tom held out his hands. Petra tutted and motioned for him to sit on the stool next to Bill. A cold draught snaked under the scullery door, but his chair was near the copper and the heat from the fire warmed his legs. Petra filled a bowl with hot water and told Tom to soak his hands. When they were clean, he held them out again for her to inspect. She patted them dry with a small towel, and smeared a yellow ointment into the cuts. '*Magia*,' she said. 'It will soon heal.' She paused and narrowed her eyes. 'What is this?' She traced a finger along the jagged scar on his left palm, the skin still raised and pink.

'I cut it at the beach last year. Down in Sussex.'

Bill looked over. 'That would have been in your fascist days, eh, Tommy? Mosley's seaside camp, was it?'

Tom tried to smile. He was used to the teasing, but after all these months it was beginning to irk. 'Something like that. It was just an accident, climbing a wall.'

'Looks like they branded you,' said Bill. He took hold of Tom's hand and angled it towards the window. 'It's the shape of a lightning bolt. Uncanny.'

'It was just an accident, I told you.' Tom pulled his hand away.

'Leave the boy alone,' said Petra. She ruffled Tom's hair. 'You know that's all in his past. He can't be helping what he was born to.' She sat down on Bill's lap and he put his arms around her pregnant belly.

Tom stood up and said in any case he ought to be getting home.

'Take care, Tommy,' called Petra, her soft voice following him as he slipped out into the darkening yard.

As he walked to the Tube, the scar began to itch. Tom tried to ignore it, kept his hands drilled into his pockets, but once he was on the train he opened his palm and scratched the skin hard. The cut had never completely healed; sometimes it woke him at night, hot and prickly, and he couldn't touch it without thinking of Hazel and what he had lost. Where was she now, he wondered? Still living in that big house by the sea? Perhaps she'd spent this summer enticing a whole procession of unsuspecting fellows over her garden wall. The thought sparked a needle of pain, and he scratched the scar harder. Then again she might have moved back to the Blooms-bury flat she'd mentioned, in which case she'd be living the high life, evenings spent up west with her rich friends. Whenever Tom went on a delivery near the British Museum he told himself to keep his head down, focus on the pavement and the job in hand. But still he found himself looking up into the windows of those red-brick mansion blocks, imagining Hazel behind the glass, gazing out with a cigarette in her hand. Perhaps even scanning the streets for a glimpse of him . . .

Well, there was no use imagining. Hazel had lied about loving him, and that was that. You were better off with a straightforward girl like Jillie Smith, someone from your own class who wouldn't let you down.

Lewisham already. He scrambled off the train and slammed shut the carriage door. It was dark now and a mist was lurking. He fancied a pint but first he'd put in an appearance at home. No doubt his mum would be going spare, wondering where on earth he'd got to.

18

'I thought I heard the door,' said Edith, hurrying into the hall. She looked at Hazel and attempted a smile. 'Thank heavens you're back. I've been listening to the wireless. Was it very frightening?'

The hallway was stuffy and still smelt of fresh paint. 'It wasn't the best afternoon,' said Hazel. 'Everything all right here?'

They walked through into the kitchen. Jasmin was sitting in her high chair, chewing on a crust of bread. She smiled and kicked her legs against the footrest. One knitted sock was on the floor; the other dangled from her pink toes.

'She's been a darling,' said Edith. 'I took her to Kensington Gardens, and after lunch she had a long nap. We've just finished tea. Poached egg on toast. I hope it was OK. I'm not much of a cook.'

Hazel lifted Jasmin from the seat. 'Thank you. It's so good of you.' She sat down with the baby on her lap, pressed her nose to Jasmin's soft hair and felt a wave of calm. 'Have you heard from Lucia?'

'She called in, then dashed out again. Everyone at HQ's trying to make the best of it. Mosley spoke in Westminster

JULIET WEST

and there was a terrific crowd. She reckons this will do more good than harm.'

'Oh? The Reds seem cock-a-hoop.'

'They would, wouldn't they? But ordinary people will be outraged when they find out how the protestors behaved. Lashing out at the police like that to stop a perfectly peaceful march. Anyway, Lucia will tell you all about it. She'll be back any minute, I should think.' Edith picked up a bracelet from the kitchen windowsill and fastened the clasp. 'If you don't mind, I'd better go. Starting to get foggy out there.'

Jasmin began to cry immediately Edith left. It was always the same. At the nursery, Mrs Allen often said what a lovely baby Jasmin was, so bonny and placid. When Edith or Lucia looked after her, she was always a darling. Not that Lucia looked after her very often. Not once, in fact, these last few weeks.

Hazel carried Jasmin into the bathroom and lay her on a towel, then reached up to jiggle the washing line that hung from the ceiling. The sight of swaying laundry generally distracted Jasmin, but this evening she rolled onto her side and began to cry harder, trying to reach a rubber ball that was wedged under the cabinet. Hazel lit the geyser over the bath, then gave Jasmin the ball. Quickly she hurried out into the narrow WC next to the bathroom, almost weeping with relief because she'd been desperate for what seemed like hours. When she went back into the bathroom, she found that Jasmin had somehow crammed the ball in her mouth. Her lips were stretched back wide, and the ball glistened shiny black above her tongue.

'No, Jasmin. *No!*' Hazel snatched Jasmin from the floor, tilted her forwards and whacked her on the back. The ball flew out, bounced once and rolled away. Jasmin began to scream.

Hazel tried comforting her, but she only screamed harder. With a free arm, she twisted on the hot tap and Jasmin quietened for a while at the sound of running water. When Hazel lifted her into the bath she cheered up, smiling and babbling, splashing the water with flattened palms. She could almost sit on her own but Hazel kept a hand on her back, and with the other hand she washed Jasmin with a sponge, squeezing fat drips of water onto her skin. Would it always be this hard, she wondered? She was doing her best, but she was so very tired.

She imagined what it might be like for other mothers, mothers with nannies and doting grandparents. Mothers with husbands. And again she heard the voice in the shop doorway, remembered the rush of relief when she thought Tom had appeared to save her. Stupid, stupid. What if the man had been Tom? Tom wouldn't want her, even if she wanted him. Which she didn't. She didn't want any man. She knew about men now, knew about power, and she knew that Mr van de Velde was wrong. Equality between the sexes? What an impossible, ridiculous idea.

19

Francine did not usually take a newspaper, but this morning she walked to the newsagent's after breakfast to buy *The Times* and the *Guardian*, as well as the *Daily Mirror*, which she tucked inside the broadsheets. It really was an unpleasant shop – a wonder Mr Arnold managed to keep any custom. The acid tang of his sweat lingered on her cashmere scarf even as she walked home.

The blackshirt business still baffled Francine. This fanatic who'd befriended Hazel – Lucia – she must have mesmerized Hazel somehow, infected her with unsavoury views. She had exploited Hazel when she was vulnerable; lured her to London just when she, Francine, had found a way to resolve the difficulty. And now there had been this shocking melee in the East End, and for all Francine knew Hazel was injured or traumatized, but she had no way of contacting her.

Francine leafed through *The Times*, stopping to read the full report on page nine. Pictures of police officers wielding batons, crowds fleeing. She scanned the faces for a glimpse of Hazel, but it seemed that most of those under attack were counter-demonstrators, anti-fascists who'd built barricades to keep the blackshirts out.

Not to know where her own daughter was living – it was

preposterous. There had been just two postcards from Hazel in the three months since she went to London, both of them bland with assurances that she was safe and well. *When I feel ready for visitors*, she had written in the second, *I'll send you my address.* Visitors? Since when did one's mother count as a visitor?

On the day that Hazel disappeared, Francine had gone to the police station in Bognor, clutching the letter that had been left on the kitchen table. The sergeant listened sympathetically but he hadn't been any help. 'She's sure to come round soon,' he said. 'Seventeen, did you say? Perfectly old enough to travel to London and stay with a friend. Modern times, Mrs Alexander, like them or not. The fact is, no crime has been committed.' Francine hadn't mentioned anything to the sergeant about the child. Would that have made him more sympathetic, or less? He was an older man with Edwardian whiskers. If he knew there was a baby involved, he would probably lose interest completely; in fact he might even deliver a lecture on the loose morals of post-war society.

Francine still felt a glimmer of embarrassment when she remembered the manner of the revelation. It had been the end of December, and she was in the kitchen with Mrs Waite, finalizing the menu for the New Year's Eve party they had decided, on a whim, to throw. Paul was back from Paris, and they'd invited friends down from London, along with a few of the least boring couples from Aldwick Bay. Christmas with Paul had been a surprising success; Francine had begun to wonder whether the marriage – or some semblance of marriage – might be salvaged after all.

The proposed menu was adventurous, given the limits of Mrs Waite's capabilities: anchovy eggs, smoked salmon canapés, cheese aigrettes and stuffed mushrooms. Afterwards there would be profiteroles and madeleines and coconut ice – a favourite of Hazel's.

Francine looked down at the list and shook her head. 'Perhaps we shouldn't have the coconut ice,' she said. 'Hazel will eat the lot and she really can't afford to put on any more weight. I wonder whether she ought to go on a diet. Could you bear that in mind, Mrs Waite? After the party, I mean.'

Mrs Waite pressed the pencil point hard into the notepad. She kept her eyes fixed on the list. 'Oh?' she said. Her cheeks flushed and she seemed unaccountably ill at ease.

'Nothing radical,' added Francine. 'But perhaps less pastry, fewer puddings? I believe there's a slimming section in one of my magazines. I'll cut out the recipes.'

Mrs Waite shifted in her seat and bit her lip. 'It might not be my cooking, Mrs Alexander,' she said. There was a grim edge to her voice.

'Yes, I know Hazel likes to buy sweets now and then.'

'Not the sweets.'

Francine stared, perplexed. 'You think she's ill?'

'Not ill exactly. In a . . . certain condition.'

There was a beat of silence, broken only by the call of a tawny owl in the trees outside. Francine put her hand to her mouth, then quickly removed it. She stood up, the chair legs rocking on the terracotta-tiled floor.

'She was mixing with some funny characters last summer, Mrs Alexander, if you don't mind me saying.' Mrs Waite didn't pause to establish whether or not Francine minded. She rushed on breathlessly, almost tripping over her words, as if the information had been festering inside her, clamouring to get out. 'My friend Ciss saw her at a blackshirt meeting at the theatre, last July I believe it was, when you were in London with Mr Lassiter. Knew it was her – recognized the ribbon on your white hat. And then I could have sworn I heard her speaking to someone, a young man's voice it was, late at night, after midnight, down at the bottom of the garden. Then there was the business of Bronwen . . .'

'Bronwen?'

'That same week Hazel said she was out with her, to the cinema, and another day for a picnic, but I bumped into the Vaughans' cook and she told me the whole family was away. Grandmother was ailing.'

'Why on earth didn't you tell me at the time?'

'I did think about it, Mrs Alexander. Tell you the truth I worried myself silly. But the girl was sixteen. I decided it was a bit of mischievousness that would blow over. I never dreamed . . . this!'

Mrs Waite's eyes filled with tears and Francine hadn't the heart to reprimand her. It wasn't the woman's fault in any case. She was a housekeeper, wasn't she? She'd never been hired as a nanny.

'Thank you, Mrs Waite,' said Francine. 'Please do not speak of this to anyone.' She paused. 'Especially not to Mr Alexander. I'd be most grateful.'

Mrs Waite nodded and blew her nose as Francine turned and left the kitchen. She stood in the winter-cool hallway and looped a hand around the banister, wondering how she could have been such an idiot, to have missed what was in front of her. Well, she wasn't the only dimwit. She was quite sure Paul had no idea either. He'd made a passing remark, *Isn't Hazel filling out?* – something along those lines – but there was no concern in his voice, only a sense of surprise at the change in his little girl.

Paul didn't know, and he mustn't know. She could only

imagine his disapproval and quite possibly his fury. And of course the blame would be laid at her door. He'd say she'd been a neglectful mother, disappearing to London to see her lover. Oh yes, it would be all Francine's fault, and then the rapprochement would disintegrate, and the word 'divorce' would be back on his lips.

Francine climbed the stairs and stood outside Hazel's bedroom door. She was playing music on the portable gramophone that Paul had given her for Christmas, but instead of the Bach and Schubert that had come with the gift, she'd taken his American records from downstairs. The mournful chords of 'Death Sting Me Blues' made Francine's heart sink.

She looked at her watch. Just after five. It wasn't too early for a drink, especially at this time of year when one could start before lunch and no one would pass comment. A small brandy, for the shock. She went downstairs again, passing the closed door of the study where Paul was checking through the accounts. In the dining room she opened the drinks cabinet and took out the Rémy Martin. She poured half a glass, sipping at first, then gulping the last mouthfuls.

The music had finished and Hazel's room was silent. Francine knocked lightly and opened the door. She still hadn't decided how she felt. She was surprised, yes, and she supposed she ought to be angry. She felt sorry for Hazel, too. And now, with the warming rush of the brandy, she couldn't deny that a small part of her was actually rather impressed.

Hazel was standing at the gramophone, winding the handle. Her blouse was loosely tucked and her skirt hung low on her hips, as if the top button was undone. Francine sat on the bed.

'What is it?' asked Hazel.

'Sit down.' She patted the eiderdown. 'I think we should have a talk.'

Hazel's face crumpled instantly. She pulled a handkerchief from her cardigan pocket and covered her eyes.

'You don't have to say anything,' said Francine. 'I've guessed.'

Hazel nodded and a sob heaved from her throat. She collapsed onto the bed, flopping sideways so that her head sank into the pillows.

Francine did her best to keep her voice gentle and delicate. 'And the father?' she asked.

Hazel cried harder and shook her head. Francine decided she wouldn't press for his name. They'd get to the truth. It couldn't really have happened last summer, could it, as Mrs Waite had suggested? She couldn't have been pregnant all this time, she wasn't nearly big enough. Francine thought of the Nielsen brothers who had both danced with Hazel at the harvest social. Guy Nielsen was the sort of young man who could charm a naive girl into bed. Yes, Guy Nielsen was the father, she felt absolutely convinced. Would he marry her? He worked at a solicitor's firm in Chichester. There could be worse fates for Hazel. Then again it would be a pity for her to marry so young, a provincial bride at seventeen. Everyone would guess the reason, and though Francine herself could shrug off the scandal, Hazel might find it trying. In which case . . . there might still be time to do something about this baby.

Francine reached across to the glass of water on Hazel's bedside table. 'Have a little sip, darling,' she said. 'We can't sort this out until you calm down.' She patted Hazel's back as she took the glass and began to drink. 'Good girl. Now, you should have waited, of course, but I'll spare you the lecture. We just have to set about solving the problem. When did it happen, do you know?'

Hazel blotted her eyes with the handkerchief and nodded. 'Summer. July.'

'Ah.'

Not the harvest dance, then. Was it safe to have an operation, five months along? One of Flick's friends had tried at around the same mark, and it hadn't ended well. Perhaps Charles's friend Veronica Cutler might be able to help? This was her field, after all.

'We'll find you a nice comfortable clinic,' said Francine decisively. 'The baby can be . . . dealt with, or adopted, and you can start afresh. If we're careful no one need know. You're only just showing now. It must be a small baby.'

'I can feel her kicking.'

'Feel "it", darling. You mustn't give in to sentiment.'

Hazel put her hands on her stomach and began to cry again. The bump was quite visible with Hazel's palms pressed to it like that. Tears dropped onto her pale young hands, sliding into the smooth dips between her knuckles, and Francine felt a sudden surge of abhorrence, to think that her daughter's hands had been wrapped around a man; hands that only a short while ago had been happy to build sandcastles or thread together a daisy chain. It was too soon. It made her feel sick and it made her feel old. Hell. She was going to be a grandmother.

No.

Francine stood, a quick flush spreading from her chest. Her thoughts whirled and she wanted only to get away from the room. But she must hold her nerve because there was more to discuss.

'I'm glad we've had this chat,' she said. 'At the moment the main thing is to keep it a secret. Your father mustn't know. He'll be safely back in Paris within the fortnight.' She bit her lip and walked towards the window, speaking to herself as much as to Hazel, working out how it would be. 'And if Paul wants to come home again soon, we'll send you away, tell him you're on a school trip. Oh, there are plenty of discreet hospitals for girls like you. July, you say, so if you were to have the baby it would be born –' she splayed her fingers on the windowsill and counted out the months – 'seven, eight, nine . . . April some time. A spring baby. Everything will be back to normal by summer next year. And you'll be almost eighteen with your whole life ahead of you – we need never speak of the trouble again. But the father . . . ?' She spun round from the window. 'Will the father make a scene, Hazel? Really, darling, you need to tell me who he is. I can't fully help unless I know what we're dealing with.'

'It's nobody you know.'

'Is it Guy Nielsen, darling? From the Fairway? Or his younger brother. I've seen you dancing—'

'No! It's someone from London. It was a mistake, in the summer. He was here on holiday.'

'A holiday romance? A fascist from London, was it?'

'What?' Hazel's face told Francine all she needed to know. 'How did you—?'

'People talk, darling. You were seen at a blackshirt meeting. Honestly, how on earth did you fall in with such an unsavoury crowd?'

'It doesn't matter. It was just a . . . fleeting friendship.'

There was something to be said for that, thought Francine. A summer passion, quickly spent. Boys like that were bound to disappear, *tout de suite*, once they'd had their fun.

He wouldn't come knocking on the door and, frankly, that was for the best.

'So you're no longer in touch?'

'No. I've never seen him again.' Hazel had stopped crying and her voice was flat and bitter. She bunched the eiderdown in her fists and her knuckles strained white. 'I'm never seeing any man again.'

'Now you're being overdramatic. We can find a bright side, darling. You were desperate to leave school anyway, weren't you? I'll tell Miss Lytton you've decided not to stay on. And to your friends we'll say you're unwell, tonsillitis – you've had it before, do you remember? – and perhaps you'll have the tonsils out, and you'll need some time to recuperate. A visit to your uncle Edward in Bristol. Don't worry –' Francine picked up a Christmas card from the sill and fanned her face – 'we'll solve this problem. I promise, darling.'

Francine sighed and pushed the newspapers away. She had done all she could to help Hazel overcome the hiccup – she'd worked out a perfectly good plan. Veronica Cutler could have taken care of everything, and when that failed there were the Misses Shaw. But no, Hazel had her own ridiculous ideas.

Yet she had seemed so compliant at the outset. When Francine suggested a shopping trip to London, a few days after the initial chat in the bedroom, Hazel had been keen, agreeing that she would need new clothes. Of course, Francine hoped there'd be no need for new clothes. She hadn't actually mentioned that their trip would include a visit to Dr Cutler; Hazel might only worry and become tearful again.

Paul waved them off from the front porch, and Francine felt curiously sentimental as she watched him through the taxi window, his smile broad and his eyes acorn-brown in the pale winter sunlight. She and Paul had been more than civil this holiday: they had actually enjoyed each other's company, and the New Year party had been a tremendous success. After the party they had shared a bed and made love in surprising ways. Evidently the spell in Paris had broadened Paul's mind, and there was no sign of the old trouble.

On the London train they settled in their compartment and Hazel took out her book. Francine remembered that she had brought the latest issue of *Theatre World*. Hazel was more keen on cinema than theatre, but Francine had imagined they might leaf through the pages together; Hazel might be tempted by one of the plays, and they might even plan another trip to London to see a matinee, once the trouble was over.

Strange, thought Francine, that this little crisis seemed to have united them as never before. It was their secret (not counting Mrs Waite, who had never again referred to Hazel's condition), and for once Francine knew exactly what to do and what to say to her daughter. For the first time, she was able to speak to Hazel as an *adult*. Perhaps this had been the problem: she simply wasn't cut out to mother a small child.

Pages and pages of *Theatre World* were devoted to pictures of Diana Wynyard and Emlyn Williams. 'Look at her divine shoes,' Francine said to Hazel, angling the page towards her. Hazel smiled and nodded, and said wasn't the dress perfect, but Emlyn Williams didn't look nearly as handsome with the moustache. Francine agreed and settled back into her seat. The train clattered along and she read the magazine to the very end, glancing finally at the restaurant directory and the miscellaneous advertisements for typewriters and clairvoyants and dry-cleaning services. One advertisement caught her eye:

> **RESIDENTIAL HOME** for Infants and Small Children. Long or short visits. Expert personal care for mothers in confinement. Special attention diet and health. The Misses Shaw, Harris Road, Selsey.

Selsey. If Dr Cutler couldn't solve the problem, the Misses Shaw might be ideal. Selsey was a little *too* close to home – gossiping distance – but it would make life so much easier in terms of visiting Hazel. And if a baby was born, the Misses Shaw could no doubt arrange for it to be taken care of. Yes, Selsey wasn't a bad idea at all. She folded the magazine and tucked it into her handbag.

The appointment in Torrington Square began well. Francine told Hazel it was a routine check-up, and everything did seem to be routine at first – blood pressure, temperature, measuring of the abdomen. It was only when Dr Cutler began to talk about *the procedure* that Hazel became difficult. There was quite a scene. A gown was flung across the room, a kidney dish tipped from its stand, sharpened instruments scattered across the floor. There was no option but to leave.

Afterwards Hazel was quite hysterical. They checked into their room at the Grosvenor, and when Hazel finally stopped crying, Francine suggested miniature golf on the roof garden at Selfridges. This set her howling again.

Later, once Hazel had had a sleep and a bath, and allowed Francine to disguise the puffiness of her face with a little make-up, they went out to Pagani's for dinner. 'All the best people come here,' Francine whispered to Hazel as the waiter showed them to their table. 'Musicians and singers and radio announcers. They troop in from the BBC.' Hazel gazed around, catching her reflection in the long mirrors that were painted with climbing flowers on gilt trellises. A man dining alone at a nearby table also saw Hazel's reflection, ogling for a little too long so that Francine had to fix him with a stare. He couldn't be blamed: Hazel did look lovely in the mauve dress, and the golden wallpaper and low lighting gave her face a gorgeous luminescent glow. Even Hazel's hair was behaving itself, now that Francine had taken her to the hairdresser for a proper wave. The man couldn't see Hazel's thickening waist, of course, because she was still clutching her coat across her middle.

They were finishing their soup when Francine spotted Charles at the door. Her heart leaped and she hated herself for it. Hadn't she and Paul just enjoyed a marvellous few days together? Still, she shouldn't be surprised to see Charles at Pagani's. It was his favourite restaurant, after all; she was quite aware of that when she asked the hotel to book the table.

Charles was chatting to the maître d', gesturing towards a table near the window. In came a much older, hunched man who walked with a stick. Charles and the old man made slow progress to the table. As Charles was about to sit, he noticed Francine and peered in surprise. He said something to his dinner companion and handed the waiter his coat. Oh Lord, now he was coming over.

Francine pretended not to have noticed him, so that when he arrived at their table she exclaimed in amazement,

'Charles! This *is* a surprise.' She looked pointedly at Hazel. 'Isn't it, darling?'

'Yes,' Hazel replied, grabbing up her napkin and pressing it to the corner of her mouth.

Charles looked down at Hazel. 'Wonderful to see you,' he said. He rested his hands on the tablecloth and lowered his voice. 'I would love to come and join you but it's my father's New Year outing. Trying to keep the old boy sweet.'

'Your father?' said Francine. She looked sideways towards the table, and then turned her head quickly back. 'I wouldn't have recognized him.'

Charles pulled a face. 'Shadow of a man,' he said. 'Come over and say hello?'

'Charles, I couldn't possibly . . .'

'No. No, of course. Look, telephone me once you're home. You can tell me how it went with Dr Cutler.' He slid his hand towards Francine's so that their fingers were touching.

Hazel coughed and her spoon dropped into the shallow bowl. There was a loud clang of silver against china and the diners at the neighbouring tables turned to stare at the young girl crying into her soup.

On the journey home the next day Hazel barely spoke. She was tired, she said, and she fell asleep soon after the train left Victoria. They had shopped for several hours – the new clothes would be needed after all – and the trail around Oxford Street had not been without tears. Francine looked through the train window at the electric lights already burning in the back rooms of dreary terraces. Her view was obscured by a small rectangular sign that read NON SMOKING on the outside of the glass, and NO SMOKING inside.

She wondered at the dull little railway committee agonizing over the wording, some self-satisfied pedant explaining the grammatical niceties. She lit a cigarette. If the guard came she would simply say she hadn't noticed the sign.

Francine's head buzzed. Seeing Charles last night had razored her nerves. She had been feeling so much more in control, so . . . *serene*, almost, to think that Paul might come back and she might have a second chance at being a wife and mother. She felt she was ready to play the part; might even attempt to become more domesticated, more like Bronwen's mother who baked cakes and telephoned through her own weekly orders, and managed with that funny little cook rather than a live-in help. Francine drew hard on her cigarette, tapped the ash on the floor and attempted to kick it under the seat opposite. Hell. Two minutes in the company of Charles had made the domestic life seem laughable again.

She pulled down the compartment window and tossed her cigarette end onto the track. A London-bound train whistled past, but the noise and the blast of dirty cold air did not wake Hazel.

'More coffee, Mrs Alexander?'

'What?' Francine hadn't heard Mrs Waite creep in. The woman was like a skinny old cat, slinking around. 'No, no, thank you.' Francine frowned at her ink-smudged hands. 'I'll go up for a bath, I think.' She had read enough about Cable Street. She looked out to the garden, where the leaves on the pear tree were already starting to mottle and fall. It would soon be winter. If Hazel refused to send her address, Francine would just have to find her. Next time she was in town she would go to the blackshirt headquarters and ask if they could put her in touch with Lucia. Surely that way it would be possible to get a letter through?

Of course there was another option – to give up on Hazel completely, to accept that she had ignored all sensible advice and gone her own way. But Paul was putting on pressure, accusing Francine of being an irresponsible mother, hinting that it would not look good in the divorce courts. So much for salvaging the marriage. Their union was sunk for ever, that was certain now. Francine preferred not to remember that Saturday in March when Paul had arrived home from Paris unannounced. She had tried to steer him into the study, but he had marched into the living room where he found Hazel, huge in a plaid smock dress, and Charles out on the terrace, drinking brandy from Paul's best crystal.

Mrs Waite fussed around, clearing away the figs, the toast rack. Francine stood up. 'I'll be leaving for town tomorrow, Mrs Waite.' She handed over her coffee cup. Yes, she'd go tomorrow. Charles could drive her to the blackshirt head-quarters. The address was there in the news reports: Great Smith Street, Westminster. 'I'll be gone for a few days.'

'Is there any word of Hazel?'

'Not yet,' said Francine. She couldn't blame Mrs Waite for asking, but it was irritating all the same. 'Do listen out for the telephone while I'm gone, won't you?'

'And the doorbell. She might appear any day, tail between her legs.'

'Thank you, Mrs Waite.' Francine brushed past her into the hallway. How presumptuous of Mrs Waite to speak about Hazel like that. Francine imagined the chatter around the estate, the hushed conversations of domestics on their half-day outings. Let them gossip and judge; let them cast her as the faithless wife who couldn't keep her husband, and you can only imagine the effect it must have had on the poor daughter. Small wonder the girl had got into trouble and run away.

Francine told herself that the gossip didn't matter. What mattered was getting Hazel to see sense. By now she might have tired of motherhood. She might be exhausted by the reality of caring for a baby with no money and no one to support her but a crowd of ludicrous zealots.

Hazel might be ready to accept that Francine was right all along.

20

It was before six and Jasmin had started to snuffle and kick her legs. She was getting too big for the Moses basket. Lucia had promised to buy a cot, but Hazel didn't like to remind her because she had already been so generous, insisting on paying the rent, bringing home extravagant treats from Fortnum's food hall. Lucia had even offered to pay for a daily, but Hazel was firm about that. She didn't want a maid in the flat. It was a relief to be free of Mrs Waite – why risk another pair of disapproving eyes? Hazel could clean and shop; her wages covered the grocery bill at least – the everyday food that Lucia never thought to buy. It wasn't exactly an equal arrangement, but it was the best Hazel could offer.

She got up from her bed and began to potter around the room, folding clothes, pairing bootees. The noise seemed to soothe Jasmin, and she quietened back to sleep. Hazel looked through the window into the small patch of communal garden, the mansion block rising behind. How strange it still seemed to be in London, to call this city her home once more. She thought back to July, to the single staccato rap of the door knocker that had sounded her salvation. Mrs Waite had answered, and from the top of the stairs Hazel was astonished to hear Lucia's voice. She raced down to see Lucia on the doorstep, her shirt as black as the look on Mrs Waite's face.

Lucia lifted her sunglasses and smiled at Hazel. 'You're still alive, then.'

'Lucia! You're in Aldwick—'

'Another year, another jolly camp.' She fluttered her lashes, exaggerating the movement as if she were a doll blinking. 'Can you come out to play?'

Mrs Waite, who had not let go of the door, began to edge it shut. 'Hazel's been unwell,' she said through the gap. 'I'll have to ask her mother.'

'Mother is away for the weekend,' called Hazel, grabbing the door and shouldering past Mrs Waite. 'Yes, I'll come out. Shall we go into town?'

Walking the beach path into Bognor, Hazel felt almost breathless in the warmth of Lucia's friendship, the relief of conversation after so many months of secrecy and loneliness. She'd given up calling on Bronny. Mrs Vaughan would answer the door, her fixed smile polite but firm, and the script always prepared: No, Bronwen was busy with an essay. Sorry, Bronwen was horse riding with Patricia. Asleep in the garden. Now here was Lucia, glamorous in her dark glasses, saying how simply glorious it was to see her, and forgiving her absolutely for not replying to the letters.

'I'm sorry I lost touch,' said Hazel. 'I haven't been well – Mrs Waite was right about that.'

'Poor thing, you do seem rather low somehow. Here, shall I buy us an ice? You can tell me all about it.'

They sat under a beach shelter east of the pier. Hazel began hesitantly, skirting around the truth, muttering about missed monthlies. Lucia soon drew out the meat.

'You mean you fell pregnant?' she asked, in too loud a voice. 'Who's the beau?'

'There's no beau,' replied Hazel quietly. 'It was no one special. A mistake.' She remembered her mother's comment about the Nielsen brothers. 'A boy I met at a dance, we got carried away, and, well . . .' Hazel glanced at Lucia's wide-eyed stare. There was something admiring in her gaze, envious even, and Hazel had the horrible feeling that Lucia was going to start quizzing her on the particulars of the act. Sure enough, the question came.

'Do tell. What was it like?'

'I don't want to talk about that, if you don't mind,' Hazel said. 'I'm trying to forget it.' She told Lucia instead about the miserable Christmas, the visit to Dr Cutler, her banishment to the Misses Shaw.

'But where is the baby now?'

'She's still there! With the ghastly Shaw women. I'm allowed to visit once a week. And by the end of the month Jasmin will be gone. Adopted. I won't even know her new name.' She began to cry into her half-eaten cone.

Lucia put her arm around Hazel. 'Adopted against your will?'

'Oh, I'll have to sign the papers, but what else can I do? Mother won't have Jasmin in the house. Father's in Paris with his mistress. He can't even bring himself to speak to me. There's nowhere I can go, Lucia. I'd leave home, I'd sleep on the streets, in this shelter – under the pier, for heaven's sake! But how can I with a baby?'

'They'd take you into one of those homes for fallen girls,' said Lucia, flicking away some cone crumbs that had fallen in her lap. 'Or the poorhouse.'

Hazel cried harder, and Lucia's arm tightened around her shoulders.

'Don't be upset, dearest Hazel. I have an idea. Listen, I've been desperate to move out, find a flat, but Father won't let me leave unless I have a flatmate, and not one of my friends has the gumption. Edith's so *safe*, you know?'

Hazel's head lifted. Hope flared in her chest, though she tried to beat it down. 'But he won't let you move in with me, will he? A girl with a baby?'

'We won't mention that bit.'

'What if he visits?'

'Unlikely. Barely moves from his chair. But if he does turn up, we'll find some story. You might have a married sister, mightn't you, a little niece come to stay?'

Hazel nodded, unable to speak because she was too terrified the moment might somehow disappear, that Lucia would laugh and say it was a mad idea after all. But Lucia didn't laugh. She gave Hazel a tender pat on the shoulder, then stood up with a smile.

'Come back to camp with me now,' she said. 'We can chat it through while we're walking. And there's a meeting in the marquee at five. I'm one of the speakers, can you believe? Do come, Hazel. It might take your mind off everything. It'll be just the tonic you need.'

It was part of the bargain, Hazel realized, her contribution along with the housework. And she was happy enough to become a blackshirt; it seemed a natural thing to do. Lucia was right: when she was at meetings or drum practice, her thoughts never wandered to darker territory. Her mind was focused, organized, looking only to the future, the next beat in the bar. It was a relief to have something to believe in.

The first fortnight in the flat had been dream-like, settling in to her new room with Jasmin, the two of them together, properly, for the very first time. Lucia looked after Jasmin while Hazel went for job interviews, and when she was offered a post at Morris & Weaver, Lucia found the nursery for Jasmin. There'd been an article about it in the *Blackshirt* – a new crèche just half a mile from their flat, open from seven-thirty in the morning till six at night, founded in memory of Sir Oswald's late wife. 'Poor Cimmie loved children,' said Lucia. 'Such a tragedy she was taken so young.'

Early-morning shadows played on the ceiling. Jasmin began to whimper – a yell was imminent. Hazel tiptoed across the cold cork tiles into the kitchen. She lit the gas ring, poured milk into a small pan and placed the pan over the heat. Half-awake, she opened the cupboard for a bottle, and it was only then that she noticed the letter on the table. It was addressed to her, and there was a note from Lucia scrawled in pencil across the front of the envelope. *Your mother appeared at HQ,* Lucia's note read. *She left this letter. PS Back v late, please don't wake me in the morning.*

Hazel picked up the envelope and held it for a while. She put her finger into the top corner but could not bring herself to break the seal.

The milk puffed and sizzled and boiled over onto the stove.

She reached the crèche just after eight and rang the bell. Mrs Allen answered, a stout woman and a dedicated blackshirt. Jasmin put her arms out and Mrs Allen took her with a smile. 'Here's my pretty girl,' she said, trying not to wince as Jasmin tugged at an ivory clasp that fixed the bun in her thick greying hair. Mrs Allen produced something from her pinny pocket – a crudely jig-sawed animal that could have been a lion or a horse – and Jasmin's fist curled around it.

'She'll only try to eat it,' said Hazel.

Mrs Allen laughed, pushing the hair clasp back into place. 'I know, I know, everything in the mouth. She's teething, bless her. Look at her little face.'

Hazel looked. Jasmin's cheeks were bright red and her nose was running. What could that have to do with teeth?

'Does it hurt her?' asked Hazel. 'Only . . . well, she cries a lot at night.'

'Some of 'em breeze through it and others aren't so lucky. You'll find powders and potions at the chemist,' said Mrs Allen. 'And we all have our own pet remedies. My mum swore by an egg in a sock, hung above the cradle. Ask your mother, dear. She'll remember what worked for you. And your husband's mother, if you're close?'

Mrs Allen cast a sly glance downwards. Hazel put her hands into her pockets, cursing herself because in the daze of the morning she had forgotten to put on the wedding ring. The fiction had been Lucia's idea, to stall any gossip. Hazel had a husband, a ne'er-do-well who'd let her down. The word 'abandoned' was not to be mentioned, but that would be the unspoken truth, should anyone cast for details.

'Yes, good idea. I'll ask my mother.'

'Leave the pram there, dear. Poppy will put it under the awning later. Running a little late, are we?'

Hurrying to the bus stop, Hazel brushed herself down and checked for any signs: splodges of sicked-up milk on the shoulder of her coat, or a smear of Germolene on her wrist. Usually she would remove the wedding ring once she was safely on the bus. Morris & Weaver did not employ married women, still less an unmarried woman with a baby. This morning, at least, the ring was one less thing to remember.

Morris & Weaver sold high-class wallpaper and soft furnishings, with a shop in Tottenham Court Road and offices in Pimlico: a Regency house over three floors. There were two rooms on each floor, and Hazel worked in accounts, the top room at the back of the building, above the light-flooded studios where the designers sketched and coloured. From the window she could glimpse the pale brick of the Tate Gallery, and she was half tempted to visit in her lunch hour, but she never quite dared because there was a chance she might run into her mother or one of her friends, visiting the latest talked-about exhibition. Instead she wandered along Millbank and ate her sandwiches on a quiet bench. It was best not to take lunch with the other girls from the office. They tended to ask questions that Hazel did not want to answer. She kept her story simple: she was Miss Alexander, up from Sussex, studying accountancy in the evenings, which meant she was too busy to go out to concerts or dances after work. As a result the girls tended to leave her alone and the office manager, Mr Boyne, seemed grateful to have a junior who was so sensible and who didn't tip in with giggly tales about the previous evening's high jinks.

The chimes of Westminster struck the half-hour and Hazel quickened her step. She tried not to think of the letter from her mother which she'd stuffed unopened into the pocket of her dressing gown. Another image came to mind: an egg in a sock. She almost laughed, but then her throat began to tingle and when she breathed in, the air seemed sharp, as if it were stuck with pins. Not now, she thought. Please not now. She dodged into a narrow alley between two buildings and lit a cigarette. The smoke soothed her throat. She remembered the Irishman patting her between the shoulder blades, and fought back the echo of his words. *You've buried it deep.*

Hazel waited until that evening to read the letter. Jasmin was finally asleep and Lucia had gone to a meeting at HQ, emergency planning after the events of the weekend. Lucia was certainly in demand at head office. She said it was marvellous the way the movement promoted women – the blackshirts were far more modern than the Nazis on that point. Hitler would have all German women dressed in dirndls, their faces scrubbed of make-up, but Mosley liked his women to be strong and glamorous. Look at Diana Guinness. You couldn't imagine anyone *more* glamorous.

Hazel lit a cigarette at the table in the living room and sliced at the envelope with Lucia's silver letter opener. The letter was brief, all of three sentences. Francine wanted to meet. Sunday 11th – this Sunday – 3 p.m. on the steps of the Tate Gallery. The Tate, of all places. Had Francine discovered that she worked nearby, or was it simply chance? A coincidence, surely. It was the kind of place Francine would suggest.

Ash flakes dropped from Hazel's cigarette onto the letter, obscuring her mother's signature, the three lavish kisses inked below her name. Outside, the autumn night was drawing in and loneliness yawned in the dark space between the undrawn curtains. Hazel ran her finger along the sharp edge of the letter opener. She had been so grateful for Lucia's friendship, for her assurances that she would always be there to help. But Lucia was less and less interested in Jasmin – seemed jealous, almost, of the time Hazel had to spend with her daughter, and the nights when she went to bed at nine because she was simply too tired to stay up chatting or listening to the wireless.

Tears pressed at Hazel's eyes. She needed someone, something. What was it Mrs Allen had said? *Ask your mother, dear.* Perhaps it was time to forgive Francine.

They were back in the summer house and she could feel the weight of him, his breath sighing into her hair. She kissed his neck, tasted the salty sweetness of his skin. A piano was playing, Brahms's Lullaby floating through the black sky. Was that a gull she could hear, crying into the night? The noise grew more insistent, and Hazel woke suddenly to the sound of Jasmin wailing, her small body thrashing in the basket.

She sat on the end of the bed, lifted Jasmin and pressed her close, aware of their heartbeats, wild and unsynchronized. She rubbed Jasmin's back and began to sing under her breath. '*I had a little nut tree, nothing would it bear. But a silver nutmeg and a golden pear . . .*' She couldn't remember the end of the rhyme. There were nursery books in Aldwick, on her bedroom shelves. Her mother would know the words. Singing was something she'd been good at: she liked the sound of her own voice.

Jasmin only cried harder. She must be hungry. Hazel's breasts ached but any hope of feeding her baby had been long abandoned. The Misses Shaw insisted on bottles – it was more sensible in the long run, they said. Mothers were less emotional once their milk had dried up.

The night-time bottle was standing on the marble shelf in the larder cupboard. Hazel lay Jasmin on the bed and quickly went into the kitchen. As she closed the larder door she heard a dull thump. There followed a beat of silence, and then a scream. She flew to the bedroom. Jasmin was lying on her face where she had fallen onto the cold floor. Hazel picked her up and tried to soothe her, rubbing her back. *There, there. There, there.*

It took forever to calm her, but finally Jasmin took the bottle and Hazel could check her face in the lamplight. There was a small mark on her left cheekbone – a bruise would surely follow – but apart from that she seemed unharmed. As Jasmin guzzled the milk her little fist reached up and grabbed a curl of Hazel's hair. She twined her fingers into it and pulled hard, so that Hazel's head sank lower and lower until their cheeks clamped together, hot and tearful.

At last Jasmin slept but Hazel knew her night had ended; she would be awake now until it was time to get up for work. The dream had stayed with her – it was as if Tom was by her side, his breath trapped in the room. She thought of the last time they had been together, the storm baying outside. The promises they had made.

Perhaps she had been too quick to lose faith, to believe the other words, those words that came later in the dread quiet after the storm.

She would never trust a man again, that was the vow she had sworn. And yet the dream, the memory of that moment when she had believed love was possible: here it was, like a silken thread swaying, almost within her grasp.

On her dressing table was the reply she had written to her mother. She dropped it into the waste-paper basket, picked up a fresh sheet of notepaper and slowly began to write.

From the steps of St Paul's she could hear the organ playing: a fugue she didn't recognize. It was five past three and she resolved to wait ten more minutes. If he hadn't arrived by quarter past she would go back to the flat and burn the un-answered notes and the scrap of paper with his scrawled-on address, and she would never, ever think of him again.

The day had felt cool when she left Kensington, but now the sun was struggling through the clouds, warming the streets. She looked towards the statue of Queen Anne, the four carved figures at her feet. There was Britannia, naked to the waist, her small breasts exposed to the weak sunshine. Hazel flushed and bowed her head. To think that he had seen her undressed, pale as stone in the moonlight . . .

Still, what did it matter? He wasn't coming anyway. She sat on the granite steps, shielding her eyes from the sun.

The fugue ended and a stillness fell over the city. At the foot of the steps a huddle of tourists gazed up at the cathedral. They looked at Hazel, too, as if she were part of the tableau. She angled her body away from them, hugging her knees closer to her chest, trying to make herself smaller.

If Tom came, would he appear from the east or the west? She could see down Ludgate Hill well enough, but there was no sign of anyone who looked like Tom.

'Ah, you meant *these* steps.' Suddenly he was next to her, his hands in his pockets. He wore a white shirt, open at the neck, and his skin was tanned from the long summer. 'I was waiting round the other side.'

She rose quickly, smoothing the creases in her skirt. 'I didn't think you were coming.'

'I don't like to let people down.'

The barb hung in the air. They stood awkwardly, looking down the steps rather than at each other, and then they spoke at the same time, and stopped at the same time, and returned to silence for a pained second until Tom asked whether she might like to go for a walk or a cup of tea. She nodded, and they took the steps slowly, Hazel assessing each one, concentrating, because she felt certain the slightest distraction might cause her to trip and tumble, to knock herself out, and eventually she would wake and Tom would no longer be by her side.

They crossed the road and headed towards the river, past St Benet's Church and the wharves of Upper Thames Street. White Lion Wharf, Horseshoe Wharf, Puddle Dock. The weather was pleasant for October, they agreed. She asked if his parents were well and he said that they were.

'And yours?'

'Fine.'

She looked across the water to Bankside, to the jetties and the coal hoists, the dark buildings with their rows of black windows like unblinking eyes.

'You wanted to meet,' said Tom, slowing almost to a halt as they approached the path under Blackfriars Bridge. 'Was there any particular reason?'

She turned her head to him but his eyes remained fixed on the shadowed arch ahead. 'I wanted to apologize,' said Hazel.

'Oh?'

'I'm sorry I didn't see you again after that night, didn't write. Everything changed. My . . . circumstances changed,' she faltered.

A small child ran under the bridge towards them, stout pink legs and scabbed knees. He was chasing pigeons. His parents followed, a young couple, arm in arm. 'Slow down, sausage,' shouted the father. Tom seemed to be watching the little boy with a tenderness in his expression, the trace of a smile on his lips. And at that moment Hazel decided. She would tell him today. Yes, she would tell him everything.

They passed the couple and the man nodded an 'Afternoon.' Beyond the bridge was a refreshments kiosk. Hazel insisted she would buy the tea, and so Tom found an iron bench and sat down as she queued.

A hazy film of cloud hung low in the sky and there was barely any wind, not even this close to the river. They sat side by side on the bench, clutching their cups of tea, blowing the surface of the liquid, trying to coax away the heat. A jackdaw flew from a plane tree and landed on the low river wall. The Thames flowed smooth and fast and Hazel felt a rush of emotion towards Tom. Her love was an undercurrent, forever tugging. But she needed more than love; she needed belief, the certainty she'd held dear for that short precious time. She must try to recapture it, for Jasmin's sake. There would be no better time than this.

'What happened last summer—' she began.

'Don't worry,' he interrupted, holding up his hand as if to dismiss her apology. 'Your circumstances have changed, you said. Mine have changed too. My politics, well – I told you about that already. I've swapped sides. And I'm off to Spain soon.'

'Spain? But the war . . .'

'The war, exactly. I'm going to fight Franco.'

'Fighting?' She gripped the teacup but found no comfort in its warmth. 'What do your parents think?'

'Oh, I haven't told them yet. Mum's still a devoted Mosleyite.'

A bell began to ring at the fire station next to the bridge, and a volley of shrieks sounded inside her head. How could the conversation have turned to Mosley? To the war in

Spain? She breathed deeply, trying to dredge up a reasonable response. 'Lucia says the communists and fascists actually have a lot in common. We both want what's best for the working man.'

Tom tapped a foot on the pavement. 'Is that right? I think you'll find Franco has some strange ideas about the working man. He's a bloody murderer. And meanwhile Britain stands by and refuses to help.' He put down his cup, scratched the palm of his hand and flinched.

Hazel looked up at the dull sky and the grey cloud pressing down. How could she possibly tell him now? He was fixed on Spain, that was clear. Dear God, had she actually thought they might be together?

'When do you leave?'

'End of the month, if all goes to plan.'

She paused, dared herself to look directly into his eyes. 'Can I write to you while you're away?'

He returned her gaze and moved his arm as if to reach for her hand, but then pulled back and picked instead at a frayed thread in the seam of his trousers.

'I suppose you could . . .' He took a deep breath. 'And your boyfriend wouldn't mind?'

'Boyfriend?'

'Your circumstances. I assumed . . . a boyfriend or a fiancé or something.'

She shook her head. 'There's no boyfriend. I'm too busy for that. I have a job now, and there's the movement. I'm in the new drum corps, the women's section. Lucia roped me in but it's actually good fun.'

She stopped. Tom's face had hardened at the mention of the movement. How idiotic of her to gabble like that. He checked his watch, then stood up.

'Perhaps it's best if I write to you first, once I know where I'm based,' he said. 'Can you give me your address?'

She hesitated. Yes, it was the fairest way. If he had her address, he held the cards. It would be her turn to suffer and wait. Because there would be more suffering, she knew that now. She could burn anything she liked, but she could not simply forget him.

'I don't have a pencil, I'm afraid.'

'Just tell me. I'll remember.'

As he repeated the address, despair invaded her body like a terrible sickness. She realized she had been picturing a future with Tom – a quiet wedding in the register office, a modest little house in Lewisham – when of course all she could hope for was a room in Lucia's flat, a narrow single bed and the endless frightening nights waiting for the crying to begin . . .

'You're living with your mother?'

The question surprised her somehow. To think he knew so little. 'No, I'm sharing with Lucia. You remember her?'

'Oh, yes.' He gave a sarcastic laugh. 'It was Lucia on Aldwick beach, wasn't it, took all the credit when you saved that little lad from drowning?'

Hazel nodded. She had forgotten entirely about the boy, the way he had dragged her down, the horrible panic as the seawater closed over her head. She felt again the weight of the water, the sensation of being crushed. 'I believe Lucia was there that day, yes. She's been very good to me.' *Very generous*, she was going to add, but that might set Tom thinking, might make Hazel sound as if she was desperate or needy, and then he might start asking questions. No, she must attempt to be breezy. She stood up beside him and stuck out her right hand.

'Very best of luck in Spain,' she said. 'I'll wait for your letter.'

They shook hands, his fingers warm and firm around hers, and she felt the shock of contact as their eyes met again.

'I must be mad,' he said, and walked away.

21

Housework was her only release, and Bea embraced it with vengeful energy. She lifted a cushion from the fireside chair, plumped it with a punch and dropped it back on the seat. Kicking away the footstool, she rolled up the front-room rug, hung it outside over the washing line and walloped it with the carpet beater. Dust clouds billowed into the sky. She took a hankie from her housecoat pocket, sneezed and blew her nose. She thought she had finished crying, but the dust had set her off again.

She blamed herself. It was her fault because she had brought Tom up to be interested in politics, to stand up for what you believed in. Now – God knows how – he'd decided that he believed in Karl Marx and the communist claptrap. Months, this had been rumbling on, but when the trouble started in Spain he began bringing home the *Daily Worker*, and as they sat reading after tea he would hold the paper up to his face, muttering over Franco and the poor Republicans and what he called the scandal of non-intervention. He tried to start arguments about Spain, but she and Harold had agreed they wouldn't rise to it. She couldn't bear the house to become a battle zone. 'It's a hot-headed phase he's going through,' Harold said. 'Best thing is to humour him.'

But that was August and now it was October, and Tom's mind was made up. He was going.

He'd announced his intentions on Monday, after they'd finished their tea and Mr Frowse had gone out for his evening walk up to Blackheath. Tom insisted that no amount of pleading would prevent him; in fact it would only make him more determined. Bea wondered what she could have done to make him hate her so much that he would volunteer to fight for another country's war, when all she had wanted was to protect him from becoming a soldier.

'You're only eighteen,' she said. 'You're too young.'

He told them about a boy called Ronnie Burghes who was already out there, and he was only seventeen. Burghes's mother was a communist, he added, and *she* supported her son all the way.

Bea had cried then. What chance did she have in the face of such wickedness? Tom had crumpled a little, tried to comfort her. He'd held her hand and said he was truly sorry, but it was something he had to do. She couldn't bear him to be tender; that was worse. If he felt a scrap of genuine love or tenderness towards her, he wouldn't be going at all.

Bea left the rug airing on the line and went inside to reheat the mince. Harold would be home at any moment. She held the match to the gas and watched the flames leap into a ring of fire. It was too cruel, she thought. Just when Harold had a job back at the factory and life was looking up, Tom had ruined everything with his fixation on Spain.

She tasted the mince and added another spoonful of salt. Perhaps it was just talk and he wouldn't go after all. And how would it look at the branch? Her own flesh and blood fighting for the Reds? She'd keep it quiet for as long as she could, but it wouldn't be easy. *Please*, she prayed silently. *Please, God, let him change his mind.*

The back door opened and Harold came into the kitchen. He was carrying a large brown-paper bag.

'Thought these might cheer you up,' he said, putting the bag down on the table.

'Biscuits?'

'Bourbons included.'

She was holding a wooden spoon. She didn't know whether to take a swipe at Harold or to strike her own head with it. She took a deep, shuddering breath. Stirred the mince.

'Lovely day,' he said. 'Been busy, I see.' He nodded towards the garden where the beaten rug hung on the line.

Something bubbled and shrieked inside her. And when she spoke her voice was strangled, high-pitched. 'You think a bag of broken biscuits will cheer me up? Make things right?'

He looked down at the biscuits. 'I didn't mean it like that, Bea. I just thought . . .'

Tears sprang again to her eyes. Her head swam and the anger seemed to drain from her. She didn't have the strength for a fight. 'He's going, Harold. Our boy. He's going.' She let the spoon drop into the pot and sat down hard on the kitchen chair. 'Maybe there's still a way to stop him. Speak to him again, can't you?'

'I can give it another go, love. But it's like he said. The more we try to persuade him, the more determined he'll be. Give him a few weeks and he'll soon grow sick of it. He'll be home and we can get back to normal.' He chuckled. 'We might even find it funny in years to come—'

'What?' She raised her voice. 'Funny? You actually think

this could ever be—' She shook her head. 'I've heard it all now. You promised you'd love him the same, Harold. You promised. But you can't. How can you? Oh, I knew it would come home to roost in the end. This pain –' she slapped a hand to her heart – 'I swear it will kill me. And in you come with your bag of biscuits . . .'

She began to unbutton her housecoat, fingers clumsy, head shaking. She would go out this minute, take a walk around Manor Park, let Harold serve up his own dinner. Harold stepped forward and put his right hand on her shoulder. As her trembling fingers struggled with the last button, there was the sound of footsteps on the stairs. They turned in surprise.

'Mr Frowse?' asked Harold under his breath.

Bea shook her head. Mr Frowse always had a meal at his work canteen. He would have said if he was coming back for dinner.

The kitchen door opened. Tom stood with a bulky envelope in his hand. He looked pale as milk. 'Just some paperwork I needed,' he said, lifting the envelope. 'I forgot to take it this morning.'

Bea wiped her face but she knew it would be red and puffy and Tom would see that she had been crying. Had he heard their argument? She tried to recall exactly what had been said, but her brain felt flat and dead. She was so tired.

'Have some dinner, will you?' she said, taking three plates from the rack. 'I'm just serving up.'

'I can't. Sorry. Work's busy this afternoon.'

'Suit yourself.' She slid one plate back. It cracked against another and a flake of chipped china dropped onto the drainer.

'See you tonight then.' He nodded and disappeared.

Bea looked into the garden at the yellowing leaves drooping from the Bramley. What did it matter if she was outside at Manor Park or inside eating dinner with Harold? Tom would be going just the same. She took the cutlery from the drawer and laid up for two.

The morning after he left for Spain, Bea picked through the large cardboard box on the landing. Outside, a church bell was tolling a funeral, each low note measuring out another endless second. She wondered about the mourners inside the church and whether their grief could be as deep and as wretched as her own.

'I've sorted through my room,' he'd said. 'Some of the stuff might do for a bazaar. If not, put it out for the bins.'

She took each item from the box: comic books; a wooden boat without a mast; his old Boy Scout uniform. A bazaar? Unthinkable. She would keep the lot. There'd be room for another box under their bed, Tom's things pressed up against Jack's.

His room was cold with November air. She wiped a little condensation from inside the window, held damp fingers to her lips. Moisture from his own breath. What had he decided to keep, she wondered? His collection of birds' eggs was still on the shelf. She took down the wooden box and opened it. The eggs were nestled in their beds of cotton wool, and below each one Tom had recorded the name and the date and the place where the egg had been found. The last was a bullfinch egg. *Aldwick Bay, Sussex, July 1935.* Their summer holiday at the blackshirt camp. It was around that time he went on the turn. What had happened to change him so completely? She picked up the egg and held it in the palm of her hand, amazed at its weightlessness. As she replaced the egg she saw there was an envelope tucked into the side of the box, almost hidden by the fluffy white layers. She slid the envelope out. Blank. Opening the unsealed flap, she drew out a single sheet of white paper. It was dated last year, *September 18th*, and it began, *My only love Hazel.*

No, she mustn't read it.

Bea replaced the letter and put the box back on the shelf. She sat on the edge of Tom's bed. He had pulled over the bedspread but the linen was rumpled underneath. She ought to strip the sheets this morning. Give everything a thorough clean.

Anger rose, tight in her throat. It seemed to come in waves, back and forth like a tide. When the tide was out, she felt only emptiness and grief. When it rushed in, her body swirled with such fury she felt giddy. Bea twisted a strand of thread on the tasselled bedspread and looked up again at the box of birds' eggs. Why should she bother with niceties and respect when Tom had shown her neither? She would read the letter, yes, she'd read it now. She snatched the box down from the shelf and pulled out the envelope.

> *My only love Hazel,*
> *I've thought about nothing else. Why didn't you meet me that night? Did you get my notes, the letter? I've tried to work out how I might have given offence or whether I did or said something that changed your mind. If you would only explain, then at least I could understand. Until then, nothing can sway me. I think you are the most beautiful girl in Aldwick and the world, and I love you.*
> *Tom*

A girl in Aldwick? Who on earth could she be? There was no one called Hazel that she could remember at the camp.

Bea read the letter again. Well. If this Hazel wasn't at the camp, she must have been an outsider, a local from the village. Perhaps she was the one who put the communist ideas into Tom's head. It made sense, the timing was right. She was to blame! Bea wished there was an address on the envelope, because if there had been, she would take the train down to Sussex and have it out with Hazel and her family. No doubt Hazel was at the heart of the whole Spain calamity. He was trying to impress her, prove that he was true to her and true to the cause. Oh, it all made sense now. Bea sat on the bed and let the letter float down to the bedspread. A queer calm washed over her. If it was all for a girl, surely there was more chance he'd see sense, once he'd accepted that she didn't want him and no amount of bravado would win her over? Yes, that was it. He'd acted impulsively because he had a broken heart, and soon it would mend and he'd be home. Now she wished desperately that she had found the letter sooner: she could have talked it through with Tom, and that might have been enough to keep him in London. Then again . . . better this way. Let him come to the decision himself.

She tucked the letter back into its place and looked again at the untidy bedclothes. Poor boy. To think of him lying there, lovesick. When he came home she'd make more effort to understand him and in time they would become great friends again, just as they always had been.

22

He'd palled up with a chap called Jacob, a ruddy-faced clerk with a thespian bent who claimed to be bound for theatrical glory until the Spanish cause beckoned. Jacob was partial to poetry: he kept volumes by Charlotte Mew and Francis Thompson in his knapsack, and he often quoted lines from poetry or plays that Tom vaguely recognized from English lessons at school.

They'd met in a Newhaven cafe, sailed together on tourist tickets, then taken the train from Dieppe to Paris where French comrades were waiting. In Paris they were given their itinerary. They would journey into Spain with a band of fellow volunteers – Americans, Mexicans and Australians. *We few, we happy few*, said Jacob.

A small bus rattled them over the border into Spain. As Tom looked out of the grimy window at the snow-topped peaks of the Pyrenees, he thought how proud Bill and Petra would be to know he was finally here. Was that why he'd done it, to prove to Bill that he was a serious communist, that his blackshirt days were truly over? Bill had been doubtful when Tom first said he wanted to go to Spain. But once he was certain of Tom's commitment he'd helped him get the necessary papers – a backdated union membership card and a letter from a Communist Party stalwart to vouch for his trustworthiness and dedication to the cause. Dedication – yes, he was proving that all right! There could be no more ribbing about his fascist past after this. Tom remembered the trace of envy he had seen in Bill's eyes when he went up to Limehouse to say farewell. 'I'd be coming with you, comrade, if it wasn't for this.' Bill stretched out his hand and rested it on Petra's swollen belly. She'd smiled and clasped her husband's hand. 'Please be careful, Tommy,' she'd said, then stepped forward to kiss his cheek. Tom turned away so that they couldn't see the blush creeping up his neck.

The bus left them in a tumbledown village, where locals gave solemn clenched-fist salutes and girls handed out mugs of strange coffee and shrivelled oranges. A lorry drove them on to the barracks at Figueras. Uniforms, of sorts, were issued. The next morning they climbed back into the lorry and travelled south in convoy to the training camp at Albacete. They hadn't been at the camp long when the ¡*Avión!* whistle sounded and they were shouted at by a furious Spanish corporal for failing to take cover. Tom pulled Jacob down, diving just as the planes appeared overhead. Daring to look up, one cheek planted into the cold wet earth beside a water trough, Tom saw that they were German aircraft, Junkers and Heinkels heading north. He thought of the girls with the oranges, the white terrier pup that had bounded by their sides.

The barracks were full, so they were to build their own makeshift shelters from pine branches. They worked together – Tom, Jacob and two miners from Derbyshire – and when it was finished their four-man shelter was surprisingly welcoming, the straw palliasses snug against each other, a space behind the head of each for their scant belongings.

'How long do you think we'll be here?' Tom asked one of the Derbyshire men.

'Fortnight at least.' He took a screw of tobacco from his breast pocket and began to roll a smoke.

Jacob whistled. 'We'd better make ourselves at home.' He paused, and Tom imagined that his comrade was searching for some apt line, but evidently none would come.

Tom was woken from a dead sleep by the call of a bugle. His eyes flew open and he was startled not to see the white canvas of a bell tent. The pine-branch roof sent his mind into a spin. Where was he? Where were Fred and Jim, where was that rough bastard Beggsy? He turned to one side and saw the back of Jacob's head, and a jolt of fury shot through him. For pity's sake. He'd trekked all those miles across Europe and still the blackshirts claimed him!

At the water trough he splashed his half-naked body, trying to cleanse the memories of Sussex that had plagued him afresh these past few weeks. It was Hazel's fault, asking to meet up at St Paul's that afternoon, looking so sad and beautiful as she offered her half-baked apology. Seeing her again had dragged everything up, and now the ache from last summer was as keen as it ever had been. How foolish to say he'd write! He'd honour his promise of course – he wouldn't be able to stop himself – but then he'd be the one waiting again. Waiting and waiting and never knowing.

'Oh, that this too, too sullied flesh . . .' said Jacob, rubbing his skin with a tatty flannel.

'Speak for yourself,' said Tom.

Jacob threw the flannel at him and they might have wrestled like schoolboys had not the squat *cabo* been standing on the other side of the trough, surveying his latest recruits with a weary frown. They fell silent, and Tom heard the drumming of a woodpecker in the pines just beyond the camp. He looked up to see another bird circling high in the cloudless sky; it was some kind of raptor, most likely an eagle. The *cabo* might know the name of the bird, but Tom wouldn't dare ask. For the first time he felt homesick: to be in a country where the birds were a mystery. His ignorance unsettled him more than he thought possible.

After breakfast a British commander appeared on the parade ground to brief the new arrivals. A fresh consignment of rifles was on its way, he said. Full training would be given – target practice, skirmishing, trench digging, grenade throwing. In rest periods there would be political lectures from the battalion commissar. All men were encouraged to write home. 'Not just to your loved ones but to your local parties, your MPs and your newspapers,' said the commander. 'We must keep the cause in the public eye.'

Tom listened carefully. He'd write home all right. But it wouldn't be simply a letter to the *News Chronicle*, it would be a full-blown report. Mr Crow knew he was out here, had even wished him luck on his last day. 'Keep in touch,' Crow had said, and Tom wouldn't let him down. He'd already been promoted from messenger to copyboy. If he could write some decent stuff out here, get a piece published, he might be given a chance as a reporter once he got back home.

'Make no mistake –' the commander's voice was grave now – 'this is a dangerous war, a lethal war, and many loyal comrades have already laid down their lives. But we have something that Franco's forces will never have. We have democracy and freedom, and above all, we have the will of the people on our side!'

The recruits cheered and raised their fists into the air.

'Written to your mother yet?' asked Jacob. They had finished another game of cards, and the Derbyshire boys had drifted off in search of more wine.

'Not yet. You?'

'She thinks I'm acting in Paris,' he laughed. 'Suppose I'll have to own up sooner or later. What did you tell your lot?'

'The truth.' It hadn't occurred to Tom to lie to his parents. But Jacob was an actor, so presumably he'd be good at spinning a line. 'Might have been kinder to lie, now I think of it,' added Tom. 'The old girl wasn't best pleased.'

'I'll bet. And what about sweethearts? Someone pining for you back in Lewisham?'

He thought of Jillie and her big pleading eyes, Jillie plucking at his shirt and begging him not to go to Spain.

'Her name's Hazel,' he said, closing his mouth in surprise.

'What's she like?'

Well, he'd said it now. And what a thrill it was to speak her name aloud! Hazel, Hazel.

'Ginger Rogers. But from Bognor.'

Jacob laughed. 'You're lucky then. I had a fiancée but . . . it wasn't to be. *For Fate with jealous eye does see Two perfect Loves, nor lets them close: Their union would her ruin be, And her tyrannic power depose.*' He pulled a piece of straw from his palliasse and put it between his teeth. 'Marvell.'

'Perhaps it's easier not to have anyone,' said Tom, though he realized as he spoke that he was wrong. Love was painful, but it was a pain you had to bear. It was a pain that meant you were alive.

The shelter felt colder that night and Tom found it difficult to sleep. His palliasse butted against the sloping timber wall, and a keen east wind blew in through the gaps. Tomorrow he'd stuff up the holes with twigs and pine leaves. He wished he'd drunk more wine; Jacob and the Derbyshire pair had downed flask after flask, and they seemed to have drifted off without any trouble. Queer the way they let you drink at the camp. It was the Spanish way, he supposed. Wine was like water.

He turned onto his back and looked at the starlight blinking through the shelter roof. Tom wondered whether it might get boring at the camp if they were stuck here for weeks. There was nothing much to do until the rifles arrived, and nothing much to write yet for the *Chronicle*. He decided that tomorrow he would write his letters home. One for Jillie – a brief note would do, she wasn't much of a reader – one for Hazel and one for his mum and dad.

Something was nagging at his brain but he couldn't pin it down. A scene at Boone Street, a conversation with his mother. No, not a conversation, an argument he'd overheard. He'd been creeping down the stairs with some papers that Bill was waiting for. His mum was agitated. *You promised you'd love him the same, Harold.* And then something about coming home to roost. What was coming home to roost? She was rambling, upset about Spain. In truth she'd become a little hysterical.

He pulled the thick blanket tighter around his body. He'd been so determined and bloody-minded before he left; there'd been no space in his mind for guilt. But now, when he thought of his mum, his conscience got the better of him. Still, there was nothing he could do about it while he was here. Best to put Boone Street out of his mind. Silently he began to list his egg collection in alphabetical order. He was asleep before he reached the jay.

23

How quiet the house was without Mrs Waite. Francine heard a *tap-tap* and listened – someone knocking at the door? – but it was only a hot-water pipe clicking in the bathroom. She sighed and drew a line of black kohl under her right eye. The skin puckered and dragged.

When her lips were done she picked up the postcard that was propped against her dressing-table mirror. It was a picture of the Grenadier Guards leaving Buckingham Palace. She turned over the card and read the message again. *Just another note to let you know we are well and happy and there is no need to worry. I will be in touch properly soon. Love, Hazel.* No mention of the letter Francine had sent, no apology for failing to meet her that Sunday at the Tate. Still, *Love* was an advance on the previous two *Regards*.

What on earth would she do with herself today? She lay the postcard down and reached into her jewellery box, tilting her head to clip on an earring. She combed her hair and arranged the curls to mask the grey strands that had begun to appear at her temples. A colour rinse would solve that: she reminded herself to speak to her hairdresser. There. At least she would be presentable if anyone should call.

Downstairs, she drifted into the kitchen. How she hated

these dark November mornings. There was a thin band of light to the east but it had a cruel edge to it, like the pale glint of marble in a cemetery.

Mrs Waite's parting gift two days earlier had been a pork casserole, *Best with mash*. There was a full sack of King Edward's in the garage, she'd added. The casserole remained untouched on the cool shelf; Francine had lifted the lid once, and the sight of the grey meat entombed in tomato-tinged fat had made her nauseous. Instead she had snacked on wrinkled apples and overripe Conference pears, thin slices of Cheddar layered on crackers. Well, she would be in London again at the weekend. Perhaps, once back with Charles, her appetite would improve.

Not that there would be a great deal of time for dining. So much to do! If Charles wasn't too busy with appointments he might come flat-hunting with her and with luck, she would be able to move by the end of the month. Francine tried to feel excited. After all, she would not be sorry to leave Aldwick; it was especially soulless during the winter, apart from the tolerable fortnight of gaiety over Christmas.

Christmas. What on earth would she do this year? Charles would be with Carolyn at their Gloucestershire house. Harriett and Jeremy would be in Highgate with their children. Happy families gathered together – she couldn't possibly impose. Paul with Adriana in Paris. She thought of Edward and immediately dismissed the idea; she would not be welcome. Her brother's life was a mystery to her. She had tried, over the years, to maintain a friendship with him. When she telephoned he would answer with a breezy 'Well, he*llo*!', delivered in high camp as if the caller might be some exotic thespian friend – Noël Coward himself, perhaps, ringing to suggest a weekend in Monte. And then she would say,

'Darling, it's Francine,' and the response would be a flat 'Oh.' His voice became dull and ordinary, and she was always sorry, because she didn't mind the camp, couldn't care two pins how he chose to live his life or whom he took as a lover. Why should it matter at all, especially now that their parents were dead? There was no family reputation to protect, no one who might disapprove.

Christmas on her own in a cheap London flat. It would be somewhere dismal, she supposed, like Shepherd's Bush or Hammersmith. East London was unthinkable and south . . . Unless she considered Barnes or Wimbledon, but really one might as well be living in the suburbs. If Paul could only get the tenants out of the Bloomsbury flat, but even when that happened he insisted the place must be sold. She'd have her share in the end, he promised, and she trusted his assurances. But right now everything was horribly uncertain.

She pictured the type of place she could afford: a cramped third-floor flat in a Georgian terrace, a shilling-in-the-slot meter and a communal hallway. Christmas Day alone with a plate of cold ham and a bottle of cheap wine chilled on a window ledge.

From the fruit bowl she took a small pear and placed it on the chopping board. Why should she spend Christmas Day alone? She had a daughter, for heaven's sake, and she would find her and they would enjoy Christmas together. She sliced into the pear and cut it into quarters, licking the sweet juices from her fingers. Yes, she would write again, and this time her letter would be more conciliatory. Of course she'd have to back down over the baby, accept that Hazel would not take the obvious route, the sensible route, and that she was determined to shackle herself to a fatherless child and end her life before it had even begun. Somehow

– she did not know how – Francine would have to swallow that and pretend in her letter to be happy for Hazel.

The next day she began to sort through the packing cases in the attic. Edward had wanted nothing to do with their dead parents' belongings. Knick-knacks, he called them. They both knew that anything of real value was long gone – sold to pay off her father's City debts. For three years Francine had tried to ignore the cases sitting up here in the box room, but now the job simply had to be done.

In one corner Francine made a pile of the few things she thought might interest the antiques dealer: a collection of paperweights; two crystal ashtrays and a bronze *pétanque* set. There was a hideous green vase that her mother had always loved – Chinese, probably – but it had been chipped years ago and the restorer had botched the repair.

The final chest contained books – a set of Shakespeare plays and various volumes of Victorian poetry. Francine decided she would keep these for the new flat: books always helped to warm a room. The chest was almost empty now. Delving between the screwed-up pages of newspaper, she pulled out a foolscap box, something she'd used to store sketches and letters when she was a girl. It had been hidden at the back of a drawer in her childhood bedroom; she must have left it behind when she went to Paris. Francine unwound the string fastener and opened the lid. There was a watercolour of the bridge at Lostwithiel and a pencil drawing of a cat. More sketches, some postcards, a programme for *A Midsummer Night's Dream*. As she leafed through the programme a small blue envelope slid out.

She unfolded the two sheets of notepaper. It was not so much a letter as a short essay, dated *August 6th 1910*. Underneath the date was an underlined title: *A Confession*. Then: *Ever since your visit last summer I have been in a kind of agony. Have you guessed?*

Had she guessed? She had suspected – hoped – but she had not been sure.

When they'd arrived that summer Charles had been his usual unwelcoming self, slouching in the hall against the yellow-striped wallpaper, scowling at his baby brother Lawrie when he toddled in tooting his little wooden whistle.

That night she had been sitting at the dressing table staring at her reflection when she saw the blue envelope slide underneath her door. She smiled as she read it, and afterwards she lay on her bed, inhaling the scent of Mrs Lassiter's roses which drifted in from the open window.

By morning she was breathless, too nervous, almost, to go down to breakfast. When she took her seat and Charles passed her the sugar caddy, her nerves stirred into a fury of excitement. As their parents discussed the news of the day – the latest on the Crippen case, the launch of the battleship *Orion* – Charles touched her thigh under the table. He let his hand rest for a moment, and she crossed her legs, trapping his fingers. Mrs Lassiter pronounced on Crippen's lover. 'She dressed as a boy, they say, but not a soul was fooled. Still, it's hard to feel sorry for any of them. The murdered wife had taken up with a lodger . . .'

'Most unsavoury,' said Francine's father, coughing into his teacup.

Lawrie dropped his bread and began to cry.

Charles smiled as Francine uncrossed her legs.

Would he be amused to see the letter, after so many years? No. It belonged to another time, a summer turned black, a tragedy they had tried so hard to forget. She refolded the paper and slipped it back inside the programme. Lostwithiel was not to be mentioned. Charles lived in the present, and she must strive always to do the same.

24

'Darling, what a beautiful coat.'

Hazel turned and saw her mother. She seemed thinner; her shoulders were swamped by a black fur stole, and her hair had been coloured. The shade was redder than her natural auburn, and it looked peculiarly harsh in the winter sunlight, set off by a mink pillbox hat to which Francine had attached a small spotted feather. She was like a creature in the zoo, an exotic animal that had somehow fetched up in the shadow of Marble Arch.

'Your hair,' said Hazel. 'It's—'

'Just a little tint.' Francine patted the waves around her ear with a gloved hand. 'Do you like it? Anyway, come here. How wonderful to see you at last. And in such a lovely ensemble.'

Hazel accepted her mother's kiss but kept her fingers tight around the handle of the pram. 'Lucia gave me the coat. She says green doesn't suit her.'

'It certainly suits you.' Francine took a slight step back and her face became very serious. 'How are you, darling?'

If she cried she would be furious with herself. She swallowed and looked away for a moment, focusing on a paper bag scudding along the gutter, and opening her eyes wide so that the cold wind could bite. 'I'm very well. I'm enjoying being back in London.'

'I'm sure. And Jasmin?' Francine looked into the pram for the first time. The baby was fast asleep with her plump chin tucked into her neck. 'Oh, that little bonnet!' said Francine. 'Adorable. My goodness, she's grown.'

'Eight months old now.'

'And is she a good baby?'

An impossible question. Jasmin cried at night because she was teething. Did that mean she wasn't good – that she was *bad*?

'Of course. She's absolutely perfect. Fast asleep as you can see – this cold air has knocked her out.'

'Jolly good,' said Francine, then added hurriedly: 'But she'll wake soon? I simply can't wait for a cuddle. Aren't you excited, her first Christmas coming up?'

Hazel thought how painful this must be for Francine, all this pretend cooing, the talk of cuddles and Christmas. She would see what it was her mother wanted and then get back to the flat.

'Let's walk into the park,' Francine suggested. 'Have you travelled far, darling? I still don't know where you're living. You *have* been a dark horse.'

Hazel relaxed her grip on the pram handle as they crossed into Hyde Park. Her mother seemed so harmless: diminished, somehow, with her garish hair and winter-pale cheeks.

'It's a garden flat in Kensington. Just off the High Street.'

'The chances!' said Francine. Her voice was shrill and an elderly woman walking ahead turned to look.

'Chances of what?' Hazel stopped, a ripple of alarm spreading through her body.

'We're almost neighbours. My new flat. It's in Earls Court

– the Kensington side. It must be only a short walk from you. *Quelle coincidence.* To think we came all the way to Marble Arch!'

Hazel couldn't look at her mother. Instead she stared into the pram and saw that Jasmin's eyes had flicked open. Francine's shriek had probably woken her, and now her nose was screwing up and she was about to cry.

'I didn't know you were moving.'

'Your father insists the Aldwick house must be rented. Holidaymakers, seaside breaks, you know? So I found a little flat, for the winter months at least. I picked up the keys just yesterday. There's an awful lot of building work going on at the exhibition hall but I'm told that will finish soon.' She nodded towards Jasmin. 'Oh, the sweetheart. Has something upset her? Look at that, she has your colouring. Pale one minute, puce the next.'

They walked quickly towards a bench under a willow tree. Hazel lifted Jasmin from the pram and her cry quietened as she blinked into the sunlight, reaching a tiny hand towards the swaying canopy of thin branches.

'Did you want to hold her?'

Francine sat down and tossed one end of the stole over her shoulder. 'Of course,' she said, patting her lap. 'Pop her here.'

Wind rushed through the branches, and for a moment Hazel hesitated. She watched a dead leaf spin down from the willow. Francine had done everything she could to obliterate Jasmin from their lives. The appointment in Tavistock Square, the hideous Dr Cutler with her white coat and her weasel words, telling her it would be the work of a moment and no one would feel a thing . . . And later, when Hazel was with Jasmin at the Misses Shaw, Francine had made a point of ignoring her granddaughter. She would bring a green apple and a magazine for Hazel, and disappear after twenty minutes with the excuse of a headache, or a haberdashery order that needed urgent collection, or a train she simply couldn't miss.

Jasmin's breath was warm on her neck. Months had passed since that time – it was possible that her mother had had a genuine change of heart. What was the point in agreeing to the meeting if she wasn't willing to give her a chance? Hazel bent down and put Jasmin on Francine's lap. Jasmin squirmed, turning and reaching up towards the black stole. She grabbed a handful of fur and tugged.

'She's strong,' said Francine. Jasmin smiled and babbled, 'Mamama.' 'And she's speaking already?'

'Not really.'

'But almost. You were a very early talker, darling. *Duck*, at seven months old. Nanny Felix was ever so impressed. You had a duck in the bath every night, you see, painted white with a yellow beak. A present from your uncle Edward. Probably the only present he ever sent . . .' Francine lifted Jasmin upright so that their faces were level and Jasmin's legs bounced down on her grandmother's thighs. Jasmin smiled again, her bottom lip glossed with dribble. 'Two teeth! I expect the nights are hellish?'

'I bought some teething powders.'

'Nanny Felix was all for a tot of brandy but your father wouldn't have it. He was ever so good with you, pacing up and down when Nanny needed a rest. I just didn't seem to have the knack. Does Lucia help out, darling, when the nights are bad?'

'She's marvellous.'

'It's very good of her, I must say. And you plan to stay with Lucia?'

'Of course.'

'Well, now we're neighbours I shall be able to give you a little break every so often. Yes, I shall, shan't I?' She addressed this last sentence to Jasmin, speaking in a girlish baby voice and planting a kiss on her cheek.

Hazel began to cough. She took a packet of cigarettes from her bag.

Francine raised her eyebrows. 'A smoker, now?' She laughed and shrugged her shoulders. 'Perhaps you wouldn't mind sharing? I left my cigarette case at Charles's.' She stood up and settled Jasmin back into the pram, tucking the crocheted blanket around her. Jasmin grabbed at the blanket, poking her fingers through the holes. 'What a sight we shall be, smoking together on a park bench like navvies!'

Hazel lit her mother's cigarette, then her own. Smoke mingled with the icy air, sharp at the back of her throat. Charles was still around, then. She would not have her mother turning up at the flat, calling in whenever she felt like it. Her mother and Charles. There would need to be some kind of arrangement. A regular date. Francine wouldn't like that, she'd say it was a bore, she liked spontaneity, not timetables. But that was too bad. If she wanted to make amends it would have to be on Hazel's terms.

Jasmin began to cry again, arching her back and kicking off the blanket. She would be getting hungry. Hazel looked in the bottom of the pram for the rusks and the cup of milk, but the bag wasn't there. She must have left it on the kitchen table in her hurry to leave the flat.

Francine took a drag from her cigarette and then balanced it on the arm of the bench. 'I almost forgot,' she said, blowing the smoke in a thin plume as she reached into her handbag. She pulled out a tarnished silver rattle and jangled it. 'Sorry it's not polished,' she said. 'I had to let Mrs Waite go, you see. I searched everywhere for the silver cloth but . . . anyway, I thought baby might like this.' Francine leaned across to the pram, shaking the rattle, and Jasmin quietened at the sound of the tiny bell. 'I finally unpacked the cases from your grandparents. I believe this belonged to my mother, and then to me. An heirloom!'

Jasmin reached out and drew the rattle towards her mouth, grazing it with her two bottom teeth. Francine smiled and let go of the handle.

'The tarnish,' said Hazel. Jasmin was gnawing at the rattle as if it were an apple. 'It might make her ill.'

'Oh, you mustn't fuss about that. You'll turn into one of those over-protective mothers. I gather that's all the rage, nowadays. Too much attention is not good for children.'

Hazel dropped the cigarette and stepped on the end with the sole of her boot. So her mother was an expert on babies now? She took a deep breath and stifled a cough. 'It's time I left,' she said. 'Jasmin will want her lunch soon.'

'You're walking back to Kensington?'

Hazel nodded.

'I'd go with you but I promised to meet Charles at Pagani's. Unless you'd like to join us, of course, but I'm not sure –' she waved in the direction of the pram – 'whether they welcome babies.'

There was a pause, a chill between them. A black Labrador bounded up to the willow and began to bark at a squirrel.

'And what about you?' asked Hazel. 'What's your view on babies now?'

'Please, Hazel. Don't use that abrasive tone. We had enough of that—'

'I'm curious, that's all. Why the change of heart?'

'Darling, I just want us to be friends. It's not been easy for me. Have you stopped to think how I've felt, not knowing where you were or what you were doing? Running away like that with Jasmin. The Shaw women were frantic, and as for the poor couple, I'm told it was a terrible shock for them.'

'Doubtless they've found another baby to adopt. An unwanted baby.' Hazel kicked the brake off the pram wheels. It had been a mistake to come. She had been weak and stupid to answer her mother's letter.

'Darling, please wait.' Francine rushed towards her and held on to the pram hood so that Hazel had no choice but to stop. 'I'm so sorry, I didn't mean to upset you. You did what you had to do, I understand that. At least, I'm trying to understand, I really am. And now I've seen Jasmin again, well, she really is marvellous. I'm proud of you, Hazel, truly. I'm proud of you and I'm proud of my . . . my grand-daughter.'

Hazel tried to speak, but a sob rose in her chest with such force that she could not hold it down. Francine embraced her, and Hazel cried into her mother's shoulder until the fur stole was spiked wet with tears.

Jasmin shook the rattle. The wind had dropped away, and the silver bell chimed in the wintry air.

'It's definitely true,' said Lucia. 'He married her in Germany. In Herr Goebbels's drawing room. And it was weeks ago. Just after the Cable Street fiasco.'

Lucia flopped onto the sofa, disconsolate. They had all heard the whispers, but Hazel still wasn't sure whether to believe the story. It didn't matter to her in any case. Lucia was the one who had harboured dreams of being seduced by Sir Oswald and becoming the next Lady Mosley. He was an incorrigible philanderer, everyone knew that, so it wasn't too far-fetched to imagine his eye might fall on a loyal blackshirt girl who was devoting her life to the cause.

'Of course Diana Guinness is terrifically rich, and well connected in Germany,' Lucia sighed.

'Not forgetting her intelligence and dazzling beauty,' said Hazel.

Lucia turned her head sharply. 'Meaning?'

'Meaning nothing.' Hazel tried to laugh but she could see that Lucia had somehow taken offence.

'Philip is forever telling me how beautiful I am,' she said, tipping up her chin with her forefinger. 'And I like to think I have a reasonable intellect.'

Hazel had not yet met Lucia's lover. Philip was a married economist who was an adviser at HQ; he had taken Lucia to nightclubs in Soho which Sir Oswald frequented, and Lucia freely admitted that she spent those evenings trying to catch O.M.'s eye. Once, he had asked her to dance, and pronounced her a 'handsome filly' as she rejoined Philip at his table.

'Of course you are . . . and you do. You're as good as Diana Guinness any day. But if it's true, why are they being so secretive?'

'He doesn't want the press finding out. Diana is very private. If I married Sir Oswald I'd be yelling from the rooftops. Just imagine.' She pushed off her heels and lay back on the sofa. There was still an edge to her voice: it would probably last for the whole evening. 'Get me a cup of tea, would you? I'm shattered. Any thoughts about dinner?'

'You're in tonight?'

She nodded. 'Philip's back in Surrey with the family.'

'There's ham. I could make omelettes, once Jasmin is in bed.'

'Omelettes, yes.' Lucia turned to look at the baby. She was sitting on the rug in front of the fire, playing with the rattle. 'That's a very tinkly toy,' she said. 'It's going right through me. I barely slept last night.'

'It was a gift from my mother.'

'You've seen your mother?' Lucia propped herself on an elbow and frowned. 'You didn't say.'

'I wasn't sure I would be seeing her. I dithered until the last minute.'

'And?'

'We had a walk around Hyde Park. It was bearable. Civilized.'

Lucia was silent for a moment, then her voice softened. 'Please don't tell me you're going back to Sussex? I couldn't possibly live here without you.'

'Of course not. Mother has left Sussex, in any case. She's back in London. Earls Court.'

'So close?' Lucia rolled her eyes. 'She won't interfere, will she, Hazel? I'm surprised you'll have anything to do with her. You said she was demented.'

Had she said that? Yes, she remembered telling Lucia about the scene in the clinic, Francine's refusal to accept that Hazel could possibly want to keep her baby. 'I think she's calmed down. Got used to the idea, I suppose.'

'So long as you're not planning to desert me.' Lucia twisted the ring on her finger. 'We're a good team, aren't we? I couldn't manage without you.'

'I'm not deserting you, Lucia. Where on earth would I go?'

'Quite.' She shivered and rubbed her eyes, child-like, with

the heels of her hands. 'Now be an angel and turn up the fire.'

The kettle took an age to boil. When Hazel carried the tea tray through to the sitting room, Jasmin had crawled closer to the electric fire. Her cheeks were flaming pink and her arm was stretched out towards the metal casing, almost touching the bars. Hazel dropped the tray onto the table, the cups skidding off their saucers as she grabbed Jasmin clear.

Lucia's eyes flew open and she put her hand to her forehead.

'Goodness,' she said. 'I must have dozed off.'

The Saturday post brought a third letter from Tom. The previous two had been short and factual; friendly but not familiar. He made life in Spain sound like an enjoyable adventure, describing the everyday things – the food and the friendships, the strange birds and the scenery. He was still at a training camp, learning drills and tactics. Hazel had responded with similarly light-hearted replies, trying to make something interesting of her life so that he would not be bored. She told him amusing stories about uptight Mr Boyne the office manager, whose right ear turned scarlet when his in-tray filled up, or the girls at work, pretending she had been out to the cinema or to dances with them. Some nights she dreamed she *was* that unfettered person, and when she woke to Jasmin's crying, the familiar dread dropped like a stone in her stomach.

Hazel stood in the cold hallway holding Tom's letter, aware of its weight in her hand. It felt different from the other letters. Heavier. Carefully she opened the envelope. There were three sheets of notepaper; his handwriting wasn't neat and stilted as it had been before, but slanted across the

page in hurried rows. She drifted into the kitchen and began
to read.

Dearest Hazel,

    *Your letter was wonderful but it made me
melancholy. Perhaps I will regret replying in haste,
but you would be surprised how little there is to do
out here, and that is why I have time to think and
write. Truth is, I think about you more than I should,
Hazel. I picture you at the cinema with your friends,
or at the Saturday dance, and I'm ashamed to say I
feel envious to imagine those men lucky enough to be
close to you, to hold you in their arms as I once did. I
know I shouldn't press you, Hazel, but I cannot rest
until I know your thoughts. This politeness is all well
and good but how do you feel about our – what to
call it – our courtship? Were we too young, too rash, is
that why you chose not to keep in touch? Yet you wrote
again after a year, but when we met at St Paul's you
seemed ill at ease. Tell me, did I do something wrong?
If it's some silly thing, easily mended, please, please let
me know and I can put it right.*

    *Maybe this life in Spain is getting to me. I told you
about Jacob, didn't I? Chap loves to spout poetry, he
must be turning me into a romantic. Not that I need
much prompting when it comes to you, Hazel. I only
have to think of that first time I saw you – half saw
you. But even in the dark I knew you were knockout.
It still amazes me, how brave you were to talk to the
stranger crouching on your garden wall in his
pyjamas. I must have looked a prize idiot, but what a
sight for sore eyes you were, standing there, smoking*

your cigarette! I'm getting back into the habit over here, by the way. Not that there's much tobacco about, but what we do have we roll into twig-thin smokes and we count ourselves lucky.

More than anything, I want to see you. I'd come home to London if I could but it's impossible. Deserters are liable to be shot and in any case, I've no intention of deserting. Things might be quiet right now but battle plans are being drawn up. There's talk of something big. We hear such stories about the fascists, pure evil. I believe I should be here, I believe it with every bone in my body . . . but now I'm on to politics and that won't do. It's an odd thing between us, isn't it? But we mustn't let politics divide us. I want to know what's in your heart.

I suppose I should tear up this letter and throw it onto the fire that I'm huddled around. It's getting very cold here now. This morning we woke to a fall of snow.

No, I won't tear anything up. I'll seal this and give it to the clerk. Because really I have nothing to lose. I love you.

Tom

She dragged her eyes from the last page and stared beyond the kitchen window. The rowan tree was rimed with frost, berries red as blood. Tom's words sang in her mind, lifted her heart, and yet her heart could not stay lifted: there was always the answering plunge of despair. How much could she tell him, truly? She wanted to be honest, but to be too honest was to risk losing him completely.

'Is there tea?'

She hadn't heard Lucia come in. Clumsily she folded the letter and shoved it in her skirt pocket. 'I'll make a fresh pot.'

'Heavens, that must have been exciting post. You're bright red!'

'What? Oh, nothing that interesting.'

Lucia sidled up, took her hand from her dressing-gown pocket and tugged one of Hazel's curls, teasing it straight. 'Come on, tell all.'

For once Hazel was happy to hear Jasmin's yell. She jumped up from the chair. 'Honestly, it's just a letter from a cousin. Boring. Sorry, you'll have to make your own tea.'

25

Bea preferred not to go into town when the weather was so wicked, but she couldn't let her branch down. The Christmas bazaar depended on the goodwill of women from the districts, and Lewisham had been tasked with providing items for the knitwear stall. She had been knitting circle-and-flash tea cosies for weeks.

The rain was icy, and the fierce wind meant there was absolutely no point battling with an umbrella. By the time she arrived at Great Smith Street her coat was soaked through and the damp had seeped into her shoes and stockings.

A haughty girl brandishing a clipboard let her in – Bea recognized her from the summer camp and from HQ meetings where she sometimes gave an address. She stared at Bea as if to say, *Look what the cat dragged in*, then took her name and directed her to the cloakroom where she could hang her coat. 'Try not to drip on the parquet,' said the girl. 'We wouldn't want the wood to warp.'

The knitwear stall turned out to be over-staffed, and Bea was asked to help in the kitchen because the leader in charge of refreshments had been taken ill. Bea would have preferred to stay in the main hall, amongst the hubbub of the stalls, but there it was, she couldn't very well refuse.

The haughty girl introduced her to the other kitchen helpers. 'Eleanor, Alexia – this is Mrs Smart. Oh, let's not be so formal. What's your Christian name, Mrs Smart?'

Bea bridled, but tried not to show it; she could be modern, if pushed. 'Beatrice. Bea.'

'Bea. You'll be handy with a dishcloth, won't you, Bea?'

'I've had plenty of experience if that's what you mean.'

'Wonderful. Here's Hazel now.' A blonde girl came out of a storeroom carrying a large pat of butter. 'Hazel, this is Bea.'

Bea looked at the young girls – not one of them more than twenty years old. They seemed the types who'd never washed up a breakfast bowl in their lives, let alone laid on teas for a Christmas bazaar. It was just as well she'd been drafted in.

The clipboard girl – Lucia, she was called – strode off and the one with the butter went back into the storeroom to find a spare apron. Bea realized she'd forgotten their names already. Lucia had thrown her with the Christian-name carry-on.

'You'll have to remind me of your name again,' she said to the blonde girl as she came out of the storeroom.

'Hazel,' she said, handing over the apron.

Hazel. It struck her, then. Hazel wasn't a common name. Bea tied the apron strings and tried not to stare.

By six the bazaar was closed and they had almost finished clearing away. Bea was terribly tired but her heart felt glad as she swept the kitchen floor. Hazel was the girl from Tom's unsent letter, she was sure of it. She was a pretty young thing, and although her face was pale she had a lovely smile. Best of all she'd turned out to be a good little worker, unlike Alexia who'd twice pleaded stomach pains and had disappeared into the cloakrooms just as the queue was at its peak.

Yes, this must be the Hazel that Tom had fallen for. *The most beautiful girl in Aldwick.* Bea found it funny to think she'd had her down as a communist, a communist who'd lured Tom away from the blackshirts, when all along she was one of the party faithful. A member of the women's drum corps, no less.

They'd had a very nice chat at the sink earlier on. Bea washed, Hazel dried. It was an easy way to talk – eyes on the job, a steady rhythm between them as they ploughed through the piles of dull green crockery.

'You're from London?' asked Bea.

'Originally, but we moved to Sussex. And now I'm back in London again.'

At this Bea felt a twist of excitement. She *was* from Sussex, then.

'I was down in Sussex the summer of last year,' Bea said. 'For the blackshirt camp. Near Bognor?'

Hazel paused for a moment, her tea towel wedged into a cup. 'Aldwick Bay. I used to live there.'

'Smashing spot. Perhaps it was your family that came up with the idea, invited Sir Oswald down?'

Hazel gave a short laugh. 'Oh, no. My family aren't supporters. I went to Sir Oswald's talk at the theatre, sort of by accident, and that's how I met Lucia.'

Bea was tempted to mention Tom. She could simply say that her son had talked of a girl called Hazel, and might she by any chance know him? But something had gone on between Hazel and Tom – that was clear from his letter. She'd let him down in some way, for whatever reason, and it might embarrass Hazel if she brought his name into the conversation. Better to keep quiet for now, she sensed, and wait for the right moment.

'So your family has moved back to London?'

Again Hazel hesitated. For all her pleasantness, there was something guarded about her manner. 'I share a flat with Lucia,' she said.

Ah. Bea couldn't help feeling surprised. Hazel was young to be living away from home, sharing a flat with another girl. Perhaps she'd fallen out with her family – they may have disagreed over her politics. There were plenty of families split in that way. Mrs Beggs's brother, a diehard trade-union man, hadn't spoken to his sister in over two years.

'That must be great fun,' said Bea, dunking a sticky plate in the water.

'Yes,' said Hazel quietly.

'And I expect you have a sweetheart?'

'No . . . not at present.'

Hazel pulled a plate from the draining rack and Bea turned to look sideways at the girl. It was unmistakable. There were tears in her eyes, and she was blinking them back as fast as she could, but it was no use because a great fat one had already dropped onto her cheek.

She was a lost soul, poor thing. Bea wished she could do something to help. But it was unlikely they'd meet again soon, not unless Bea joined the drum corps or started coming up to HQ more often. Neither option appealed. But she knew she must somehow stay in touch with Hazel. It was clear to her now that there had been a mix-up or a misunderstanding between Hazel and Tom. She seemed too sweet and sincere to have let him down purposely. Perhaps she, Bea, could set things right between them. It was just a case of treading gently. Smoothing the way, without interfering. What had he written? *If you would only explain, then at least*

I could understand. She could try to understand on his behalf. And then, tactfully, she could let Tom know.

Bea put the broom back into the store cupboard and untied her apron. Now that the idea had taken root, she felt happier than she had since October when Tom announced he was leaving. Surely he'd come back from Spain if he thought Hazel was waiting for him? The winter was getting cold out there, and although she tried to avoid all news of Spain, it seemed the Republicans were struggling. He stayed cheery in his letters, of course, just as Jack had when he wrote from Flanders.

In the kitchen Lucia was holding court, her posh voice echoing off the scrubbed white tiles.

'Takings for the refreshments are good,' she said, clanking coins in a canvas money bag. 'Up on last year. Bric-a-brac is down. Overall a success, but did you see those women haggling over the prices?' She sighed and wrinkled her nose.

'Did somebody let the Semites in?' said Eleanor.

Alexia snorted. 'I thought there was a strange smell at one point. Blasted cheek, coming here.'

Bea flinched. She thought of Mr Perlman and the two frightened children, great-nieces of his late wife, who had arrived from Germany the previous weekend.

'Quite,' said Lucia. 'But apart from that unpleasantness, it was an excellent afternoon. Well done, ladies.' Lucia leaned towards the girls. 'See you on Wednesday evening for envelope duty?'

'Envelope duty?' asked Bea.

'Oh, just a little gathering at my flat,' she said with an airy wave of her hand that made it clear Bea was not included. 'Stacks of members' Christmas cards to address.'

'I'm happy to help,' said Bea.

'You?' Lucia looked at her as if she doubted her ability to write.

Hazel broke the silence. Her cheeks had pinked – at least she had the decency to feel embarrassed, thought Bea. 'That's very kind, don't you think, Lucia?' said Hazel. 'Many hands and all that.'

'Yes, I suppose an extra pair of hands . . . It's Kensington, though. You're from the districts, I gather?'

'I can find my way around town, dear.'

'Of course. We'll look forward to seeing you.'

It was a pig of a journey but she arrived in good time. The flat was on the ground floor of a mansion block, just off High Street Ken, a nice part of town. Bea rang the polished brass bell for Flat 1, and stood waiting on the chilly doorstep for half a minute. She was about to ring again when the door was opened by Hazel, dressed in a velvet evening gown with a green silk corsage pinned to the collar. One half of her hair was styled and curled, the other half frizzed in all directions. A cigarette dangled from her left hand.

'Bea,' she said. 'Please come on through. I'm sorry I look such a sight.'

'Not at all. That's a lovely dress.'

She wondered why Hazel was dolled up, and why her nerves seemed jangly, but there was no need to ask because Hazel began to gabble, all the while standing at the hall mirror fiddling with the corsage between puffs of her cigarette.

'I got completely muddled with my dates,' said Hazel. 'My mother's coming in half an hour. She's taking me to dinner, so I can't help with the envelopes after all. Thank goodness you volunteered. I don't have to feel so guilty.'

Oh, glory, thought Bea. The whole point of the exercise was to get to know Hazel better. Now she was going to be stuck for the evening with Lucia and the other two.

'Not to worry,' she said. 'I suppose you can't let your mother down.'

Hazel smiled and showed Bea into the living room. The girls were sitting at a table where cards and envelopes were stacked in a dozen or more piles. 'Here's Bea, good as her word,' said Hazel. 'Got the hair irons on in the bedroom. Must go.'

Bea took off her headscarf and unbuttoned her coat. No one offered to take her things, and so she laid them on the arm of a settee. She noticed something silver wedged under a cushion. A baby's rattle? Queer.

With her stockinged foot, Lucia nudged out a chair from under the table. 'Do take a seat,' she said. 'We're drawing up a system. You can be R to Z.'

Bea felt in her bag for her fountain pen, marvelling at the manners of these supposedly well-bred girls. She hadn't even been offered a cup of tea. Still, she was here now, and she'd have to get on with the job in hand. At least it was warm in the room, with the heavy brocade curtains drawn and all the bars glowing on the electric fire. Unscrewing her pen lid, she took her section of the list and began to copy out the first address. She was proud of her handwriting – it was better than Alexia's untidy scribble – but then a loud bell sounded and her pen jumped with the surprise, splodging a blob of ink directly on the H of Hillingdon. She reached for the blotting paper.

'The door again!' said Lucia. 'Hazel's mother must be early. Alexia, can you let the witch in?'

Bea's back was to the living-room door. She twisted around

in her seat, ready to smile at the woman as she walked into the room. *The witch.* There was a man beside her. The ceiling light was bright, and the table lamp was burning. There could be no mistaking this couple. Immediately she turned away, staring back down at the envelope, pressing the blotting paper onto the smudge of black ink and praying that Lucia would not suddenly remember her manners and introduce Bea to the visitors.

'Mrs Alexander, how lovely to meet you,' said Lucia. 'Hazel won't be a moment.'

'You must be Lucia?' said the witch. She pronounced it *Looseeya.*

'It's Lucia, actually,' she said. '*Ch.* Italian.'

'Very well.' She sniffed. 'Please don't let us interrupt anything. Just that I thought if I were a little early I might see Jasmin.'

Bea's cheeks blazed. Jasmin? Who might Jasmin be? She wanted to look around the room again – had she missed someone? – but she kept her eyes fixed downwards, her fingers firm on the blotting paper.

'She's fast asleep,' said Lucia. 'I doubt Hazel will want to wake her. Oh, here she is now. Your mother's arrived, with—'

'Charles. Charles Lassiter,' said the man. His heels clicked on the floor as he stepped forward. 'Charmed to meet you, the mysterious Lucia.'

Bea's spine stiffened. She realized she was holding her breath and she exhaled, quietly, quietly, praying again that no one would notice her. This prayer, at least, was answered.

Sleep was impossible. Harold was dozing, sick with a winter bug, a fever that wouldn't go away. He slept on his side without his pyjama top, the skin loose and wrinkled on his back, and she could feel the heat from him creeping along the sheets. In the early hours she slipped out of bed and wandered onto the landing. There was no sound but the slow whirr of the meter wheel in the cupboard. She wished for something shocking and sharp: spears of rain attacking the windowpane; a cat fight; even a dog whining to show that she was not the only creature awake and suffering. It was a cold night but her skin was burning hot. Perhaps she was catching Harold's bug. She would get into Tom's bed. The linen was freshly made up; the sheets would be cool.

There was a time when the memory of Charles was something to savour, a treat Bea might allow herself on those long afternoons when Tom was at school and Harold was working at the factory.

To see Charles again, to be in that warm room with him – it was too much to take in. He looked a little older, of course – the fair hair had darkened, and his skin was weathered – but in essence he was unchanged. Had he noticed her, sitting at the table, gripping her fountain pen so hard that her thumbnail scored the barrel? No, he wouldn't have noticed her, same as he hadn't noticed her in the Aldwick pub, and even if he had he wouldn't recognize her because she looked decades older – transformed into a dumpy sack of a woman whose long shiny hair had become an unkempt bob flecked with suet-grey strands.

Tom's sheets were too hot now. Hot and damp and heavy. She tiptoed downstairs and into the front room. On the mantelshelf was the photograph from Margate – Tom in the middle holding their hands, the wind blowing his fringe across his eyes.

Next to Margate was the snap taken by a street photographer in Greenwich: Harold with his arm draped around her shoulder, a few months after he'd been sent home from the war. They were standing near the river, a barge drifting behind them. They looked happy, and she supposed they were, in a cautious kind of way. Harold's injury was a terrible pity but they were making the best of it. Bea felt she could manage without the act itself, and in any case they could still be close: a kiss and a cuddle and other things she'd never known about in their newly-wed days.

What she couldn't manage was the thought that she'd never be a mother, and it was worse to bear because she'd once come so close, the summer of 1914. Perhaps it was the shock of the war being declared, the worry that Harold or her brother might have to fight, that led to the disaster. The poor scrap was born four months early. She'd caught a glimpse of its tiny body as the doctor wrapped it in muslin and hurried out of the bedroom door. 'A boy or a girl?' she asked the doctor when he came back into the room empty-handed. 'Best not to ask,' he answered. 'Least said soonest mended.' Oh, how she wished that were true.

Later, when Harold was called up, they convinced themselves that losing the baby was a blessing in disguise. All those mothers around the world, driven half-mad trying to cope single-handed. It was hard on the kiddies without their dads around. No, there was plenty of time to start their family after the war. It would happen eventually.

Harold never saw the front line because of his poor eyesight. They had him working as an orderly at a military hospital near Rouen. He wrote letters from his dorm in an old chateau. There were some terrible goings-on, he said, but weren't they lucky that he was safe here, miles behind the line, though often you'd feel the ground shake with the shelling.

Meanwhile Jack was in the thick of it, a gunner in the Royal West Kents. From his postcards you'd think he was on a jolly to Brighton. Bea knew the forced cheeriness meant things were really bad, because Jack was a serious boy in truth. He wasn't given to daft jokes.

Their parents were both dead and Jack wasn't married, so Bea was down as next of kin for her brother as well as for Harold. That meant double dread when she heard next door's terrier barking: the signal that the postman was on his way.

The first letter was typewritten and signed by Jack's C.O. *It is with the deepest regret that I have to inform you . . .* Poor, poor Jack – the sweetest baby brother. Eyes the colour of lightest amber, dimples to melt your heart. She felt the grief might end her. There was only one way of coping, she discovered, and that was to pretend it wasn't true. She collected Jack's things from his Catford lodging house and stored them under the spare bed, ready for the revelation – the stories weren't unknown – that the C.O. had got it wrong, mixed up the identity discs in the chaos of battle.

And then came the telegram. Harold had been injured and he was on his way to a hospital in England. Bea sat on the bottom stair and cried. The injury was grave, they said, but his life was not in danger.

It was not until he came home, just before Christmas 1916, that Harold was able to explain. A patient in the hospital, a young Frenchman, had taken against Harold, something to do with a sleeping draught and Harold not fetching a nurse quick enough, and the patient had somehow hidden a knife beneath his sheets. When Harold came up to his bed to take away a screen, the Frenchman attacked him with the knife, plunged it right into Harold's groin and another cut down his thigh. The patient stabbed himself next, straight through the heart, which finished the job at least, said Harold, because if he hadn't done himself in, it would have been the firing squad.

Bea replaced the Greenwich photograph and went into the kitchen to drink a glass of milk. Moonlight fell through the window onto the table. There was her purse, the coins for the milkman stacked neatly beside it. The old magazine advertisement was still hidden inside, behind a sewn-up tear in the purse lining. *Wives of Wounded Soldiers: Discreet Fertility Service Offered.* She had cut the advert out with kitchen scissors and kept it under the cutlery tray for weeks. Eventually she found the courage to show Harold. He scanned the clipping, then handed it back in silence. 'Is it worth writing off?' she asked. He said he wouldn't object, if it was what she wanted. And so it began.

'Charles Lassiter' was the name he'd given to Lucia. Bea had known him only as Charles. She'd asked the woman who ran the clinic, Dr Cutler, whether it would be possible to arrange a prior meeting, just so that she might have some knowledge of the man before the meeting proper. Dr Cutler said it wasn't usual, and frankly it was inadvisable, but not to worry because she had no doubt that Mrs Smart would find Charles charming, courteous and utterly alive to the sensitive nature of the situation.

They arranged to rendezvous outside a small hotel in Bloomsbury, a short walk from Russell Square station. He would be wearing a red-and-white polka-dot handkerchief in his jacket pocket, Dr Cutler said, and a homburg hat. Bea's heart reared up when she turned the corner into Bedford

Place and saw a young man in a homburg leaning against the hotel's iron railings. It had to be him. He turned to look at her, tipped his hat, and then it was too late to change her mind.

They shook hands and she smelt a drift of citrus-scented cologne. 'Charmed to meet you, Mrs Smart,' he said, as the concierge held open the door into the lobby. They went into the bar, and to her surprise no one took any notice of them. She thought she would be shown up in her home-sewn evening dress, but it wasn't such a flashy place after all, and of course the war had kept everyone to a certain level. She had her mother's necklace, at least, and the moonstone earrings that Harold had brought back from France, wrapped in a twist of soot-blackened newspaper. Her long hair was piled into a bun, and her dress was laced at the back, pulled tight against her curves. Perhaps it was even possible that Charles found her attractive.

A port and lemon was what she'd normally have, but when he suggested gin and vermouth, she nodded and said that would be lovely. He chatted about his travels in Europe, and the war, and how it might be over soon, now the Americans were in. His manner was gentlemanly, almost condescending, yet she was certain he was younger than her, twenty-six or twenty-seven, perhaps. Bea wondered why he wasn't fighting and Charles must have read her thoughts, because he briefly mentioned something about war work – an administrative role, he said. Rather confidential. Never once did he ask a question about her own life. That was part of the understanding, and she was glad of it.

The room was on the second floor. She was breathless when they reached the top of the stairs, her blood rushing with the gin and the strangeness of the evening. He unlocked the door and pushed it wide. When Bea hesitated he smiled: a kind, encouraging smile. She met his eyes and stepped over the threshold.

Quickly she glanced around, taking in the large bed with its cream embroidered linen, the vase of long-stemmed lilies in front of the fireplace, the silver ice bucket in which stood a bottle of uncorked wine.

'I took the liberty,' said Charles. 'Trebbiano?'

She felt tipsy already yet she nodded, hopeful that one more drink would offer the courage she needed. He poured two glasses and handed one to her. Bea stepped towards the window. He followed and stood at her side, parting the delicate lace curtains to reveal a tall chestnut tree that filled the hotel garden. The branches were so close to the window, it was almost possible to reach out and touch the May blossom. Bea's eyes were drawn to the pink flush at the base of the ivory petals. Such pretty flowers; she had never noticed their beauty before.

She took a sip of wine. 'Spring is my favourite season,' she said.

Charles made no reply, and she knew that the time for talking was over.

Afterwards, they had lain in the bed for almost an hour. Charles put two pillows under her thighs. 'Tried and tested,' he explained, 'Helps the fellows on their journey.' She blushed at the reminder that this was something Charles had done goodness knows how many times before. It hadn't felt like that, earlier. It had felt as though they were truly intimate. The way he had touched and kissed her . . . it had been all she could manage not to cry out. If this was an act he was a terrific actor, and she did not regret one penny of the ten pounds she had paid to Dr Cutler.

She sat up and drank the last of her wine. Charles reached out and touched the lobe of her ear. 'Beautiful earrings,' he said. 'French?'

Bea nodded. 'My husband brought them back—' She blushed again and bit her lip. It seemed wrong to have mentioned Harold, yet after all he was the reason they were here. She pictured him for a moment, sitting at home with a glass of Watney's and the evening paper, trying to ignore the ticking of the clock.

'Well, your husband is a lucky man,' said Charles. 'And I have no doubt that you would make the most wonderful mother. Here's hoping, eh?'

She nodded, and felt her throat swell with emotion. A baby. Please God, a baby. It was likely, surely, after all Dr Cutler's talk of dates and optimum times, her temperatures and her charts. Everything had been so precise.

Bea tore open the purse lining and took the advert from its hiding place. She'd kept it all these years, just in case, but in the event she'd never dared to suggest a second visit; a brother or a sister for Tom. Standing over the sink, she lit a match and touched the flame to the corner. The paper burned yellow, a sudden star tilting at the moonlight, fading quickly and fluttering to ash.

It was too awful to contemplate, the thought of Tom getting involved with Hazel's family and finding himself in a room with Charles. Lucia had gossiped that Mrs Alexander was going through divorce proceedings. Charles was the woman's beau. It wasn't fanciful to imagine he might become Hazel's stepfather.

JULIET WEST

In the morning she would write to Tom. She'd mention in passing the bazaar, and the envelope night, how she'd got to know a few of the blackshirt girls, and that all those rumours of loose morals amongst the young women at HQ were certainly true. She composed the sentences in her head: *A girl called Hazel Alexander is the most notorious. She's carrying on with a district commander (married), and by all accounts there are two other poor unfortunates dancing to her tune . . .*

That should do it. Any fond thoughts he might still have of Hazel would be well and truly squashed. It was harsh but it was necessary. Especially if, as she suspected, the girl had a baby and goodness only knew about the parentage.

She was sorry for Hazel, really she was. But as she rinsed the ashes down the plughole, she whispered, 'It must not happen.' Tom and Charles must never meet.

If that meant leaving the movement, well, she would leave.

Whatever it took to protect her boy, that is what she would do.

215

26

'Take cover!'

Armistead's shout echoed in Tom's ears as he flung his body flat to the hillside. Take cover – what a bloody joke that was. How was a scraggy olive tree going to protect him from Franco's machine-gun fire? Their own machine guns were useless – he cursed again to think of whoever it was who'd loaded the cartridge belts with the wrong ammunition. Six hours they'd been on this ridge, attempting an advance. Every time they moved a few yards down into the valley, they lost another ten or twelve men. Three men for every yard, he reckoned. He'd tried to help his comrades, dragged one lad behind a blackened bush and gave him water, but the blood pooled in a red halo, and his eyes closed before he could even swallow. There was no saving him.

Yet Tom had survived this far. Jacob too, and now night was falling and Armistead told the company to dig in. It was February and the ground was hard, but they made a foxhole of sorts and collapsed, back to back, hugging their legs, resting their foreheads on their knees.

Jacob's voice had dulled. There was no longer any humour in it, no lines of poetry. 'Wrong bloody bullets,' said Jacob.

Tom could feel the back of Jacob's head, slowly shaking from side to side. 'Wrong bullets.'

'We'll be all right,' said Tom. 'New ammunition's on its way. Reinforcements.'

''S'good . . .' His voice tailed into sleep.

The valley was almost silent, just the occasional sniper shot into the darkness and the faint sound of the Jarama river rushing below. Tom screwed his eyelids shut. This was what he'd wanted, wasn't it? Proper action, a real show? He'd been desperate to get out of the training camp. They'd spent too long there, long enough for those letters to arrive. Long enough for Hazel to make a fool of him once more.

He should never have written that daft declaration of love. Oh, she'd replied quicker than he could have hoped, and she swore she loved him too. There were complications, she said, but she would explain everything once he was home. Complications? Wasn't everything that was worth fighting for bound to be complicated? They could overcome any obstacles, he was certain of that. For a fortnight he treasured her letter, hurled himself back into love with a kind of violence that gave him strength. Hazel's love was something to fight for, and when he sang the 'Internationale' after morning drill he felt boundless as the eagle which circled above, sovereign of the skies.

Christmas at Albacete had been almost enjoyable. There was a barrel of brandy, chicken stew, chocolate bars and almonds. Tom had a good feeling about the coming year. Battles would be won in 1937. The *Chronicle* would publish his eyewitness reports. He would return home and Hazel would be waiting. His mum and dad . . . well, they would forgive him.

The letter from his mum came on the last day of the year.

Jacob tossed it to him as he crouched in the shelter, polishing his disassembled rifle. He put the rifle back together before opening the envelope. The usual small talk, and then the bullet. *A girl called Hazel Alexander is the most notorious.* He tried not to believe it at first, but it was no use. What reason had he to doubt his own mother? She had no grounds to invent such a story. Of course it was true! He knew for a fact that Hazel was easy – hadn't she given herself in the summer house that stormy night? Kissing him, unbuckling his belt, letting him take her without so much as a murmur of protest. At the time he'd convinced himself it was something more than sex; it was an act of love between them, beautiful and unstoppable – sacred – but now he saw it was nothing of the sort. Not for her, anyway. *By all accounts there are two other unfortunates dancing to her tune.* What an idiot he'd been! At least now he understood the 'complications' she'd mentioned. The complication was that she was a faithless tart.

'Tom!' Jacob was shaking him, kicking him in the back. 'Jesus Christ, Tom, wake up!'

He blinked and scrambled to his feet. The drone of engines from the west was unmistakable. Heinkels, flying low. Where was their air cover, the Russian fighters? The machine guns were no use – they'd have to defend with their rifles. It would be funny if it wasn't so deadly, so pathetically serious. Around him he could see the shadows of men taking up their positions. He could weep at their bravery. Giants, these men, every one. Whatever happened, he would never regret coming here. He would be a communist till he died, a defender of the people . . .

Bombs dropped on the neighbouring hill. The air seemed

to scream before the dull burst of the explosion. Now the planes were overhead, the German gunners strafing. Tom turned as he heard Jacob's cry, saw his body thrown into the air. He crawled, cursing, on his stomach towards the spot where his friend had landed. Jacob's guts were open to the sky, wet and pulsing, coiled like a thrown-down skipping rope. Pages of poetry flapped and scudded over the hard earth and Tom scrabbled to retrieve them, trying to keep the pages flat, the verses true. And then the gunners fired again and there was nothing but darkness.

27

At last Jasmin had started to sleep through the night. She was walking now, toddling around the flat at astonishing speed. Mrs Allen at the nursery said she kept them all on their toes. 'Fanny Fanackapan', was Mrs Allen's nickname for Jasmin, spoken with a half-smile that seemed to mask a grimace.

Edith rarely called at the flat. She was engaged to a banker named Martin and spent all her time on long walks and picnics and boating on the Serpentine. Edith barely gave two hours a week to the movement. If she wasn't careful she'd get her service badge taken away, said Lucia, and then it would be the uniform – not that their uniforms counted for much now they'd been banned in public – and then Lucia would begin a rant about government crooks and the outrageous attacks on civil liberties.

It was a shame about Edith. Hazel had never much liked her, but she'd always been willing to mind Jasmin on drumming nights. Fortunately, the porter's wife from along the road had stepped in. She loved babies, she said, which was lucky because Lucia never seemed able to help out. She'd screwed a bolt to the inside of her bedroom door so that Jasmin couldn't toddle in. Sometimes Hazel wondered whether Lucia would ask them to leave the flat, but there had never yet been any hint. Hazel made sure she was useful: if it wasn't for her, the place would be an awful tip and there'd never be any proper food or a clean pair of drawers.

'Good-ger,' Jasmin babbled, placing another wooden brick atop a wobbly tower.

'Good girl,' said Hazel, looking up from the ironing board. 'Good girl!'

Jasmin laughed and clapped her hands, but her fingers brushed against the tower and the bricks crashed down. She began to wail.

'Shhh, shhh. We mustn't wake Lucia.' Hazel unplugged the iron and lifted Jasmin from the high chair, putting her hand over her mouth to stifle the yell. It wasn't nine yet but perhaps they could have an early walk. Jasmin liked to watch the squirrels in Kensington Gardens, and by mid-morning the older children would begin to arrive at the pond with their little sailing boats.

She opened the larder cupboard to check there was enough milk and bread for Lucia's breakfast, and found a biscuit to keep Jasmin quiet while she tidied the kitchen, emptying the leaves from the teapot and rinsing out her cup. Sometimes Philip stayed on a Friday night, but she was certain that Lucia had come home alone last night. She laid out breakfast things for one.

There was a letter face down on the doormat in the hall, a small creamy-coloured envelope of the kind Tom had used. She snatched it up, but the letter was addressed to Lucia. The postmark was from Germany – it would be from one of the fascists she'd palled up with on her trip to Berlin.

She let the envelope drop back to the floor. Idiot. Tom had not written since December – not for eight whole months – so why would he suddenly write now? It was a good thing, she reminded herself, that the letters had stopped. He must have regretted his outburst of affection, felt overwhelmed, perhaps, by her gushing reply. In any case, the correspondence had been a deception, at least on her part. If he ever came back from Spain, she would have to carry on the lie, the pretence that Jasmin didn't exist, or else she could tell the truth, with every chance then that he would disappear for good. He didn't want to be tied down with a child. Hadn't he told her that when they were first together? He'd shuddered to imagine being stuck in a room with a screaming baby. Perhaps, somehow, he'd got wind of the truth, and that was why the letters had stopped.

Every day she bought a paper and scanned the pages for news of the Spanish war. It was not going well for the Republicans. British casualties were published regularly in the *News Chronicle*, and to date his name hadn't appeared. She even went to King Street once, to the communists' head-quarters, thinking she would go inside and ask if there was any news of Thomas Smart. But she lost her nerve – a black-shirt at Red HQ! – and left Covent Garden with a pound of apples and a bunch of spring violets. On the bus home, she reassured herself that if anything had happened to Tom, there was certain to be gossip at party meetings. A turncoat blackshirt, killed fighting the fascists in Spain? People would crow and say it was just deserts. No, Tom was all right. He might even be back home, in love with some other girl.

It didn't matter. She and Jasmin would manage, because Hazel had a plan. Each week she saved a little money. She'd even stopped smoking, adding the extra pennies to her tin.

Her throat felt better for it, too; she hadn't had a coughing attack in weeks. In two years or so she would have enough money to rent a flat, or a decent-sized room, just her and Jasmin. Pimlico was the plan, somewhere close to work, which meant she would save money on buses and Tubes, and Jasmin could go to the infant school which was close to her office. Two years seemed a horribly long time, but Hazel liked having the goal; it buoyed her on the darkest nights, gave her a focus when she lay in bed trying not to listen to Lucia in the bedroom with Philip, the cries that might have been pain or pleasure and seemed, in some strange way, designed to mock Hazel as she attempted to sleep, alone in her small bed.

It was cloudy but the air was warm. She walked quickly along the High Street towards the Gardens, ignoring Jasmin's pleas to be let down from the pram. 'Down, down!' she cried, kicking out her legs and twisting against the harness. Passers-by smiled sympathetically at Hazel, and as she waited to cross the road, a tall thin woman struck up conversation. 'Little one looks determined,' she said, dipping her head towards the pram. Jasmin quietened at the sight of the woman's old-fashioned hat with its bunches of waxed fruit, the little fake bird stuck with dull black feathers.

'She's desperate to see the squirrels,' said Hazel.

The woman shifted her gaze to the pram handle – to the fingers of Hazel's left hand.

'Your little sister, is it?' she asked.

Dear Christ, thought Hazel, I'm sick of this. To her work colleagues she was a single girl. To the blackshirts she was an abandoned wife and mother. Always playing a part, just to make other people feel better. She was eighteen now, old enough to be her own person, to stand her ground. What would happen if, for once, she played herself?

'My daughter.' Hazel caught the gleam of judgement in the woman's eye and felt a snip of sudden rage. 'If it's my wedding ring you're wondering about, I'm not married.'

The woman jerked her head back as if to deny that she had been ogling Hazel's naked finger, and her eyes darted across the road and up towards Kensington Church Street where a soldier stood sentry outside the army barracks.

'And this is what our laddies fought the war for, is it?' she said. Her soft voice became coarse and loud. 'So that hussies like you could swan about with their –' she hesitated, her lips forming the B and then pulling back to show a ragged line of teeth with sharp brown canines – 'with their *offspring*, and not even an ounce of shame does she show.' The woman was addressing the wider street now, shaking her head so that the bird on her hat seemed to peck and scold in time with her wagging finger.

Hazel stood paralysed for a moment. What had she been thinking, goading the woman like that? She could not muster a response; she wanted only to disappear. Spinning the pram on its back wheels, she began to run, turning right onto Palace Gate and then down Gloucester Road. She almost tripped over a man sweeping litter from the doorway of a pub. 'Mind yourself, darling,' he called. Jasmin thought it was a great adventure and she clapped her hands, screeching 'Mumumumum!' as they raced along the pavement. At the bottom of the road there was a newsagent's shop. Hazel left the pram outside, ignoring Jasmin's shouts. In the shop she bought a packet of Pall Malls, a box of matches and a bar of Fry's.

She gave Jasmin the chocolate and lit a cigarette. She

would smoke it here, on the street corner, in this seedy neighbourhood, because that was where she belonged. The sole of her shoe stuck to the pavement – there was a broken bottle, a dried-up puddle of orangeade, insects crawling at the edges. An ant ventured onto her shoe, her stocking, but she didn't bother to brush it off. She remembered what Charles had told her. She was a slut, a whore.

The air here stank of motor fumes and morning-after booze. She smelt the whisky on Charles's breath, felt his hand gripping the top of her arm, pushing her back into the dark summer house. His clothes were wet from the storm. Soaked through.

He had been spying. Had he seen everything?

She was nothing but a whore, he slurred, and she deserved all she got. If she ever played around with that young lad again he would have him in court for rape. And then he stared at her, silently put a hand to her cheek.

'What about you?' Hazel had asked afterwards. 'What if I told the police about you?'

Charles was quiet for a second and Hazel wondered whether he might have sobered up, whether he might feel any remorse for what he had just done. But then he ruffled her hair and laughed. 'Oh, I don't think the police would believe a silly sixteen-year-old with a crush on her mother's lover. Do you?' His laughter died away and he shook his head in mock-seriousness. 'Imagine the humiliation. You'd be the talk of the town.'

'But—'

'Don't bother denying it. I've seen you looking at me. I know what you've been reading this summer.'

He picked up the book from the floor and placed it on the tea chest.

Hazel wanted to rip the book to pieces. How foolish she had been, to believe van de Velde's words. Charles had revealed the truth to her. Sex wasn't about love and equality. It was about humiliation and pain.

She lit another cigarette and stared down at her daughter. The yellow cardigan was covered in dribbles of chocolate. 'Good girl,' said Hazel, turning her head to blow a stream of smoke up towards the sunless sky.

Ridiculous to think she could ever get a flat on her own, to imagine that she could exist without lies. No respectable landlord would rent a flat to an unmarried mother. She supposed that Charles was right: she was no better than a whore. She needed Lucia. She needed the movement. This was her family and she must be grateful for it.

28

'Tonight?'

'It can't be helped, Frangie. I'd rather spend the evening with you, naturally, but Veronica says this client is absolutely desperate.'

'Aren't they all?'

Charles sighed and reached for Francine's hand across the narrow kitchen table. He had called round to Earls Court unexpectedly, and she was still in her nightgown, uncomfortably aware that yesterday's eye make-up would be smeared into the creases around her eyes.

'Timing is everything. You know how precise Veronica likes to be.'

She sniffed and told herself that she must try to smile, try to be gracious.

'It's no fun for me,' he continued. 'She's another of Veronica's social cases. I have to get them to bathe first.'

'Don't!' said Francine, pulling her hand from his grasp. 'It's too squalid.'

'But Frangie, you've always been so understanding. Open-minded. I rely on you—'

'You say Veronica screens them, but how do I know?

Sooner or later you'll pick up some vile disease from these slum women.'

'Not exactly slum women, darling. The fee is still considerable. Vee's not running a charity.'

'You just said yourself they're filthy! They need to bathe before you'll bed them.' She stood up and walked to the kitchen window. Labourers were dismantling the scaffolding from the roof of the exhibition centre: the building work was finally coming to an end. She thought of the day ahead – stuck in the flat with the scaffolding clank-clanking; workmen yelling and catcalling whenever a woman passed; the man in the flat above practising on his wretched oboe – and now not even the prospect of dinner with Charles to look forward to. She felt a twist of anger as she turned back to look at him. He was fiddling with a cufflink, and there was a look of weariness – or was it boredom? – upon his face.

'You don't care where these women are from, do you?' she hissed. 'You don't care what they look like or smell like. You fuck them for money and you love every single minute of it. All those babies, those children running around London. You must have hundreds of them now.'

'Two hundred and eighty-two,' he said in a faraway voice.

'What?'

'Two hundred and eighty-two, since 1916. One child a month, near as dammit. At least, those are the successes we know of. Not every woman keeps her follow-up appointment.'

He smiled and her rage flared brighter.

'This is a joke to you?'

'Frangie, really,' he said, rising from the table. 'If you're having a bad day I think it's better I leave. Though I must confess I had hoped—' He reached out and pulled at the silk cord of her dressing gown. The bow slowly unlooped.

She looked down at his hand, felt the light pressure of the cord against her waist. He smiled again and stepped towards her. She caught the scent of his cologne.

'Had hoped?' she asked.

The cord slid to the floor and he stroked a finger along her bare collarbone.

'I might fuck them for money. But I fuck you for love, my darling.'

When he kissed her she felt the rage melt away. It would be all right. He still wanted her. The other women meant nothing. They were simply . . . business.

There was no food in the flat, so she walked to the Italian delicatessen on the Cromwell Road. The grey skies had lightened and the temperature was rising. Perhaps it would be a sunny day after all. In the delicatessen Francine bought bread and tomatoes for lunch. She hesitated over a tray of pastries decorated with glazed apricots and strawberries.

'*Tre . . . grazie*,' she said, pointing to the pastries. Jasmin had a sweet tooth, just like Hazel, of course. She'd pop by and surprise them. The delicatessen sold wine, too. Hazel wasn't keen on wine, or any alcohol, it seemed, but it would be a shame to arrive without a respectable offering. She bought a bottle of Chianti, and the shopkeeper parcelled everything up in brown paper.

The walk took twenty minutes, and she wished she'd worn different shoes, or hailed a cab, but the wine would have to serve as her extravagance for the day. How tiresome this money situation was. The Aldwick house had not been let as frequently as expected, and the last guests had refused to pay the balance because the water heater had broken down on the third day.

She passed a solicitor's office, its brass plaque glaring in the sudden dazzle of sunshine. She had not yet heard from Paul's solicitor. Paul was chasing recompense for a cancelled contract; it seemed he couldn't afford the time or the money to invest in a divorce. Everything hinged on selling the Bloomsbury flat, but that was far from straightforward. Property in town was hardly the most desirable, with all this tiresome talk of war.

Hazel looked unwell, thought Francine. When she answered the door her face dropped, and she gave a guarded glance over Francine's shoulder, asking whether Charles was on his way.

'Charles is busy today. I'm feeling a little lonely, as a matter of fact. I've brought us some treats. Have you had lunch?'

She held up the paper parcel and Hazel opened the door a little wider.

'Not yet . . . We've been out. Come in.'

Jasmin's face broke into a wide grin when she saw Francine. She was wearing a knitted yellow cardigan that looked as if it was covered in mud or chocolate, and her face was just as grimy. 'Nee-nee,' she called, clapping her hands. 'Nee-nee.'

How sweet, thought Francine. Jasmin seems to have decided on her own name for me. Nee-nee. Yes, that was much better than Grandma or Granny. Clever little girl. She bent down and stroked Jasmin's head.

'It's Nee-Nee come to visit, that's right. Haven't you grown?'

'You haven't seen her for a while.'

'Isn't it silly, darling? I honestly have no idea where the time goes. Of course there was the fortnight in Biarritz – it was so kind of Deborah to invite me. Dreadfully hot out there, though. As much as one could manage to take a dip in the pool.' She looked down again at the parcel and handed it to Hazel. 'Just a few luncheon things. And a bottle of *vin*. I'm ever so thirsty.'

Hazel mumbled a thank-you and disappeared into the kitchen. Francine sat on the edge of the sofa, surveying the room. It was an odd set-up. Rather bare and unfeminine, considering the occupants were two young women. A dining table was pushed against the back wall, and on it were several foolscap files, piles of papers and a coffee-stained cup and saucer. In the corner next to the table was a standard pole with a huge flag wound around it. Francine didn't have to unfurl the flag to know it would be emblazoned with some ghastly fascist emblem. She had given up trying to fathom why Hazel found the Mosley party so attractive. The way the man preened and strutted; he was plainly ridiculous.

Next to her on the sofa was a copy of the *Blackshirt*. She glanced down at a cartoon on the front page that showed a group of Jewish bankers, stunted and grotesque. The image made her feel queasy. Was it possible that Hazel found this loathsome Jew-baiting amusing? Francine knew it was the kind of thing her dead father would have admired, anti-Semite that he was. She'd managed to hide Paul's ancestry from him, but there'd been a suspicion from the start. 'Always imagined you with a taller fellow,' he'd sniffed. 'Rather exotic isn't he? Interesting face . . .'

Francine folded the paper and slid it underneath the sofa, out of sight.

'Nee-Nee.'

Jasmin had pulled herself up and now she was toddling over to Francine, her chubby button toes splaying on the rug with each wobbly step.

'Clever girl!' said Francine, holding out her hands. 'Clever girl has learned to walk! Come to Nee-Nee, that's it.' Jasmin lunged towards her, almost overbalancing, but Francine clasped her under the arms and lifted her onto her lap. 'We'll have a little song, shall we, Jasmin? Now let's see . . .' She began to sing: '*Daffydowndilly has come to town, sweet and fresh as a country breeze. In a yellow petticoat and a green gown, daffydowndilly has come to town.*' At the end of the song she blew into Jasmin's hair, and her wispy curls lifted in the stale air.

''Gain,' laughed Jasmin. ''Gain!'

'Again? How about Nee-Nee's favourite? Mummy used to like this one, too.' Francine began to rock Jasmin. '*Bye baby bunting, Daddy's gone a-hunting, to fetch a little rabbit skin, to wrap his baby bunting in.*'

Jasmin's warm body melted into hers; she lay in Francine's arms staring up with devoted eyes.

'That's meant as a dig, is it?'

Hazel was standing in the doorway holding a glass of wine, her face pinched and angry.

'A dig?'

'Daddy's gone a-hunting.' She slammed the glass down on the table so that the wine sloshed over the edge.

'I honestly didn't give it a second thought, darling. It's just a nursery rhyme. You're being ridiculous. Oversensitive.'

'If you're so desperate to know who the father is, I'll give you a clue,' said Hazel.

She strode across the room, lifted Jasmin from Francine's lap and held her against her hip.

'There are two possibilities,' said Hazel. 'And one of them is Charles.'

Francine sat motionless, allowing the seconds to pass until Jasmin began to cry and squirm in Hazel's arms. She stood and staggered towards the table, picked up the glass and gulped down the wine. Without a word she walked towards the door.

''Gain!' shouted Jasmin. 'Nee-Nee 'gain!'

Jean stood with her arms crossed, the hem of her drab petticoat flapping below her skirt. 'Mr Lassiter didn't say to expect you.'

'Didn't he? Oh, it's all arranged. I know he won't be back until later but I found myself at a loose end.'

Francine's legs were trembling, but Jean didn't seem to notice. Grudgingly, she let Francine through the front door and showed her to the sitting room. 'I'm in the scullery,' she said, 'in case you need anything.'

'Actually, I might go up for a lie-down,' said Francine, putting her hand to her forehead. 'I've this headache. It's rather close, suddenly, don't you think?'

'Heatwave coming,' sniffed Jean. 'The ants are getting ready to swarm.'

'The ants. Yes, quite.'

Upstairs, she sat on the bed and tried to summon a sliver of calm.

There are two possibilities.

What did she hope to find in his bedroom? A journal, perhaps. A list of his conquests. Letters. Proof. She began to open the chest drawers, quietly in case Jean was loitering, running her fingers through the layers of socks and underpants, shirt collars and braces. She searched through his bedside cabinet, under the mattress, under the bed. Nothing. Finally, she opened the drawer at the bottom of the wardrobe. There were some tennis whites there, and an old scuffed cricket bat. She was about to close the drawer when she saw a cigar box pushed towards the back. Inside were a few photographs – Charles as a baby in a Victorian studio, trussed up in his christening gown; a photograph of herself with Charles and Miss Heath, taken on the banks of the Fowey. On the back was an inscription in careful handwriting: *Me with Francine, Summer 1909.* It was the first summer that Edward had not come to Lostwithiel, the summer before—

She dropped the picture face down in the cigar box, and now there was just one photograph in her hand. It had been taken a year later, the summer when—

Francine gazed at the picture: a shot of Charles with his brother Lawrence at twenty months old, little Lawrie dressed in a blue linen romper, holding the red-painted toy train that Francine's mother had brought as a gift when they arrived for the August holiday.

Francine felt an icy sweat break on her forehead. Here he was – Lawrie, smiling for the photographer who'd come to the house that rainy morning. She remembered how the flashbulbs had excited Lawrie and made him giddy so that he'd refused to have a nap after lunch. The weather cleared in the afternoon and the two families went into the garden to enjoy the sunshine. Lawrie cried for his mother to put him in the hammock, and then cried for her to get him down again, and the rigmarole repeated itself until Mrs Lassiter sighed and said nannies really oughtn't to be allowed half-days. Finally, exhausted, and with the bribe of his green bedtime blanket, Lawrie settled in the hammock and fell asleep.

As the early-evening sun filtered through the oak leaves the parents went into the house to dress for dinner. 'Keep an eye on the baby, won't you, children?' said Mrs Lassiter. 'Call me when he wakes.'

They both nodded and smiled. When Mrs Lassiter disappeared Charles gave a bitter laugh.

'Children? I'm almost eighteen.'

'Wouldn't you rather they think of us as children?' asked Francine. She sat straight-backed on the rug, her legs folded sideways beneath her. 'If they had any idea, we'd never be left alone.'

He stared at her body and smiled. One hand reached out and stroked the underside of her calf. She put down her magazine.

'Not here,' she said. 'Come tonight.'

'I can't wait until then. I've been in torment all day, Francine. Agony. Just a short walk down to the field.'

'We can't leave Lawrie . . .'

They looked into the hammock. Lawrie's thumb was planted in his mouth, his blanket snuggled to his cheek. 'He's fast asleep,' said Charles. 'A kiss, that's all. You wouldn't deny me that?'

Francine slipped her shoes back on and stood up. 'I'll go first,' she said. 'Come and find me.'

The field at the end of the garden was edged with a row of sprawling beeches. She stood with her back against a beech trunk, watching a flock of half-grown lambs grazing in the distance. A tiny fly landed on her forehead and she flicked it away. When she heard his footsteps shushing through last autumn's fallen leaves she stepped on a twig to make it snap. The footsteps stalled for a second: Charles had heard. Now he was before her, his eyes locked on hers, his face grave with love.

How long were they gone – ten minutes? Twenty? Afterwards Francine went ahead, Charles promising to follow at a respectable distance. Reaching the garden, she knew before she peered into the hammock that Lawrie was no longer sleeping inside. The fabric was light and empty, the fringed calico swaying unburdened in the breeze.

Scanning the lawn, Francine quickened her pace towards the house. By the steps to the veranda she saw a flash of green – Lawrie's blanket, snagged on the wooden post. He had toddled into the house then; that was good. She would follow him inside and with luck, no one would ever know that they'd left him alone.

At the top of the veranda steps she heard Charles running up the lawn. A clot of colour hit her eyes as she turned her head. The toy train.

It was floating blood-red in the barrel that collected rainwater for Mrs Lassiter's roses. Below the train was a small pale hand, fingers reaching up like fragments of lifeless coral.

Francine and her parents had boarded the first train back to London the following morning. They sat stiffly in the carriage, white-faced with shock. A tragic accident, the police inspector had pronounced, but Mrs Lassiter had made it clear she blamed Francine for Lawrie's drowning. Charles did his best to defend her – the walk down to the field was his idea, he told his mother – but Mrs Lassiter took little notice. Charles was a boy; boys were liable to be distracted. Francine was a young woman; she would be a mother herself one day. She should have known better than to abandon a sleeping baby.

They never returned to Lostwithiel. Francine's father would bring home the occasional snippet of information, gleaned on the golf course or at bank dinners. Charles Lassiter had suffered some kind of breakdown, it was reported, and when war came he was registered unfit and shoved into a clerking role for a merchant-shipping firm. 'I'd like to know how much Lassiter paid for the psychiatrist's report,' sniffed her father.

It was Harriett who had reintroduced Francine to Charles, unwittingly, at the opening of a Sickert exhibition one summer in the late twenties. 'Have you met Charles Lassiter?' Harriett said to Paul and Francine as they stood in the gallery sipping white wine. 'Charles, this is Paul Alexander and his wife, my friend Francine.'

Lassiter. Francine looked at the blithe blue eyes and the combed hair and could see little trace of the young man she'd once known. But there was his straight sharp nose, the full lips now upturned in an easy smile.

'Charles?'

He took her hand. 'Francine. How delightful to see you after all this time.' He kissed her hand, and then both her cheeks, and she found it impossible to hide her astonishment. Even when they moved apart she was acutely aware of him: the way his face crinkled with each laugh; the sun-weathered hands which pushed through his hair; the adolescent intensity replaced with such effortless charm.

Harry thought it was marvellous that two childhood friends had been reunited, and she threw a drinks party so that Charles and Francine could reminisce at leisure. There were more drinks parties. Luncheons. Dinners. Francine tried to resist Charles's overtures, but after Paul's infidelity she saw no reason why she shouldn't indulge. And God, what a joy it had been. Just the memory of that first night together was enough to make her pulse quicken.

They had endured so much. They were bonded, even when they were apart, when she was with Paul or he was with Carolyn or his clients or any number of lovers he had enjoyed over the years. Nothing had been able to break the bond. But Hazel?

Francine lay on the bed until she heard Charles's car pull up outside, the click of his heels on the pavement and his key in the door. She hurried down the stairs into the hall and almost collided with Jean. The two women spoke at the same time.

'Mrs Alexander said you was expecting her—'

'Charles, I won't be staying—'

Charles dropped his keys next to the telephone and tossed his hat onto the stand.

'Yes, thank you, Jean,' he said, taking Francine by the elbow. 'How lovely to see you, Frangie.'

He steered her into the sitting room and closed the door behind them. 'Is everything all right?' he asked. 'You look rather wild.'

PART THREE

PART THREE

29

London, May 1940

'Do you like butter, Mummy?'

Jasmin had found a clump of buttercups in the church-yard near the nursery. Hazel crouched beside a gravestone and tilted her head back a fraction.

'You do!' said Jasmin, holding the flower under her mother's chin so that the yellow light reflected on Hazel's pale neck. Jasmin's eyes became earnest: this was a serious experiment. 'You *love* butter, Mummy.' She skipped ahead on the church path, twirling the buttercup stalk between her thumb and forefinger. The small brown box bumped against her hip. Jasmin had named her gas mask Angie, after a friend from nursery who had been evacuated to Scotland. The mask should have a pretty name, she'd announced, to stop it from being so ugly. 'Angie's like angels. Angels are always there, even when you can't see them, aren't they, Mummy?'

'Wait at the gate,' Hazel called. She preferred to walk as slowly as possible through the churchyard, and as she walked she tried to imagine that they were in the countryside rather than the centre of London. She wanted to delay the moment when they would arrive at the nursery, when Jasmin would be out of her sight, out of her reach, for another endless day. Every single air raid in the months since the war began had been a false alarm. People were calling it a twilight war, but no one believed it could last. Hazel hated the raids when she and Jasmin were apart, each in their own subterranean gloom. Mrs Allen had strung a line of bunting across the steel roof of the nursery's Anderson shelter, as if a row of cambric triangles cut out with pinking shears might ward off a high-explosive bomb.

The office was eerily hushed. Mr Weaver had been recalled to his old regiment. Ancient Mr Morris sat in his office drinking Darjeeling, speculating as to when the firm's moth-balled commissions might reasonably be revived. The girls all agreed that he was going doolally-tat: what person in their right mind would kit out a house in luxury wallpaper and velvet curtains when Jerry was about to come calling? They – the girls – might as well join the WAAF or the WAAC or move out to the country to help on a farm. Bridget had already gone. Anne had handed Bridget's latest postcard round that morning: *I'm up to my ankles in cow shit and it's glorious.*

Hazel kept quiet about her own plans.

In her lunch hour she bought a copy of the *News Chronicle*. It was a while now since she'd last seen his name, but that was no reason to stop looking. He'd been doing well – a reporter at last – and until a month ago there had been quite a few news stories written by Thomas Smart. They tended to be the less consequential stories towards the back of the newspaper – thunderstorm damage to barrage balloons, a goods train derailed – but she cut out every one and kept the collection in a Manila envelope, hidden under the seat cushion of her bedroom chair.

It was warm enough for short sleeves, and the breeze blowing off the river held the promise of summer; there was a ripe saltiness to the air, and from a distant jetty came the screech of gulls. If she closed her eyes, she could almost be in Aldwick.

The bench where Hazel usually sat was taken by two men in uniform, so she walked a little further along Millbank, ignoring the whistle from one of the men as she passed. She brushed a sprinkling of white blossom from the bench and sat down, opening the paper and scanning through the pages. Nothing. Of course there was a chance that Tom might have moved to another newspaper, but she could hardly buy each paper every single day and anyway, the most likely explanation was that he had joined up. Why wouldn't he? He'd been quick enough to fight the fascists in Spain. The only surprise was that he hadn't gone sooner.

She read through the paper again, slowly this time. There was a story about fundraising for Jewish refugees, a photograph of children who'd arrived on the *Kindertransport*. Hazel had seen the pictures many times now, girls of Jasmin's age and younger, wide-eyed and afraid, clutching their pathetic possessions. It was too awful. Hazel had tried to speak to Lucia about the Jews, of the persecution in Germany, but Lucia seemed incapable of sensible discussion. She parroted phrases from the *Blackshirt* – 'Oh, to hell with the refu*jews* and their sob-stuff, charity begins at home!' – or she repeated lines from Sir Oswald's speeches, learned from the recordings she'd played over and over on the gramophone. Hazel always backed down, let her rant on. It was easier that way because she still needed Lucia – for now, at least.

She folded the paper into her bag and wandered back along the riverside. It was low tide and the wind had dropped; the water looked calm, benign. Hard to believe that the Thames could be the Nazis' secret weapon. *London will always be betrayed by the river. At night, from the air, it reflects the moon or the sky.* Tom had written that in one of his reports on air-raid precautions. The words stuck in her head like lines of poetry.

After work she called in to Derry & Toms and took the lift up to the luggage department. The woman on the counter was pushy and tried to sell her a set of three leather cases – 'Outstanding value,' she gushed – but Hazel would not be persuaded. She chose a small blue valise for Jasmin, fitted with tiny brass clasps, and a large board-backed case for herself.

Kensington High Street seemed deserted as she walked back to the flat, an empty case in each hand. She remembered that summer Saturday, cold and wet, when she boarded the train at Chichester clutching Jasmin in one arm and a rain-soaked hessian bag in the other. She had left the Misses Shaw's pram outside Selsey bus station with a note giving the return address. She would not be accused of stealing anything, least of all her own baby. At Victoria station, Hazel had searched the crowds, fear thumping behind her eyes. But there was Lucia, next to the telegraph office as promised, forearms resting on the handle of a brand-new pram. They queued for a taxicab, Lucia giggling as they tried to lift the bassinet from the chassis, to fold down the shining frame.

The pram had been sold now, and Lucia donated the proceeds towards the latest fundraising drive at HQ. In the bottom of Hazel's wardrobe, the hessian bag still lay folded. Their possessions were few: it would not take long to pack.

'You're leaving? I don't quite – *tomorrow*, did you say?' Lucia put down her pen and stared at Hazel in disbelief. The sitting room was dark and chill despite the sunny evening outside.

'Tomorrow morning. We're going to Devon. Winnie's family have taken a pub. They've invited me and Jasmin.'

Lucia scrambled up from the table, knocking her chair hard against the back wall. 'How terribly generous of Winnie. You've had enough of my charity, then?'

'I'll work to earn our keep. It will be safer for Jasmin to leave London.'

'For heaven's sake. This obsession, this *paranoia* about the Luftwaffe—' Lucia paced across the room, stood at the window and looked out onto the street, tapping her fingernails on the wide sill. Outside, a torn-eared cat stalked across a wall, stopped on a brick pier and arched its back.

'I am grateful to you, Lucia.' She got up from the sofa and stood beside her at the window, ventured a hand on her shoulder. 'You know I am. I couldn't have . . . well, I would have lost Jasmin if it hadn't been for you. But everything has changed now. The war, the movement—' The movement has failed, Hazel wanted to say. All those meetings and rallies, the canvassing for peace. None of it had made any difference.

'So it's all about you and the shop girl now,' said Lucia, shrugging off Hazel's hand. 'I take it you and Winnie aren't inviting me along to Devon. Happy for me to take my chances here?'

Hazel hesitated. She'd assumed that Lucia would never

leave London, because London meant Philip and her work – such as it was now – at HQ. She wouldn't leave, would she? She had to be bluffing.

'I'm sure Winnie would be happy to invite you.' Hazel did her best to sound enthusiastic, cheery. 'They might be grateful for an extra pair of hands.'

Lucia whirled around from the window. 'I'd rather die here.' Her dark eyes narrowed and her lips peeled back to show her teeth. The expression was somehow familiar to Hazel – yes, it was the expression of the communist girl who'd cornered her in the shop doorway. There was the same wild loathing in Lucia's eyes, the same flash of danger.

'Don't say that—'

'Or perhaps I'll leave London altogether. I'll go back to Berlin.' Lucia's face softened and broke into a distant smile. 'He'd welcome me, you know, Karl. Our correspondence—' She stopped abruptly and walked back towards the table.

Correspondence? She must mean the Nazi commander she'd struck up with on her last trip to Berlin. A man who, Lucia claimed, worked closely with the Führer.

'Germany? You wouldn't. How would you get there, and how on earth would you get back?'

'Don't pretend to care!' Lucia's voice rose to a shriek and she lunged towards Hazel, grabbing her by the arms and digging her fingernails through the thin fabric of her blouse. 'Don't you dare pretend to care for me now, don't you dare!'

'Lucia! Of course I care.'

'Liar. I've been useful, that's all. You've used me. You don't truly believe in the movement – do you think I hadn't noticed? All this time you've used me as a cover for your sordid little secret.'

Hazel tried to shake herself free. *Sordid little secret.* Did she mean Jasmin? 'Please,' she said. 'Please don't shout. You'll wake Jasmin.'

'Jasmin, Jasmin, Jasmin.' Lucia dug her nails harder into Hazel's flesh. 'Jasmin, Winnie, the girls at work. Thomas treacherous Smart – don't think I don't know! Loyal as a pup to everyone but me.'

'Tom? How do you know—'

'It's my flat, isn't it?'

'You've been in my room, read my letters?'

'He let you down, though, didn't he? Cut you off!'

Hazel swallowed down her fury. Just for one more night, she told herself. One more night. 'I do care for you, Lucia. I owe you everything. I'll never forget what you did for me. But I have to take Jasmin away from London. I have to put her first. Surely you can see?'

Lucia released her grip and turned away with a heave of disgust. She sank onto the sofa and put her head into her hands. Her shoulders began to quiver and Hazel realized that she was crying.

'Do you remember when we met?' asked Lucia, her voice trembling.

'Of course I remember.' Hazel knew she ought to sit next to her, to comfort her, but her feet remained planted under the window. 'The rally at the theatre.'

'No. The very first time. You were watching the parade.' She looked up, wet lashes glistening. 'I'll never forget that day. I thought you were the most perfect girl I'd ever seen. I wanted us to be friends, true friends.'

'And we have been. We are. I'm so grateful.'

Lucia gave a curt laugh. 'I don't want you to be *grateful*, Hazel. I want you to love me back. The same. Instead you're betraying me. Ambushing me with your news. You must have been plotting for weeks.'

Hazel struggled to reply. It was true: she and Winnie had been discussing the move since Easter. So why hadn't she told Lucia? Because she *didn't* love her, that was why. Lucia was right. In fact, for a long time now, Hazel hadn't even liked her.

'I didn't think you'd mind so much, Lucia,' she said, forcing a note of nonchalance. 'Thought you might even be pleased. You'll have more time alone with Philip. And if you want another flatmate you'll find one soon enough. A girl with no ties, more fun than I'll ever be.'

'I don't want anyone else,' said Lucia, her voice steady now, steel-edged and low. 'I only want you.'

Winnie and her brother had promised to come at ten. They were bringing a van, and from Kensington they would all drive straight to Devon. 'We'll arrive in time for tea,' said Winnie. 'Scones and jam. Butter not marg!'

Everything had been packed, filling the two suitcases and the hessian bag, along with three apple crates from the greengrocer. That their lives could be parcelled up so simply saddened Hazel, and she wondered whether it would always be like this; whether she would ever manage to find a proper home for Jasmin – their own home with a cluttered dresser and a toy chest filled to overflowing.

'Bored,' said Jasmin. She picked flakes from a wax crayon. 'Why can't we go to the pond?'

'Sorry, poppet. We can't go out because Auntie Winnie is coming and we're going on a long drive. A holiday, do you remember? And we'll be staying in a lovely village with a great big pond with baby moorhens and coots and ducklings. Do you remember Auntie Winnie told you all about it?'

Jasmin's face brightened. 'Baby moorhens like blobs of soot?'

'That's it,' smiled Hazel. 'Scraps of soot, aren't they? All black and fuzzy.' She picked up a teddy and nuzzled it into Jasmin's neck.

'Is the holiday coming soon?'

Hazel looked at her watch. It was just after nine. 'Quite soon. Less than an hour.'

'Is Nee-Nee coming?'

'No. Nee-Nee prefers to stay in London.' Hazel picked up a blanket and refolded it so that the corners were tight. 'Now, see if you can draw me another picture. How about a lion, like we saw at the zoo?'

She drank two more cups of tea. Lucia was still in bed. Hazel didn't want to wake her, but she knew she could not leave without saying goodbye. Last night, when Lucia had finished crying, they had become oddly polite and formal. They switched on the wireless at nine and listened to the news without commenting. When Billy Cotton and his band came on, Hazel lit a cigarette, and Lucia didn't sigh or complain as she generally did.

Ten minutes to ten. Hazel hovered outside Lucia's door and raised her arm, but as she was about to knock there was a loud creak of bedsprings and an exaggerated yawn. The door opened. Lucia was wearing men's pyjamas, the pair that Philip kept for his overnight stays.

'Is it really so late?' she said. 'I'm due at a meeting. And I suppose you're— It's any minute, isn't it? Winnie and the van?'

Hazel opened her mouth to reply just at the moment the doorbell rang. Lucia raised her eyebrows. 'Right on cue,' she said. Her eyes were puffy and her lips looked dry and chapped. 'You'd better answer it.'

Jasmin had already run ahead to the front door. Hazel followed her down the dark hall passage, watching as she stretched up on tiptoes to turn the latch and pull the door wide. On the doorstep stood two men in cheap grey suits.

Jasmin shrank back and buried her head in Hazel's skirt. 'Not Auntie Winnie,' she whined.

The taller man asked Hazel if she was Miss Lucia Knight. Hazel said she was not, and she asked who might be calling. He held up a piece of paper and said, 'Police. We have a warrant to search the premises.' He spoke loudly, but Hazel wasn't sure whether Lucia could hear. She had gone into the kitchen, and the kettle was beginning to whistle on the stove.

The men strode into the living room as Hazel shepherded Jasmin into the bedroom. 'Stay in here and draw me one more picture,' she said. 'A really good one for Mummy.' She rushed into the kitchen. 'The police are here,' she whispered to Lucia.

Lucia's eyes widened. She leaned against the sink, gripping the edge.

'They asked for you.'

She half-shrugged her shoulders as if to make light of what Hazel had just told her, to pretend she hardly cared. She drew herself up and tilted her chin outwards.

'Typical of this small-minded little government,' she said. 'All the Germans and Italians have been rounded up. Now it's our turn. Fascists are patriots to the core and yet they'll accuse us of being fifth columnists.'

'Not us, surely? We're no danger—'

Lucia cut in. 'They're at the door?'

'No, they're in the flat. The living room. Apparently they have a warrant to search—'

'What?' The colour drained from Lucia's face. 'My papers!' She pushed past Hazel and ran into the living room. Hazel twisted off the gas under the kettle and followed her.

In the living room the taller policeman – the one who seemed to be in charge – was sitting calmly at the dining table, picking through the notebooks and correspondence that were stacked in messy piles.

Lucia stood in the doorway, Hazel close behind.

'Members' address list,' said the man, holding up an opened ledger. 'Damned considerate of you to leave that out.'

Lucia flew towards the table and thrust out her hand for the ledger. 'Those are my private papers,' she said. The policeman laughed, snapped the ledger shut and held it close to his chest. Behind him the other officer was unfurling the flag that leaned against the wall in the corner of the room. He whistled as he stared down at the circle-and-flash emblem. 'Christ,' he said, turning his head to look around the room. 'What sort of a place is this? A veritable fascists' coven, I'd say.'

'Now then –' the officer at the table slapped the ledger down – 'I don't believe we've been properly introduced. I'm Superintendent Farr. This is Inspector Travers. Miss Knight, I understand you're an active member of the British Union.'

'I am,' said Lucia. She straightened her spine as if on parade, unabashed by the fact she was wearing pyjamas.

'And this is . . . ?' Superintendent Farr nodded towards Hazel.

Hazel knew she was expected to give him her name, but she found herself unable to speak. She coughed, and felt her breath light and jagged in the back of her throat. Perhaps she could invent a name. Her thoughts scrambled and the only one which came to mind was Bronwen. Could she lie? It might buy her time, just until Winnie arrived. She opened her mouth, but now Lucia was talking.

'This is my flatmate, Hazel Alexander,' said Lucia. 'Also an active member.'

A shiver coursed through Hazel's body. Had Lucia really said that? Did she hate her so much? And it wasn't even true – she wasn't an active member, not any more. She and Winnie had agreed; they'd sent their letters of resignation to Mrs Dunn, enclosing their drum corps badges.

'In actual fact I'm no longer a member,' said Hazel. She croaked out the words, doing her best to battle the cough. 'I've resigned,' she said. 'I'm about to leave London.'

'I bet you are,' said Inspector Travers. 'Fortunate we came when we did.'

'No! I have a daughter, you see. We're going to the country-side. To safety.'

'And your husband?'

Hazel looked down. There was a smear of dried mud on the sole of the inspector's shoe. He would consider her to be less than the mud. He would squash her and she had no power to fight back.

'I'm not married.'

Her eyes were on the floor but she could sense the men raising their eyebrows, exchanging a glance.

'Indeed?' said Superintendent Farr. 'You're not married. And you claim *not* to be involved in the British Union. Yet Miss Knight here says you are an active member.'

'Hazel is one of the faithful – a valued member of the women's drum corps,' said Lucia. 'Along with Winifred Harris who, I believe, will be arriving here at any moment.'

Flashes of white smudged Hazel's vision. She sank to the arm of the sofa and doubled over, trying to catch her breath. 'I need a drink of water,' she gasped. 'Please?'

The superintendent nodded, and Hazel walked slowly to the kitchen. Running the tap, she did her best to conjure reassuring thoughts. These policemen are simply throwing their weight around, she told herself. They're just trying to give us a scare.

'Finished!' It was Jasmin, calling from the bedroom. Hazel gulped down the water then hurried in.

'Do you like it?' Jasmin held up a piece of scrap paper decorated with green scribbles above a wonky brown rectangle.

'A tree? It's lovely. Clever girl.' Hazel looked down at the scattered crayons and picked up a black one. 'Now listen carefully, Jasmin. I'm going to write a special message on this picture, and when you hear the doorbell ring, I want you to rush out and answer the door. It's sure to be Auntie Winnie this time and you must give her this picture right away. And then come back inside.'

Jasmin nodded solemnly. Hazel's hands shook as she wrote the message: POLICE ARE HERE. LEAVE NOW.

She folded the picture and gave it to Jasmin. 'Can you be a grown-up girl and remember what I said?'

Jasmin nodded again. 'Give the picture to Auntie Winnie when the bell rings.'

'That's right.' She turned away, tears in her eyes. 'Just wait nicely in here until you hear that noisy old bell. She'll be along any minute now.'

'Where are you going?'

'Mummy needs to talk to the visitors. It shouldn't take too long.'

They were told to sit on the sofa, to wait quietly while the documents were gathered and itemized. When the doorbell rang, Jasmin's little footsteps scampered down the hall. Hazel heard Winnie's cheery, 'Hello, love!' and then there was silence, before the front door quietly closed.

Inspector Travers went into the hall but already the van engine was revving. He came back into the room with Jasmin by his side. 'Did it, Mummy,' she smiled.

The superintendent looked perplexed.

'Did what?' asked Inspector Travers.

'Oh, she means . . . her business,' said Hazel. Her pulse hammered but somehow she kept her nerve. 'Come with me, Jasmin.' She held out her hand. 'We'll check you left the lavatory clean.'

'If that was the Harris girl she didn't hang around,' said the inspector.

'Pity,' sighed Superintendent Farr. 'But I think we have enough to keep us busy here.'

While Travers carried the boxes to the police car, another officer arrived. This one was in uniform, a tall unsmiling woman who stood with arms folded in front of the fireplace as if she were guarding the mantel clock.

Hazel sat on the sofa with Jasmin on her lap, reading a story. Lucia got up and stood at the window, tapping her foot and staring onto the street.

'Again, Mummy.'

Hazel flicked back to the beginning of the book for a third time. Slowly she read the story and turned the pages, reciting the words without registering any meaning. Her thoughts raced. She hoped that Winnie had gone on to Devon regardless. Soon the police would be finished here and she could join Winnie later, take a train instead. They'd have to leave the crates behind but that was all right, they would manage with the minimum. There would be shops in Devon. She had her savings. '*And Mr Drake Puddle-Duck, and Jemima and Rebeccah, have been looking for them ever since,*' she read. It was the end of the book again. She became aware that everyone was looking at her. Superintendent Farr was speaking, nodding in her direction.

'When it comes to the child,' he said, 'you are permitted to take her with you, although I would advise against.'

'Take her?' said Hazel. 'To Devon, you mean?'

'Miss Alexander, you are not going to Devon.'

'Where then? Where are we going?'

'Holloway Prison. We're detaining you. I'm sorry, you clearly don't understand at all, do you? Let me spell it out. Miss Hazel Alexander and Miss Lucia Knight, you are to be detained until further notice under the Defence Regulation Act, Clause 18B.'

'Until further notice?' cried Lucia.

'You might have heard of the new amendment to the law?'

'Swine!' screamed Lucia. 'We've done nothing but honour our king and country.'

'You can make your case in due course,' said the superintendent, holding up his hand. 'Now –' he turned to Hazel – 'if you don't wish the child to accompany you, I suggest you make other arrangements. WPC Gallagher here can escort you to a telephone box if necessary.'

*

The strangest thing was that the operator sounded bored. Hazel was seized by a savage twist of envy: how odd that her own life had become something surreal, something beyond a nightmare, yet this telephonist could sit on her stool and speak as if she were staring at her fingernails and wondering what shoes to wear for the weekend dance.

'Connecting.'

The line rang three times, and Hazel willed her mother to answer. It was almost midday; she might have gone on a shopping trip or a lunch date with one of her friends.

Finally, there was the click of a lifted receiver, a sleepy hello.

'Mother?'

'Hazel? Are you in Devon already?'

'No, I'm in a phone box near the flat. Can you come round, please? As soon as possible? There's a . . . problem, with the police.'

'What on earth has happened, darling? Is it a burglary?'

'Nothing like that.' Hazel looked through the glass pane of the telephone kiosk and met the eyes of WPC Gallagher. She would not cry. All that mattered was Jasmin. She had to make sure Jasmin was safe, had to be brave. Her fingers tingled and the telephone felt strange; weightless and heavy at the same time. 'Mother, they're going to detain me. Me and Lucia. They're taking us to Holloway. Jasmin is allowed to come, apparently, but I couldn't possibly – she mustn't know I'm in a prison. I need you to look after her, Mother. Can you do that?'

Silence, then the faint rasp of a cigarette lighter. Francine spoke again, her voice husky with smoke. 'I think you might have to say that again, darling. I must have misheard.'

30

Francine replaced the receiver and slumped back against the pillow. One thought dominated all others: thank God she'd stopped him from answering. He had leaned across her in the bed, and his hand had been hovering over the telephone, but she'd batted him away, assuming the caller would be Paul, and heaven knows with the divorce negotiations so fraught, she didn't need to offer Paul any more ammunition.

But it had been Hazel, not Paul. Francine closed her eyes, hoping again that she had somehow misunderstood. That this was in fact a bizarre hallucination.

Charles patted the bedcovers above her thigh. 'Well, Frangie?' he said. 'Whatever it was, it sounded weighty.'

'It was Hazel. She's . . . she's been arrested. They're taking her and Lucia to Holloway prison. Hazel wants me to look after Jasmin.' She threw back the covers and swung her legs over the side of the bed. 'I have to get to their flat right now.'

'Damnedest thing. Arresting her for what?'

'For her politics, of course. She's a fascist, isn't she? An enemy. The *silly* girl.' Her thumbnail snagged on her stocking and she cursed.

'I'll drive you.'

'You can't possibly.'

'I'll drop you at the next street. She'll think you caught a cab.'

Francine hesitated as she zipped up her dress. 'All right. But not the next street. Two streets away. If she knows I've been with you there'll be the most almighty scene.'

Cromwell Road was busy, so Charles decided to take the backstreets, the engine straining as he careered past grand terraces and mansion blocks. Neither of them spoke. Francine stared out of the window at the black railings flicking past, blinking at the flashes of sunlight that dazzled through the gaps between buildings. She wondered whether she might be able to reason with these police officers who wanted to take Hazel away, to separate a mother from her daughter. Two mothers from two daughters. Francine thought she might just hold some sway if she smiled pleasantly enough and apologized and explained that Hazel was simply an impetuous young girl. As for Lucia, well – she wouldn't speak up for her.

But what if pleasant smiles weren't enough? If Hazel was taken regardless, and she, Francine, was left to care for the child? On the telephone, she'd tried to get some idea as to how long this detention might last, but Hazel hadn't been able to say. Just a night or two, perhaps. They'd question the girls, and surely when they discovered that there was nothing dangerous or traitorous about Hazel, she would be released. But in the meantime, where would Jasmin sleep? The flat had only one bedroom. The sofa would be comfortable enough, she decided; it was small, but it should be a perfect fit for a four-year-old. And what on earth would she give her to eat? Francine tended to eat dinner in a restaurant, or not at all. Well, there was always cheese on toast. Porridge.

Marco at the deli would see that Jasmin had a treat now and again.

The car passed a man in a cravat with a newspaper under his arm. Francine thought she recognized him. He was an actor, she remembered, someone she'd met at one of Harriett's parties. She thought of the play at the Adelphi next Saturday. She would have to find someone to look after Jasmin that evening, or perhaps she wouldn't be able to go at all. She sighed, her heart heavy. There wasn't a great deal of gaiety to life these days, but what little interludes she enjoyed would now be snatched away.

'Blasted nags.' Charles swerved around a rag-man's pony, the Brough almost clipping the side of the cart. Jasmin would enjoy a ride in the Brough, but that was out of the question, decided Francine. She was such a bright little thing, chattering away like a child twice her age. She'd remember his face, and his name, and then she'd tell Hazel all about Charles once the pair of them were reunited.

It pained Francine to deceive Hazel. Deception was not in her nature. And after all, she *had* tried to break it off with Charles, hadn't seen him for three whole months after Hazel's revelation. She had lived like a nun until that Sunday evening in November when he had arrived at the flat with a bottle of chilled white wine. Perhaps it was because it was her birthday, and she was feeling particularly alone, horribly sober, in fact, after a dry birthday lunch with Hazel, that she invited him in. This time she listened. Gave him a proper chance to explain.

He said he loved her, he had always loved her. Everything that had happened, happened because of his love for her.

'Can't you see, Frangie?' he pleaded.

They were sitting opposite each other in the dull lamplight of the sitting room. Raindrops slunk down the windowpane. It was cold but she had not bothered to switch on the fire.

'Lawrie's death . . .'

Francine almost gasped, to hear Charles mention his brother's name.

'It was my fault,' Charles went on. 'I abandoned Lawrie because I loved you. I wanted you. I've tried somehow to make amends, all those extra babies, the new little boys . . .'

She couldn't bear it. Couldn't bear to hear this – what? – confession? It was the first time Charles had ever spoken of Lawrie since the accident. But why mention him now? Her thoughts hardened. This wasn't about Lawrence: it was about Hazel.

'And sleeping with my daughter? That was because of your love for me?'

Charles flinched and cast his eyes down. 'No. That was a terrible – an unfor*givable* mistake. I was drunk, Frangie. Very drunk. I don't know if you remember but you had gone to bed early that night – a rotten headache, wasn't it? I tried to sleep but couldn't, and so I went downstairs for a night-cap, sat in the living room for a while in the dark, drinking. I heard Hazel go out into the garden. I wanted to know what the girl was playing at, thought it would be a help to you, I suppose. So I followed her, saw what she was up to in the summer house with the boy.'

'Why didn't you stop them? Chase him off?'

'I kept on drinking, straight from the bottle, like an idiot in a trance. Just wasn't thinking straight, Frangie. When the boy left, scrambled back over the wall, I thought, Here's my chance to confront her. Warn her to be careful. But she wouldn't listen.' He paused, sighed. 'And the way she smiled, well, it was as if you were there in front of me, Frangie, you at sixteen, beautiful and alive, and all the desire I had felt for you earlier in the evening, somehow it overwhelmed me. I'm not proud of what I did.' He looked up, thumped his fist on the arm of the sofa. 'The fact is, I've never been more ashamed. It happened just that once. I swear to you.'

'She says you forced yourself on her.'

'Really? There was no force that I recall. But, the whisky . . . perhaps my memory . . .'

She stared down at the rug, trying to absorb his words. *All the desire I had felt for you earlier in the evening, somehow it overwhelmed me.* What did that mean?

'You're trying to say it was my fault, for having a headache that night?' she said. 'If I'd gone to bed with you it would never have happened.'

'Of course I'm not. The evening could have passed quite differently, it's true –' He looked up, and she met his gaze with a warning stare. 'But no, the responsibility is all mine. I accept that.'

'And what about Jasmin? Is she your responsibility? Hazel says you could be the father.'

'No. I don't think so.'

'Why?'

'Let's just say it wasn't my finest hour. Rather too much whisky.'

'Please.' The detail – the image – was too much.

'Jasmin is a little like you.'

'Hardly. She's fair – so is Hazel.'

Francine wished she knew what the boy had looked like. Charles had seen him, of course, but she preferred not to think of what he had seen through the windows of the summer house. She poured another glass of wine.

He sighed and reached in his pocket. 'Please forgive me, Francine. I lost you once. I can't bear to lose you again.' He held out a small box wrapped with a red velvet bow.

She took the box and opened it. Inside was a gold ring, a night-blue stone encircled by white diamonds. Francine shook her head. He couldn't possibly mean . . .

'It's a blue diamond,' he said. 'Terribly rare. Look, I can't divorce Carolyn yet. These cursed loans. But when my father finally bows out, well, the inheritance will change everything. I do want to marry you, Frangie. It's all I've ever wanted.'

Her hand flew to her mouth. 'But it's too beautiful!'

'Let me see if it fits.'

He stood and took the ring from the box, then knelt beside her. She could smell him now, feel his hands on hers, the band of warm gold slipping onto her finger. It was too much.

After that night, the ring had stayed in her jewellery box. She couldn't marry Charles, could she? Yet the promise was enough. They had made a vow.

A policewoman answered the door to Hazel's flat. 'The mother?' she asked, in a granite voice that was more statement than question. Francine nodded and the policewoman motioned for her to step inside.

In the living room, Francine's attempts to reason with the superintendent had no effect. She tried pleading and dabbing the corners of her eyes with a handkerchief, explaining that Jasmin was unusually close to her mother, that it would be utterly cruel to separate them.

'18Bs can take one child with them,' said the superinten-dent. 'They're entitled to certain privileges.'

'You'd put a child in prison, too?'

'Shhh,' said Hazel. 'She'll hear.' Jasmin was in the kitchen with a biscuit and a glass of milk. 'Jasmin mustn't know. And Mother –' she paused, trying to steady her voice – 'I want you to take her to Aldwick.'

'Aldwick? But your father's in the house now! Your father and Adriana. For heaven's sake, I can't possibly—'

'It's not safe in London. I've made up my mind to get her out. The Aldwick house is big enough for all of you. Please. It might not be for very long. I can't bear to think of her at Earls Court. Traipsing down all those stairs to the shelter.'

Francine nodded. Now was not the time to argue.

'Please. I need you to promise.'

Hell. She could raise it with Paul, at least. These *were* exceptional circumstances. And it was about time he met his granddaughter.

'I promise to ask your father. I'll do my absolute best. And try not to worry. Jasmin will be quite safe with me.'

There was a snort from the far side of the room. Francine turned to look at Lucia. She was standing at the window, biting a fingernail, manically tapping the sole of a black patent shoe. It was all Lucia's fault, thought Francine, which-ever way one looked at it. Oh, if only the blackshirts hadn't come to Sussex that summer. Why couldn't they have chosen Kent or Dorset for their wretched camp?

Jasmin appeared, half a biscuit in one hand and a small blue case in the other. She offered the biscuit to Francine. 'Want some, Nee-Nee?'

'Nee-Nee's not hungry, darling. You finish it, there's a good girl.'

'Not hungry neither. I want to go on the holiday now.' She placed the case on the floor and sat on it.

Hazel crouched in front of Jasmin and grasped both her hands.

'I'm afraid we can't go on the holiday with Winnie today.' Hazel's eyes were wet but somehow she was smiling. 'Mummy has been asked to do some special war work. It shouldn't take very long, and until I get back Nee-Nee is going to look after you. Won't that be exciting?'

Jasmin nodded, but she looked uncertain. 'Can I see the lions with Nee-Nee?'

Francine put her hand on Jasmin's head. 'We'll have all manner of adventures, darling. It will be great fun, just you see.'

The inspector coughed. Hazel put her arms around Jasmin and hugged her. 'Bye, sweet girl.' She kissed her daughter's cheek, then disappeared into the hall where the police-woman was waiting.

31

A wasp had landed near the ashtray on Tom's desk. He finished the water in his tumbler, shook the drips onto the floor and turned the glass upside down to trap it. Once this story was written, he'd open the window and set the wasp free.

'Smart!'

When the news editor yelled the whole office jumped. Tom grabbed up his notebook and pencil and strode across to the newsdesk.

'More 18Bs. Fascists, in the main. Five pars should do it.' Crow thrust the wire into his hand without looking at him. His face was set in its usual grimace, the pinched and yellowed skin stretched across his cheekbones.

'Yes, Mr Crow. And the scrap-metal story?'

'Why are you still here? File the fascists first, for fuck's sake.'

Tom hurried back to his desk. It was a hot day and the sun beat in through the fourth-floor windows. It was a terrible thing to be out of Crow's favour. All because of a tiny mistake in a story about a train derailment. Did anyone really give two hoots which class of engine had left the tracks?

He told himself to focus on the 18Bs story, to ignore the fine sweat which had broken out on his forehead. Bill Cork had never let on about Tom's past, thank Christ; if Crow found out he used to be in the British Union he'd be ripped to shreds, never mind that he'd left four years ago and that he'd only ever been dragged into it by his mother.

Amazing to think that the British fascists were all but finished now. At first there were just a handful of arrests, Mosley and other high-ups, speakers whose names he recognized from meetings and rallies. But this past week they seemed to be going for anyone who'd ever delivered a leaflet or sold the *Blackshirt* on a street corner. He thought of his mum in Boone Street, her old uniform still hanging in the under-stairs cupboard along with the winter coats. She'd be all right, wouldn't she? Surely the police had better things to do than to come after her?

He wiped his forehead with his shirtsleeve, then began to read the Press Association report. *The following members of the British Union were this morning arrested and detained under the Defence Regulations 18B . . .* He scanned the list of names. Closed his eyes as a pulse hammered below his brow.

Gerald stopped battering his typewriter keys and stared across from his seat opposite. 'All right, my man?' he said. 'You look rather rattled.'

Tom realized he was holding his breath. 'Just a bit warm in here,' he said, pulling his shirt collar away from his neck. He fanned himself with the wire, then angled it towards Gerald. 'More blackshirts banged up.'

'Good show.'

Tom swiped the saucepans story from his typewriter, wound in a fresh sheet of paper and began to type. He ignored the wasp's buzzing, the angry *tap-tap* of its body as it threw itself against the sides of the glass.

*

Gerald and the others were going to the pub at the end of the shift, but Tom didn't fancy joining them. They were decent enough but they were older men, ex-public school mostly, drinkers with dicky hearts, Great War veterans. The young and the fit had already gone.

Instead he went down to the composing room to see if Bill was around. 'Day off,' shouted old Charlie, hunched over his stone. Tom wiped his brow: even hotter down here with the heat from the machines. Each clank of a mallet was like a direct hit on his skull.

'Not to worry. I'll catch him next week.'

'You'll have to be quick. Call-up's come.'

Did he hear Charlie right over the din? Of course he did. The only surprise was that Bill hadn't got his papers sooner. Petra would be beside herself. He made up his mind to visit Bill and Petra at the weekend, use his coupon to buy the children some sweets.

In the pub opposite Lewisham station he ordered a pint, careful to keep his left hand in his pocket so as not to attract the stares of the girls who were looking across at him from the table in the window. He recognized one of them – Elsie Warlock, whose parents owned the fried-fish shop on Lee High Road. Elsie knew Jillie, didn't she? Well, he couldn't be bothered to go over, to grin through the congratulations and all that gushy stuff.

Fixing his eyes on the evening paper, he tried to read the front page but found it impossible to concentrate. His mind kept returning to the PA wire, the alphabetical list of names. She'd been there, right at the top. *Hazel Alexander.* The thing that really pained him was that when he'd read her name, he'd felt a punch of relief. She's not married then, was the

thought that flew into his mind, and now he loathed himself
for it. What could it possibly matter to him whether or not
she was married? Hazel was in prison and it served her
bloody right. She ought to be locked up along with the other
fascists, separated from her lover, or lovers – those men his
mother had mentioned in her letter. To think he'd been
taken in by Hazel a second time, had even confessed his love
in that ridiculous letter from Albacete. When he found out
the truth, the life she was really living, he'd longed for
revenge and now, in a sense, he had it. It was just a pity he
couldn't seem to summon any pleasure.

He ordered a second pint and lit a cigarette. There'd been
another name he recognized on the list: Lucia Knight. Lucia,
the snooty one who liked the sound of her own voice. Tom
had always thought she was dangerous. And wasn't that the
point of these 18B detentions, to imprison people who
might be dangerous to the State? Strange to imagine all those
posh girls slumming it inside, though. Not that the 18Bs
had it too bad. All sorts of privileges, apparently. Mosley had
denied the reports about champagne and red wine but if
Tom had learned one thing in Fleet Street, it was that these
stories were never a complete fiction . . .

'Tommy Smart!' It was Elsie, tottering up to the bar, all
heels and lipstick. 'You're a dark horse, all right.'

'Evening, Elsie.'

'When's the party then?'

Tom raised his eyebrows and Elsie elbowed him, catching
his left arm. He tried not to wince. 'Party?'

'Engagement party. You and Jillie! She came in the shop,
showed us the ring.'

'We thought we'd keep things low-key. Jillie doesn't like a
fuss.'

'That what she told you, is it?' Elsie winked and took a ten-bob note from her purse. 'You'd better start saving, I'd say.'

Tom screwed his cigarette end into the ashtray. 'Love to stay and chat but the old girl's expecting me.' He smiled and tipped his trilby, then strode four steps to the pub door. He used the remains of his left hand to pull the door open, and he could feel the girls' eyes on him. Why not let them get a good look after all? They were just the type to enjoy a freak show.

At home, his mum started up the minute he walked in the door. She still had on her best blouse because she'd been to see the Quaker minister, the Friend-in-Chief or whatever he was called.

'Ever such a simple ceremony,' she wittered. 'No pomp or fuss, and you get a lovely certificate that we all sign. The whole congregation!' She put her hand to her heart as if a signed certificate was akin to a divine blessing. 'What do you think? A Quaker wedding, will it be?'

Tom loosened his tie and draped his jacket over the stair-post. 'I don't mind, Mum. If Jillie's happy with it—'

'But I want you *both* to be happy with it. As for timings, it's whenever you're ready. Next month if that suits.'

'You know that's too soon.' He went into the kitchen and his mum followed. 'We'll need savings.'

'There's soup. Or shall I fry you egg and chips?'

'Soup's fine,' he said, reaching for the matchbox to light the ring. He tried to grip the box with the mangled stumps of fingers but it slid out of his grasp and matches scattered across the floor.

'Let me do it, love.' She'd already bent down to start picking up the mess. Christ, he hated it when she treated him like an invalid, when she clucked with sympathy. And it was a dishonest kind of sympathy, because he knew that she was absolutely bloody delighted he'd had half his hand shot off at Jarama. 'Escaped with a Blighty,' he'd overheard her telling one of the new Quaker friends, barely disguising the glee in her voice. To think how upset she'd been about him going, yet the fascists in Spain had been able to achieve what Mosley never could. They'd got him sent home and would keep him home for good. No army would want him now.

He crouched and picked up the last few matches, dropped them into the box which she held open. She was on about the wedding again.

'Maybe not next month, love, but the autumn, perhaps? September's good for a wedding. *Married in September's golden glow, smooth and serene your life will go.*' She lit the gas ring and took a bowl from the rack.

Tom sat down heavily at the table. 'Next year, more like. There's no rush, is there?'

She sighed. 'I'm looking forward to it, that's all. To having Jillie here, and God willing, you'll want to start a family. It's awfully quiet since Mr Frowse went. Can't believe I'm saying it but I miss the racket from his wireless, I really do.'

'We won't be living here permanent, you know that, Mum.'

'But a year or two, while you're saving up? And think what a help I could be to Jillie. She's a smashing girl but she won't know much about homemaking, if the mother is anything to go by. We'll be a marvellous team, I know it.'

'She's very fond of you.'

Bea smiled. 'You couldn't have chosen better.'

32

The minute he came in from work she could tell Tom was in a strange mood: jittery with the matches, snappy about the wedding. And now he'd disappeared to bed for an early night. She could hear him moving around in the front bedroom. It was a nice-sized room, there'd be plenty of space for Jillie too, and of course the box room next door would be perfect for a new arrival.

It was nine-thirty, a warm evening, and she hadn't yet drawn the blackout blinds: there was still enough light to knit by. She had almost finished another blanket for the refugee children. Poor little mites with their twiggy legs and shadows under their eyes. What a crime it was, she thought, to have bags under your eyes at the age of seven.

She'd washed the jumpers before she unpicked them but Harold's presence was there somehow, the inky smell of him mixed up with the scent of soap flakes. Even before the funeral there were mutters about clearing his clothes – Mary next door had been fixated on it, seemed to think Bea would never stop grieving until all traces of Harold had been removed from the house. But Bea had held firm and now she was glad. Harold would be pleased to think of his old pullovers helping out those unfortunate children. 'Isn't that right, love?' she said to him under her breath.

Upstairs, there was a creak as Tom climbed into bed. He'd filled out over the past couple of years. Thank heavens, because when he came back from Spain he was a pitiful sight, thin and grubby, his poor arm strapped up against a too-big white shirt donated by the Red Cross. There were tears in Harold's eyes, the day Tom arrived home. Later, in bed, Harold sobbed with relief to have him back, and Bea felt guilty for ever doubting his love for their son. Harold was very ill. The winter fever had turned out to be something much worse: a 'mass' was what the doctor called it, a mass in his lungs that would only grow bigger. They'd known nothing but fear since the diagnosis, but when Harold stopped crying that night Bea sensed a new peace in his soul. With Tom home, Harold gave himself permission to die. It was as if he had found his Inward Light, just as the Quakers described it.

Bea looked up and realized she was sitting in near-darkness. She drew the blinds, switched on the lamp and fiddled with the wireless dial. When the knock came on the door it was very quiet at first, and she dismissed the tapping as drumbeats on the music programme. But no, there was the knock again, in the silent seconds before the dance band began the next number. She lifted the edge of the blind and peered through the side pane of the bay window, onto the path. The person on the doorstep was standing close to the front door. All she could see was the sleeve of a dark-coloured jacket.

The argument had blown up over a pair of tweezers, of all things. The mother had lost the tweezers and accused Jillie of taking them, and Jillie knew she hadn't but her mother flew into a rage, lobbed a high-heeled shoe from the top of the stairs right down to the bottom where Jillie was standing in the hallway. She hadn't dodged quick enough and there was a lump on the back of her head where the heel had hit.

'Sorry to turn up so late,' sobbed Jillie. She was on the settee between Tom and Bea. 'I can't go back there. Not tonight. She's cracked.'

Tom looked at Bea over Jillie's bowed head. 'I'll walk you back home if you like,' he said. 'See if she's calmed down.'

'Nonsense, Tom,' dismissed Bea. 'You can't go out like that.' She flapped her hand in his direction, frowning at his pyjamas. 'Stay here, Jillie. I'll make up the spare room.'

Jillie blew her nose and gazed at Bea. 'Would you? Oh, Mrs Smart, I'd be ever so grateful.'

'Won't your mum worry?' asked Tom.

'I told her I was coming here. Anyway, it serves her right.' She sniffed triumphantly and circled her shoulders, stretched a hand out – her fingernails were painted cherry red, Bea noticed – and rested it on Tom's knee.

Next morning Bea watched Tom saying goodbye to Jillie on the front path. She had tipped her little face up to him, and both arms were flung around his neck. He patted her in a way that was kind but not tender. Perhaps it gave him discomfort to be embraced so fiercely; his poor arm had never completely healed, and his hand often flared up around the scars. Eventually she peeled off him, and then he pecked her on the cheek and rushed off towards the station. Jillie had to get to her job, too, but she didn't seem in much of a hurry. She checked her face in a pocket mirror, patted some powder over the spots and then sauntered towards the park.

Bea went into the box room and saw that Jillie hadn't pulled the sheets back for airing. Hadn't even drawn the curtains. The girl was under a lot of strain, bless her. She'd find no arguments once she was living here, thought Bea. No tweezers or flying shoes.

The billboard headline leaped out as she passed the news-agent's *en route* to the library: MORE FASCISTS DETAINED. Her breath quickened a little, to think what might have been if she'd stayed in the movement. Fortunate to have got out when she did, to have broken all ties. It had been difficult at the time, quite a wrench. But once she was out she'd begun to feel a giddying sense of relief. She could go to Mr Perlman's with a clear conscience. She no longer had to puzzle over the rights and wrongs of this policy or that. Harold had been pleased, too. 'Never quite trusted Mosley,' he'd muttered. And of course if she hadn't left the blackshirts, she would never have found the Quakers. Odd how things turned out.

She wasn't one for mysticism, for souls and spirituality. But the Friends talked about the spirit in a matter-of-fact, gentle fashion – nothing hellfire or hocus-pocus about it. They left you alone to find peace in your own way. *Shine a light into the dark corners of your mind* – that's what you had to do. And you could do it just by sitting quietly and think-ing peaceful thoughts. It was a kind of deliverance.

On the way home from the library, her basket weighed down with a fresh set of books, she took a detour into Manor Park. It was warm and the young squirrels played among the branches. The avenue of horse chestnuts was in full bloom, magnificent white spikes that took your breath away. For the first time in months she thought of Charles – the chestnut in flower outside the hotel window, the lilies in the vase – and she allowed her mind to drift and sway around the memory.

A memory. That's all it could ever be. She would never see him again now, she'd made sure of that. Sometimes Bea remembered Hazel, swallowed down a surge of guilt at the letter she had sent Tom, but it didn't take much to reassure herself. The means had justified the ends. As a mother, you had to do what was right, even when the right thing seemed awfully close to the wrong.

33

Jasmin had decided that she didn't like the beach. 'Too hurty,' she said, when the pebbles dug into her feet as she struggled towards the patch of sand beyond the shingle. Francine had some sympathy – she herself had always found the shingle an abomination – but she would have to jolly Jasmin along, otherwise they would be stuck in the house all afternoon and the prospect of that was enough to make Francine weep.

'We'll buy you some beach shoes for next time, darling,' called Francine. She watched Jasmin lunge forward, her tangled hair lifting in the breeze, bucket wobbling in her hand. 'There, you've made it now. Build a sandcastle. Good girl.' Francine huffed warm breath onto the lenses of her sunglasses, polished them with the hem of her dress and put them on. She would keep her eyes straight ahead, out towards the horizon, and try to believe that the world was normal. The barbed wire hadn't quite reached this stretch of beach yet. Bognor seafront looked a fright, and Mrs Waite had told her that the foreshore would soon be mined. Gun emplacements, scaffolding – Sussex was ready for the Hun.

The evacuation from France had begun at the end of May, the rag-tag fleet sailing across the Channel while at home anyone with a traitorous whiff was rounded up and detained. Infuriating that Hazel should be among them, but Francine could understand the government's paranoia. And now the troops, what was left of them, were home. France had fallen, and nothing but the sea and this *hurty* beach stood between England and the enemy. God, the irony was almost amusing. All those children evacuated from London to the south coast, yet now their parents were demanding their safe return to the capital. Perhaps, when she visited Holloway next week, she could explain to Hazel that Sussex was no longer a haven, that they'd actually be better off in Earls Court. If the Nazis stepped onto the beach at Aldwick, where on earth would they hide? In London there would be options.

Separation had been the tactic thus far – separate mealtimes, separate outings, separate rooms. Paul and Adriana had, grudgingly, conceded the master bedroom to Francine, decamping to the guest room, while Jasmin was in Hazel's old room, delighted with the teddy bears and the music box and the patchwork eiderdown sewn by Nanny Felix all those years ago. There were occasional conversations in the hallway or the drawing room, polite words masking a thousand resentments. The formality couldn't last. One more week – one more day – and the pretence would be blown apart.

She yearned for Charles. The ring was still in its box, and she took it out every night and wore it for a minute or two, flashing her hand in front of the dressing-room mirror. Marriage seemed more of an impossibility than ever, and the war was just another complication. Still, there was Tuesday to look forward to. After Holloway, she would take a cab straight to Bruton Street.

Closing her eyes, she listened to the swish of the incoming tide. It wouldn't be long before the sand was swallowed. And then it would be shingle or nothing, and Jasmin would whine to go back to the house, and Mrs Waite would pounce, fretting about what to cook for dinner and whom to serve, when and where.

'Nee-Nee, look!'

Jasmin had fished something out of the large rock pool at the base of a breakwater, and now she was waving it in the air. It looked like a tin hat, seaweed dripping from the strap.

'Put that down, darling.'

But it was too late. Jasmin had tipped it onto her head. The hat covered her eyes and rested on the pink bridge of her nose.

'Please take it off!' Francine called. 'We don't know where it's been.'

Jasmin giggled and marched unseeing towards the shingle with her arms outstretched, as if she were playing a game of blind man's buff. Her right foot stubbed up against a rock and she fell sideways, screeching as her head hit the sand.

'*Silly* girl!' Francine said under her breath. She sighed and stood up from the beach chair. Its wooden frame creaked – the old thing was on the verge of collapse. She didn't want to step onto the wet sand in her white leather shoes, but really there was no choice. Jasmin didn't seem to be getting up; she was howling, the hat still over her eyes. Gulls wheeled and screamed as Francine picked her way across the pebbles.

'Sit up, darling. Come on.' Francine crouched over her granddaughter, grasped her shoulders and pulled her up to sitting. It was only then that she noticed the holes on one side of the hat, the side where Jasmin had fallen. Like bullet holes, she thought, and then with a twist of fear she realized that in all likelihood they *were* bullet holes, and for all she knew the hat might have company; there could be a dead soldier or a mash of brains or any monstrous sight washed up by the hideous tide.

Carefully she tried to lift the hat but it was strangely resistant. One of the holes was almost triangular, folded inwards. Francine edged the hat to one side and felt a lurch of nausea as she realized the bent metal was wedged into Jasmin's scalp. Gently she pulled, and as the hat finally came free there was a sickening slicing sound. Blood spilt from the deep wound, darkening Jasmin's blonde tangles. Francine let the hat drop, heard it thump to the sand. A hush fell over the beach – the waves, the gulls, Jasmin's cries; all were silent – and Francine looked around in bewilderment at the sudden, terrible peace.

34

It was like living inside Schoenberg's head. Mornings were the noisiest. Metal doors clanked, keys jangled, Blakeys on boot heels struck like tolling bells on iron spiral staircases. The clash of chords would echo in her ears even after the morning had quietened.

Hazel looked down at the mug of weak cocoa. A layer of grease floated on the top. Soon, when she could summon the strength, she would take her spoon and skim off the grease, clasp the handleless mug, like a child, and gulp down the lukewarm liquid, trying not to taste or to smell. Trying not to gag. Then she would chew the bread – ignoring the flecks of unidentifiable grey – and wait to be let out for the half-hour's exercise. In the yard she would walk slowly with her eyes raised to the sky. She would not look at Lucia, she would not look at the Holloway ground. Only the sky above gave her comfort. It was not part of this place; it was free and belonged to her as much as it belonged to Jasmin. A brief moment of sharing.

Sixteen days. Sixteen days she had been imprisoned and still no date for her appeal to be heard. She hadn't been charged, had barely been questioned. It didn't matter how much she pleaded, the wardresses just stared stone-faced, parroting the same lines about 18Bs and the Advisory Committee and backlogs and *patience*.

F-wing's cells had been recently whitewashed. She was lucky, one inmate had told her, to have escaped the filth of other wings, where mushrooms and rats were liable to spawn overnight. But the whitewash masked nothing. Already it was flaking, wet with damp, impervious to the hot June sun and the tantalizing summer breezes that swooped into the exercise yard.

She had dreamed, once, that this cell was the summer house – its size was similar, she supposed – and she was with Tom, could feel him inside her, his skin welded to hers, their bodies moving like a tide, and the moment was coming, that indescribable moment, when their love would be equal and pure. She felt the truth even for a fraction of a second after the air-raid siren wailed and she woke to see the dim blue landing light seeping beneath the cell door.

Warnings were frequent; some nights she could hear aircraft overhead. But still no bombs.

'Hazel, please.'

Lucia had fallen into step beside her and she was trying – again – to strike up conversation. Hazel dug her fingernails into the palms of her hands, kept her focus on a faraway cirrus cloud, ignoring the crunch of pain in the muscles at the base of her neck. Never again would she speak to Lucia. She would not speak to any of the fascist women, the believers, the defiant inmates who clustered in the yard and around the trestle tables at mealtimes, humming fascist anthems when they thought the wardresses weren't listening. They feigned cheerfulness, affected a kind of camaraderie. Mrs Dunn had appeared for the first time a few days previously and there was a round of quiet applause as she took her seat on the bench, her right arm lifted in a coded half-salute.

'All right, you won't speak to me,' said Lucia. 'But that doesn't mean I can't speak to you.'

Hazel watched the cloud drift southwards. It was shaped like a swallow on the wing. Its shape would change, it might divide into two, or three, but later Jasmin might look up and her eyes might fix on the same patch of moisture and air.

'I should have covered for you when they came to the flat. Hazel? I know I shouldn't have mentioned the drum corps. But they probably would have taken you anyway, don't you see? Forgive me? I can't bear to see you punishing yourself like this.' She reached out her hand and touched Hazel's elbow.

Hazel stood still in the yard and screamed.

It was Tuesday and her mother was visiting later in the morning. The wardresses listened in on conversations, made it clear that they would be writing reports. Hazel saw this as a good thing: they could listen and report as much as they liked, because then they would learn that she should not be here, that she had only become a blackshirt because she needed a home for her daughter. What a cruel bargain that had turned out to be.

Lying on the rough-woven blanket, she began the ritual mental torture, the game of *if onlys*. If only Winnie had arrived fifteen minutes earlier. They would all be in Devon by now; the police wouldn't have bothered coming after her there, would they? If only they'd gone the week before, the date Winnie had first mentioned, and that Hazel hadn't said she'd need a little more time to tie up her work in the office, because it wouldn't be fair to leave Mr Boyne high and dry.

If only Lucia had been a true friend. Hazel understood her now. Lucia wanted someone she could possess, a kind of pet, dutiful and loyal. Yet she had chosen badly – first Hazel, and then Philip, each with ties beyond Lucia's control: a daughter, a wife. No wonder she was bitter.

With a blunt fingernail Hazel picked at a flake of white paint on the wall, exposing the murky red brick beneath. No. The *if onlys* were an indulgence, an attempt to mask her own culpability. No one had forced her to join the movement, had they? She had been intrigued by it, flattered by Lucia's friendship that summer when she was sixteen and hopelessly bored. And the following summer, when she was so desperate to keep Jasmin, sharing a flat with Lucia had seemed like the perfect solution, a wonderful blessing. Blackshirt meetings were a distraction; she had looked forward to drum practice with Winnie, the weekend parades, the escape from her relentless routine. She had learned to salute along with the rest of them, found herself swept up in the speeches and the singing. Oh, she had never swallowed the rhetoric, had never shared the obsession with the Jews, but she had gone along with it, and perhaps that made her worse than the others. She had marched and cheered, but she had never truly believed.

Would she have joined the movement if it hadn't been for Jasmin? She turned away from the brick wall and faced the crooked chair in the corner of her cell. It was a hard question, but she was getting closer to the heart. And in the heart, that black heart, lay Charles. It was Charles who had changed everything, twisted her mind, turned her against the truth. Against Tom.

If only she had never known Charles.

'Alexander!' The wardress threw the door wide and stood back. 'Visitor waiting.'

Her mother looked surprisingly undecorative. She wore a mustard-coloured sundress with a plain silk scarf and no jewellery. She had taken off her hat, revealing grey roots around her temples.

As Hazel approached the table, Francine stood up. There was a pained expression on her mother's face. No doubt Francine was shocked to see how thin Hazel had become over the last fortnight, how lank and untidy her hair had grown.

'Darling,' said Francine. There was a handkerchief in her hand. Hazel felt dazzled by the whiteness of the cotton, its purity against the grime of this low-ceilinged room. The handkerchief was wet, she registered. Her mother had been crying. It was not like Francine to cry.

'What is it?' asked Hazel, leaning across the table to grasp her mother's arm. 'What is it? Not Jasmin?' The pitch of her voice rose and heads turned towards them. 'Jasmin?'

A voice called out from behind her. 'The prisoner must sit!'

Hazel dropped into her seat. Hysteria bubbled in her chest and her breath came in gasps. Nothing had been said yet. Nothing. She was being ridiculous.

Francine dabbed at her eyes with the handkerchief. 'I'm afraid there's been an accident,' she said.

Flashes of sun-white light pulsed across the room. Hazel heard her mother's words as if through a distant gramophone. The skin on the back of her neck tightened and froze.

'Jasmin is in the hospital. She's going to be all right, we . . . we think. The doctors are very positive. It's a cut to her head, a piece of metal on the beach, silly accident, happened in a heartbeat, there was nothing I could have done. One of those silly, silly things.'

'A cut?'

'Well, it's rather deep, they worry about infection. But darling, honestly, she's in the right place. Your father is with her today.'

'She needs me.'

'In an ideal world, of course, but –' She twisted one corner of the handkerchief and wound it around her forefinger.

Hazel clutched at the table, fixing her eyes on a cigarette scorch in the wood, willing the prison walls to crumble into dust. She would go insane if she could not be with Jasmin. She wanted to run to the wardress, to shake her and demand to be released that very second. 'They have to listen,' she said, her voice rising again. 'There must be a way . . . some compassion. Please!' She scraped back the chair, stepped across the floor to face the wardress. She was a middle-aged woman with a crescent of small moles on one cheek, not so hard-faced as some of the others.

'Let me see the committee. Please.' Hazel laced her fingers together, prayer hands pleading. 'I must see the committee.'

The duty doctor gave her a sleeping draught but it did nothing to still her mind. Back in her cell, Hazel stared at the 25-watt bulb burning in its metal cage. Twenty minutes till lights out. A letter, that was her only hope. There was time to write a letter, if she was quick. Tom worked on a newspaper, didn't he? He would have connections. They would vet the letter but it would get through, so long as she kept it superficial, said nothing about the prison or the conditions.

Gripping the pencil, her hand began to tremble, and as she wrote, a dreadful weariness trickled and dripped through her limbs.

35

'Post for you,' his mum said, nodding towards the rack on the wall where they kept the keys and the letters.

It had been a difficult day at work. Crow on the rampage again – no one was safe from his curses. All Tom wanted was to unlace his shoes and stretch out on his bed, drift off to nothingness. But no, here was a letter and his mum was clearly curious. He took the envelope from the rack. You couldn't blame her for hovering. The writing wasn't familiar and the postmark was faint, impossible to distinguish in the gloom of the hall passage. He balanced the envelope on his knee and tore it open with his good hand. Shaking out the letter, he scanned down to the name at the bottom.

'Not bad news, I hope?'

'What?' He fought to unscramble his brain, to counteract the shock. 'No . . . a comrade from Spain. He might be passing through London.' Tom refolded the letter and stuffed it into his jacket pocket, searching for the right words, the small talk to stall her interest. 'Warm again, eh?' he said. 'I'll have some lemonade if there's any left?'

'Just about,' she said, disappearing into the kitchen. 'Last of the lemons, though.'

He went into the front room and sat on the settee next to

a stack of neatly folded blankets. Strange to see his father's pullovers reconfigured: those familiar earthy colours – brown, beige, moss green. He chewed his lip as he pictured the grave, new grass grown over the mound, lush and thick. He walked across to the window. Quickly he took out the letter again and read through the short paragraph. She wanted him to visit her in Holloway. *An urgent family crisis. Please believe I do not ask this lightly.* And then that strange phrase, the writing growing fainter, weakening. *It is of your intimate concern.*

The nerve of her! He ought to rip the letter to pieces, pretend it had never arrived. It would be easy enough to ignore, no harm done. For all she knew he no longer lived at Boone Street. Yet she had remembered the address, must have kept the notes that he'd stuffed under the summer-house door. It had been – what? – over three years since they were in touch.

Bea took a coaster from the mantelpiece and set the glass down on the side table. 'Seeing Jillie tonight, love?'

Jillie. What had they arranged? 'She's coming over, I think.'

'Off out?'

'We'll stay in with the wireless, Mum. Keep you company.'

'You'd better have a shave. She won't think much of you looking like that.'

In the bathroom, he lathered his face with shaving soap. His left hand ached; there was a pain in his missing fingers, and the scar on his palm itched. It had been joined by other scars, a criss-cross of shrapnel wounds working their way up his arm, yet this one was still distinct, still had the power to set his teeth on edge. Her phrases dangled and looped. *It is of your intimate concern.* What the hell was she talking about? He drew the razor across his skin. Through the open window, he heard a woman laugh. Water splashing onto a parched flowerbed. He rinsed the blade in the sink, turned his face to shave the other side. Perhaps he *would* visit her, and he'd do it soon. Yes, he'd see if he could get a visiting order. After all, there might be a story in it, he might be able to stand up those tales of luxury living for the 18Bs. God knows he could do with getting into Crow's good books.

The order was granted, no questions asked. All right, he wasn't a famous reporter, hardly a household name, but he'd thought someone in the prison might run a check, discover that he was a journalist for the *Chronicle*. But no, here he was on the number 29 bus, the visiting pass folded inside his shirt pocket. He could feel the friction of the paper, the heat of it. It might be dangerous, he knew that. It might as well be ticking.

The bus passed St Pancras, close to the tenement block where Jacob had lived. Tom had visited once, when he was just home from Spain. On the hillside at Jarama, he'd pieced back together the Charlotte Mew, and now he felt that Jacob's family would like to have the book, with all its scribbles and underlinings, the jottings of Jacob's own poetry in the blank pages at the back. There were photographs to pass on too, and an old pocket watch that had somehow survived the attack.

Arriving at the flat, Tom had seen that the blinds were still drawn. Inside, Jacob's mother greeted him with an embrace. A young woman, the ex-fiancée, was there too. 'He often spoke of you,' Tom said to the girl, and she had pawed at her heart as if it would break.

Holloway loomed, ugly and ornate, its Victorian turrets and crenellated walls deep red against the morning sky. He'd never been inside a prison before, assumed it would be nothing like he'd imagined, but in fact it was exactly as he'd imagined: bunches of keys hanging from the belts of unsmiling guards; gloom and damp; a stink of boiled cabbage and disinfectant. He was patted down and shown into the visiting room with the others who were waiting. They were women in the main, some higher class, others down-at-heel in threadbare cardies hugged to their skinny bodies. It was cold in here, despite the June sun blazing outside.

He took his seat on one side of a wooden table and waited. His tactic, he'd decided, would be to say very little. To let her speak and see what came out. Then, once the ice was broken, he'd steer her in the direction of his hoped-for story. *So, how are they treating you? Plenty to eat?*

The prisoners began to file in. A scrawny girl with dark hair scraped into a bun drew out the chair opposite him. He rose, meaning to tell her she'd made a mistake, that he was waiting for someone else, but then the girl's mouth opened in a half-smile and he saw the chip on her tooth.

'Hazel?'

Her smile disappeared as she sat in the chair. She looked a decade older, her face too thin and her forehead screwed into a frown.

'Your hand?' she said.

Damn. He'd meant to keep it on his lap under the table. But of course he'd stood up and now the mangled lump was on display.

'Wounded in Spain.'

'I had no idea. When your letters stopped. Well –' she took a deep breath – 'now I can see why.'

'Oh, I'm not left-handed. I can still write.'

There was a pause, a spike of silence between them.

'But you chose not to.'

'I'm surprised you noticed,' said Tom. 'I heard you were rather busy entertaining at home.' Christ, so much for his tactic, for laying low, letting her speak. Turned out he couldn't keep his bloody mouth shut.

'Entertaining? You mean – what do you mean?' Her eyes seemed to ignite, a flash of understanding. 'Entertaining lovers?'

'Apparently so.'

She swallowed and looked over to the clock on the far wall. 'There isn't time to go into much detail, Tom. I have no idea what you've been told, or by whom.' She gave a bitter laugh. 'There haven't been any lovers. What I'm going to tell you now is the truth. I swear it on my daughter's life.' She put one hand to her heart and sobbed.

Tom reeled back in his chair. A daughter? So she *had* been about! Why, she even had a bastard to show for her efforts.

But he was here now, so he would have to listen. He folded his arms, right over left, so that she would not stare or be tempted to show him any pity.

Light a cigarette and keep walking. Turn south down York Way towards King's Cross. He recited instructions as he walked. If he were a machine, it would be easier; moving parts and cogs that didn't have to think. But his legs only grew more unsteady and his heart roared louder than the stoked furnaces in the engines beyond the high station wall.

Turning into a side street, he saw a pub with its doors just opening for the lunch-time trade. He ordered a brandy and downed it at the bar, almost choking as the heat flared in his throat. Next he ordered a pint, and took it to a tucked-away table near an open door which led onto the yard. A dog was tied up, asleep in the shade of an old advertising hoarding. MY GOODNESS MY GUINNESS.

It was the detail of Hazel's story that made him dizzy. Only a lunatic could have made all that up. She was frantic, that was clear. Beside herself with anxiety. Not a lunatic, though. It was hard to believe she was mad.

Impossible to stop his thoughts racing. Charles. The mother's lover. The swine had forced himself on her, threatened to have him – Tom – arrested for rape. Told her she was a whore. It was no wonder he'd never heard from her again that summer. Girl must have been terrified. He'd thought it was the start of something wonderful, turned against her when the promised letter never arrived. He should have tried harder to get to the truth, should have persisted, shouldn't have been so proud. And then when they *did* meet, when she was all set to tell him about the daughter as they sat drinking tea by the Thames, he'd boasted about Spain, took pleasure in surprising her with the news. He'd relished the opportunity to let *her* down, to get his own back.

Oh, he'd softened soon enough, treasured her letters when they began to arrive. But when his mum's letter came, pride kicked back in. He never seriously questioned the truth of Bea's gossip.

He swigged the pint and felt his shoulders begin to loosen. Of course he'd believed his mum. There was no reason not to: she had never lied to him before. And what if Hazel was lying again today? She was desperate, wasn't she?

Prison could do strange things to your head. There were comrades who'd been in Franco's camps, still struggling to recover. Focus on the facts: he knew for a fact that Hazel was easy, she'd proved as much in the summer house. Slept with him – when? It was only the fourth time they'd met. There'd been no persuasion on his part, no weasel words. The sex had happened, natural as breathing. At the time he'd thought it was something beautiful and magical between them, a pact of love. Now here she was, saying he'd been right all along. It *had* been extraordinary, she had felt the same. She had never loved anyone else.

The child. Jasmin. He tested the name, repeating it under his breath. She was four years old, born April '36. He counted back again. The dates were right. 'She has blonde hair and a dimple,' Hazel had said, and Tom had put his hand to his own face. 'I believe, I hope, that Jasmin is your daughter . . . but I can't be sure. So I kept it a secret. I was ashamed. And you didn't want children. You'd said that.' She stared down at her fingernails.

'Why are you telling me this now?' asked Tom.

'Jasmin is very ill in hospital. An accident, some kind of infection. I have to get out of here. Tom, please, if there's anything you can do . . . Any influence you might have. I thought – with your job on the newspaper?'

The wardress had coughed and tapped her foot on the oilcloth floor.

That was the reason she'd summoned him, then. The daughter was ill. She believed he might be of some use.

He went out into the pub yard and found the privy, knees almost buckling as he took a piss, the last remnants of energy draining from him. If Hazel's story was true, then he should try to help her. He could speak to Gerald. Gerald was well-connected. Old school tie and all that, played golf with a cousin of Churchill's. But did he want to confide in Gerald? Christ. It was tempting just to stay here, to keep drinking until his brain was flat. But he had to get back to Lewisham. There were a few questions he needed to ask his mother.

At Charing Cross the trains were delayed; a signalling problem outside Peckham. He stood against a pillar near the tobacconist's stand, keeping his head down because the last thing he needed was to see anyone from work. He'd swapped his day off with Gerald, said it was to take his mum to a hospital appointment.

An older man in a tan jacket ambled up to the stand, bought twenty Viceroy and walked off in the direction of Villiers Street. The man was about his dad's age, fifty-odd. He wore the same kind of boots, dark brown and polished to such a shine you could see the girders of the station roof reflected in the leather. Grief dropped an iron weight on his chest. His dad had been dead three years, and some days Tom found it easy to forget. Not on a day like this, though. A day when he discovered that he might be a father, that his dad might have died without ever knowing he had a grand-daughter, a little fair-haired girl with a dimple in her chin.

He waited until after tea, when they were settled in the front room. 'I've been looking through my old letters,' he said. 'The ones you wrote to me in Spain.'

'Best forgotten, I would have thought.' Bea shook her head. 'Dreadful days.'

'Worse to come.'

'Not for you, God willing.'

294

'Do you remember writing to me about the blackshirt girls?'

'Not especially.' The click of her knitting needles slowed. The question had unnerved her, he could sense that.

'You mentioned a girl called Hazel Alexander. You said she was notorious, men dancing to her tune.'

Bea replied that she couldn't possibly remember. It was years ago, a different time. But her cheeks had coloured, there was a hesitancy in her voice, and in that moment Tom felt certain that his mother was lying. She had lied about Hazel going with other men. Why? Had she got wind of his correspondence with Hazel, tried to sabotage their love? My God. She was jealous! Jealous of his relationship with a better class of girl. Did she think she'd be left behind?

Tom stood up and turned off the wireless; Elgar crackled and died. 'Tell me why you lied about Hazel.'

'For goodness' sake, Tom! I've no idea what you're talking about.' She leaned over and dropped her knitting on the lid of the sewing basket. 'You've spent too many hours up the Gaumont, gawping at films. All this melodrama –' she folded her arms against her bosom – 'my own son calling me a liar!'

He crouched at her feet and put one hand on her knee, speaking in a low voice and in a tone that seemed to come from a dark place that neither of them knew existed. 'Mum. If you can't give me a good explanation, I swear I'll never forgive you. You can't know how important this is. It's the most important—' His voice cracked and he stood up quickly. 'I'll move away, I swear. Don't expect to come to the wedding.'

Her face paled. She was silent for a moment and her lips moved soundlessly, as if she was trying to remember something, and then she cleared her throat and began to speak in a jumble of words. 'Hazel, you say? No, no, thinking back I must have made a mistake, got my names muddled. So many of them at HQ, it was a Christmas bazaar, I think, when we met. Perhaps Hazel might have been the wrong name – it was the friend who was a strumpet. Fancy name. Lucia, was it?'

'Oh Christ, Mum.' Tom groaned and paced over to the window, balled his hand into a fist and held it against the glass. 'Mum, what have you done?'

'What on earth does it matter?' She raised her voice, trying to keep it strong, to mask the tremble. 'Those girls are nothing to you. You have Jillie!'

The air-raid siren answered, a wail that claimed Jillie's name and seemed to twist and toy with it as they made their way wordlessly to the Anderson shelter in the back garden. Tom fumbled with the matches and managed to light a candle, then wedged the door shut with sandbags. He glanced at Bea's face in the candlelight, caught the look of alarm in her eyes. It didn't make sense. His mum was good with names, always had been. Now she was staring at the photograph hanging on the shelter wall – the family snapshot taken at Margate; Tom in the middle, his mum and dad either side.

'You did it deliberately,' he said. 'Why? Why did you lie about Hazel?'

The siren stopped but the silence was more threatening. Tom waited for his mum to answer the question. 'I didn't see it as a lie,' said Bea, finally. 'A white lie, maybe. I was trying to protect you.'

She perched on the edge of the straight-backed chair, her eyes still focused on the shadowy photograph. Her hands were slotted under her thighs and she rocked a little, forwards and back, forwards and back. Tom stood, his heart knocking in his throat, swallowing down his rage.

'Go on,' he said.

'I found a letter you'd written to Hazel in your bedroom, tucked in a box of birds' eggs. So I knew there was something between the two of you. And then I met her at the bazaar, and I saw the set she mixed with, and, well, I took against them. I'm not ashamed!' she burst out. 'They're ill-mannered, for all their money, and Lucia was the worst of them, gadding about with married men. Hazel was Lucia's friend so it stood to reason . . . I didn't want you to get hurt.'

'It was none of your business,' said Tom. 'You should never have interfered.'

'I'm sorry. I didn't see it would harm, honestly I didn't.'

'You don't see much, do you?'

Bea started at the crump of a direct hit, a few streets away to the west. The glass shook in the Margate photograph. Tom knew he couldn't stay here, no matter that there were bombs dropping outside. He had to get out, get away from his mother and the oppressive shelter walls. He kicked aside the sandbags, wrenched open the door and banged it shut behind him, ignoring Bea's cries as she pleaded with him not to leave.

The house seemed sticky in the honeyed twilight. A trap. In the front room he lifted one of the folded blankets from the settee and held it to his nose, inhaling the faintest scent of his father. He ought to go back to Bea, ought to watch over her, but the betrayal was too great. He couldn't forgive what she'd done. She deserved to be punished.

Outside, the street was empty: good citizens, hiding, all. Tom strode away from the house thinking he would go to Jillie's, but instead he started walking north, up Mounts Pond

Road, across the Heath and down into Greenwich. Aircraft whined overhead. There was the sound of machine-gun fire, shrapnel rattling off roof tiles, and his thoughts turned to Spain, to Jacob and his poems. *For Fate with jealous eye does see two perfect Loves.* Fate! His mum fancied herself as fate all right; sticking her oar in, trying to control his life.

A warden yelled at him to take cover, and he was forced to clatter down the steps of a basement shelter. When the all-clear sounded he was first out, on towards the river, pushing through the crowds spilling free from the foot tunnel under the Thames. On the Isle of Dogs he stayed close to the dock walls, kept heading north, guided by the reddening clouds to the west.

Finally, he reached Limehouse and turned in to Bill's narrow street. He tapped on the front window of the end terrace and waited until he saw Petra's face peeping from behind the blind. She squinted and he called softly: 'It's Tom.'

The front door opened and she bustled him in, kissing him on both cheeks. 'You're not well?' she said. 'Come and sit. Bill is on his late shift. His last shift too, you know?'

'I heard. I'm sorry. I shouldn't have come today.' Christ. What a shameful thing. He'd been so wrapped up in himself that he'd forgotten Bill's papers had come. He ought to leave now, couldn't possibly burden Petra with all his troubles.

'No, no. I'm pleased. The children are asleep and it's lonely. Just my stories –' She gestured at a book that lay face-down on the armchair. It would be a book by some Russian writer, ever so highbrow. The kind of book he'd like to read one day.

'Schnapps?'

He nodded. A strong drink was what he needed, the stronger the better.

She poured the clear liquid into two small gold-rimmed glasses and handed one to him. He took a sip and swallowed, enjoying the burn on the back of his throat. Petra picked up the book and sat down in the armchair. How beautiful she looked under the pink-shaded lamp. 'I think you have a story of your own?' she said, leaning down to place the book on the floor. Tom nodded and took another sip. Why not tell her everything?

Petra listened quietly, her face impassive even when he reached the most sordid part of the story. When he had finished speaking she put a hand out and touched the side of his arm.

'Do you believe Hazel now, about her love for you – that she was always faithful?'

He bowed his head and screwed his eyes shut. Yes, the truth was that he did believe Hazel. He believed every word. He looked up at Petra and nodded.

'And do you love her?'

'Yes.' He tightened his grip around the glass. 'But it can't work, can it? Not when it's such a mess. And the child. This man who forced himself upon her – the mother's lover. He could be the little girl's father.'

'Naturally it can work, if you have enough love. Look at me. My family said they would never speak to me again if I married a *goy*. They love Bill now as their own son. What is the little girl's name?'

'Jasmin.'

Petra repeated the name and smiled. 'I hope that you can see her. That she gets well.'

299

'I hope so too. Really.' He sighed and pushed back the hair that had fallen across his eyes. 'I don't know whether I can forgive my mother. The way she interfered, slandered Hazel . . . Yet I still don't think she's telling the truth. I feel there's more to it.'

'Don't seek out trouble, Tommy. Your mother has apologized. Perhaps that can be enough?'

Tom bit his lip. 'Hazel reminds me of you,' he said. Petra shifted in her seat and he realized, too late, that he had embarrassed her. 'No, I didn't mean like that. Not in looks. I mean – her spirit reminds me of you. She's different. Interesting.'

Petra nodded. 'Different to Jillie?'

'Oh, God.' He almost laughed. 'Yes, different to Jillie.'

At home he found his mother still awake, sitting at the kitchen table. Her face was blotchy and her dressing gown was buttoned up all wrong.

'I'm back, Mum.' He lingered at the threshold, watching her veined hands as she stacked and re-stacked a small pile of coins. A sudden lurch of affection propelled him forward. 'It's all right,' he said. 'Don't cry.'

She stood to embrace him, her downy cheek soft against the stubble of his chin.

'You're safe.' Her shoulders began to shake. 'The fright you gave me, disappearing like that. Oh, Tom!' she sobbed. 'I was wrong. I should never have written that letter. I can't imagine what I was thinking. Half-crazed, I was, with you in Spain—'

Her tears were wet on his skin as he drew back. 'I can't marry Jillie,' he said.

'I know, love,' she replied. 'I know.'

36

How Tom's face had changed in the years since they'd met. Bones sharper, eyes less trusting, a shallow crease between his brows. He had seemed taller than Hazel remembered. The injured arm – terrible to think of his suffering. Yet he was making a career for himself, a reporter, just as he'd dreamed. Hazel experienced a sudden glow of pride, then shook her head. What did Tom's bravery and resilience have to do with her?

He had listened to her story without making any promises, without any sign, in fact, that he believed a single word. Leaving the visiting room, he'd walked in an exaggerated straight line as if following an invisible yardstick, his spine stiff and unyielding. She'd dragged herself back to the cell with little hope, but greater understanding. One puzzle, at least, had been solved.

How did she do it? She must have found his address when she was snooping through the letters, then written to Tom pretending to be . . . goodness knows who. No, an anonymous letter – that would be it, purporting to be from a well-wisher, poisoning Hazel's reputation with malicious talk of 'entertaining'. Cowardly, devil of a woman. Astonishing, really. Hazel hadn't thought it was possible to hate Lucia any more than she already did.

Footsteps stopped outside her cell door. It would be the doctor, she imagined, with his leather bag of pills and potions. He was early, but that was good. After Tom's visit, she needed something to make her numb.

The door swung slowly open and a wardress stood, key in hand. She jerked her head to one side. 'You're to come to the front office.'

The committee had reviewed her recent letter, and they were satisfied that she did not pose any danger to the British state. Hazel listened in disbelief. She looked at the man – the governor's clerk or whoever he was – but his words swirled, as if she was underwater and he was speaking to her from a boat bobbing on the waves. She was to reside at a fixed abode, he said, and report to the nearest police station every Monday morning at nine a.m. She was not permitted to own a camera or a motor car.

'And your address?' The clerk looked up, raising his eyebrows when she failed to respond. What was her address? Not the Kensington flat. No, she needed to get to Sussex. She gave the Aldwick address and asked when she would be free to leave.

'You may leave now.'

It took a moment for his reply to register. 'Now?' she repeated. She looked around, expecting to hear sniggers, fingers pointing and the wardress laughing because she had fallen for the trick. But there was no laughter. From the road beyond the prison, motor engines chugged and a tram bell sounded. Her pulse began to race. She was free. Almost free. 'My things. My purse?'

'The wardress will fetch your belongings. Good day.'

Hazel waited behind the counter of a locker room until the wardress reappeared with a jute sack tied with a name tag and number. 'Here you are, Miss Alexander.' She handed over the sack and smiled. 'Good luck,' she said. 'I've a niece the same age.' She smiled again, and Hazel looked at her more closely. It was the wardress with the moon-shaped moles, the one who'd been supervising – listening in – when Francine had visited earlier in the week with the news about Jasmin.

'The committee, was it you . . . ?'

The wardress straightened her back and her smile disappeared. 'The committee is obliged to examine every case on its relative merits,' she said. But there was something about her manner, a hint of conspiracy.

'Of course.' Hazel wanted to take the woman's hands, to kiss them, but it would not do, she knew. It was important to keep her guard. 'Thank you,' she said, lifting the sack and clutching it to her chest. 'Thank you with all my heart.'

Outside the prison gates, Hazel fumbled inside the sack and found her handbag and purse. The money was still there, the five-pound note and the half-crowns she had saved for Devon. It was late afternoon. She would take the Tube to Victoria. And from there a train to Chichester, to the hospital where Jasmin was waiting.

Visiting hours were over, but Hazel pleaded with the auxiliary until she gave way and went off to fetch the ward sister.

'You've been away on war work, I hear,' said the sister. She looked Hazel up and down in the corridor wondering, no doubt, why she wasn't in uniform, why she looked dirty and unwashed and smelt of sour sweat. 'I'm afraid your daughter is gravely ill. The wound is infected. Sepsis.'

Sepsis. That was blood poisoning, wasn't it? A cousin of Bronny's had sepsis after a ruptured appendix. He'd died on his tenth birthday. But Jasmin would not die. Hazel would not let her die. She felt a rush of strength through her fear.

'I must see her.'

'It's a question of *infection*, Mrs Alexander. You may wish to . . . smarten up?'

'Please. Is there a bathroom here? I have clean clothes.' She had tried to hide the jute bag by dangling it over her back, but now she let it drop in front of her. The name and number on the tag glared up, stark under the fluorescent light.

'It's out of the question,' said the sister, frowning down at the bag. She looked up and met Hazel's eye. 'Mrs Alexander, it's highly irregular for you to be here at all after visiting hours. However –' she checked the time on her fob watch – 'the patient has been calling for you. A visit may result in a more restful night. If you can return within the hour I will allow you to see her briefly. Any later than ten p.m. and you must wait until tomorrow.'

Hazel turned and ran from the hospital, down the long drive, past the lawn with its towering cedars. Ahead rose the spire of the cathedral, bone pale in the fading light. An hour was not enough time to get from Chichester to Aldwick and back. Night was falling and the streets were unlit, cars crawling along Broyle Road with their headlamps dimmed. On the right of the road was a pub. She could just make out the name on the pub sign, the small board underneath pronouncing ROOMS. She would try the Bell, and if they didn't have any vacancies, the landlord might know of a guest house nearby.

'If you don't mind the attic,' said the landlady through cigarette-clenched lips.

'Is there a bath?' asked Hazel.

'Lavatory on the downstairs landing but there's a sink in the room. You can top and tail at least.'

Hazel nodded her thanks as the landlady handed over a small towel and a sliver of soap. She was so grateful she couldn't speak. If she tried to speak she would cry.

The attic was stifling hot and spiders scurried around the eaves, but after the dank of Holloway, the room seemed close to heaven.

Hazel arrived back at the hospital with fifteen minutes to spare. The sister gave a brisk nod and asked a nurse to take Mrs Alexander to Ward 3.

'Ten minutes, no more,' she said.

Night had fallen and the ward was dark, pungent with the hot sweet smell of sickness. Blackout blinds were fixed to the windows. It couldn't be right, thought Hazel, for ill children to be entombed like this, in a room with no air. The nurse switched on a dim torch and led Hazel to a bed under the farthest window.

Jasmin's head was bandaged, and she lay sleeping on her back. Even in this feeble light, Hazel could see the high colour on her cheeks, the clammy sheen above her brow.

She reached over to stroke her daughter's cheek but the nurse stepped forward, palm raised.

'Please don't wake her,' she whispered. 'Finally dropped

off twenty minutes ago and she's a devil to get back to sleep. I'll find you a chair.'

Hazel sat on the chair beside the bed and fixed her eyes on Jasmin. Her small hands lay on the blanket, fingers curling lightly upwards. She was wearing a nightie that Hazel didn't recognize, the neckline crudely stitched. Tears welled in Hazel's eyes and she was unable to stop them. This was a new kind of torture. To be so close, yet unable to touch, to embrace, to speak. But she was here. And she would be here again tomorrow, and the next day. Every day until Jasmin was better.

The minutes ticked past. Hazel shifted in her seat and the chair moved, metal legs scraping on the floor. The sound was enough. Jasmin's eyes flickered open.

'Mummy?'

Hazel put a finger to her lips, then blew her a kiss. 'Yes, it's Mummy, and I'm here for you now,' she whispered. 'Go back to sleep. You'll have a lovely sleep and I'll see you in the morning.' Jasmin smiled and closed her eyes.

Now the nurse was marching down the ward, signalling that her time was up. Hazel followed the nurse into the corridor. The floor began to vibrate beneath her feet: a fleet of aircraft passing overhead. It couldn't be the enemy or the siren would have sounded. Furies or Spitfires, scrambled from Tangmere?

'What do you do in an air raid?' asked Hazel.

'We pray.'

All night Hazel sweated and coughed in the hot attic room. She couldn't sleep but she didn't mind, didn't need the oblivion of the prison doctor's potions. By five the sun had risen and she climbed from bed. She lit a cigarette – the landlady had sold her five Black Cats from a jar behind the bar – pulled back the lace curtain and stood at the open sash window. Birdsong filled the glittering dawn. Every note imaginable, an explosion of joy. Her cough eased as she inhaled the cigarette smoke, listened to the birds – a robin's rich trill, the *peep-peep* of blue tits – then a low rumble. The sound was coming from inside the room, she realized. Her own body. When did she last eat? Well, there would be time enough for breakfast: visiting at the hospital was not until eleven. She doused the cigarette end with a trickle of water from the tap, then climbed back into bed. Finally, she fell into a deep sleep. At eight she was woken by the landlady knocking on her door, asking if toast and marmalade would be sufficient because they were completely out of bacon.

After breakfast she walked to the telephone box at the top of North Street. Her father answered after just two rings, and she felt comforted by the surprise in his voice. He sounded pleased – delighted, even – when she told him she'd been released.

'You're out? Oh, that's marvellous.' He must have muted the receiver with his hand, because his voice became muffled. 'Hazel. Released,' he called to someone – Francine? – and then he was back. 'You're in London?'

'Chichester. I caught the train yesterday evening, went straight to the hospital. I found a room for the night.'

'You should have called sooner. But how is Jasmin? Is she any better?'

'She was asleep. The nurse didn't say much. I'm visiting again at eleven. Is Mother there?'

'I thought she was at the hospital. You saw her?'

Hazel paused. 'I must have missed her somehow.'

'All-night vigil, she said.'

'We'll cross paths this morning, I expect.'

'And afterwards you must come back to Aldwick.'

'Yes. Yes, I'll see you later.'

'Shall I collect you?'

'Could you?'

The pips went and she garbled a goodbye, replaced the receiver. Her father seemed to want to see her. He had asked after Jasmin, had appeared concerned. It sounded for all the world as if he had forgiven her. That was what came of a crisis, she supposed.

There were still some coppers in her purse. The operator would be able to put her through to the *Chronicle*. She pictured Tom's face across the prison table yesterday, when she'd told him about Jasmin. The disbelief, the mistrust. Yet there was no malice. A part of him had believed her, surely?

She began to dial the operator, but her hands started to shake and in a panic she replaced the receiver. It would be better to ring Tom after the morning visit. She would have more information then. Might feel more composed.

As she walked up the hospital drive a car swept by and pulled in at the main entrance. The passenger leaned across and kissed the driver, and he put his hand up to her face, caressed her cheek.

Hazel was closer now, and as the woman climbed from the car she recognized the white sandals, the flower-shaped buckle at the ankle. The engine revved and the car spun around in a U-turn. Hazel kept her head down as the Brough passed. Now Francine was just a few paces ahead; she was climbing the stone steps up to the hospital entrance, adjusting her hat to the required angle. Why wait and let her go in first? Better to meet now than inside the hospital where people would be watching, listening.

'Mother!' Hazel called.

There was no response. Francine lifted her hand towards the brass door plate.

'Francine!'

She turned around this time, narrowed her eyes and then gasped. 'It's Hazel! Darling, how . . . ?' She flew down the steps and kissed Hazel's cheek. 'Well, this is wonderful. Have they let you out at last?'

'So it would seem.'

Francine took Hazel's hand. 'I'm so, so pleased. It will be a huge comfort to Jasmin. Now, darling, I must warn you, she doesn't look at all well.' She glanced down at her wrist-watch. 'We're a few minutes early, and they're terrible sticklers. Shall we take a wander around the lawn?'

Hazel nodded. 'I saw Jasmin last night,' she said. 'I came to the hospital. Father thought you'd be here, keeping vigil.'

'Did he? I *was* here. Until tea-time.'

'And then you were with Charles.'

'Ah.'

There was no sound but the whisper of wind in the cedar branches. They walked slowly beside the flowerbeds, and when they reached a sprawling hydrangea, Francine plucked at a pink petal and began to speak.

'I've been wanting to talk to you about Charles, for a long time after your –' Francine hesitated – 'your accusation. I confronted him, you know. I told him I knew what he'd done and I was appalled, wanted never to see him again. And I didn't see him for months, many months, but he came to the flat pleading forgiveness.' She let the petal drop and fingered the chain around her neck. 'He'd been very drunk that night, he said, and he was possessed by a sort of madness. Oh, it's a poor excuse, I know. I've felt so torn, Hazel, you must know that. It's been agony. But he does love me.'

'I don't want to see him, ever. I don't want him near Jasmin.'

'I can understand that, darling. Truly. Though you mustn't worry about him being Jasmin's father. He says he can't possibly be.'

Hazel stopped. Charles couldn't be Jasmin's father? How had he convinced Francine of that? Her mother began to speak again. 'He was rather blotto, you see—' but Hazel thrust out her hand, hissing at her mother to be quiet, and Francine closed her mouth with an indignant pout.

It was too hateful to speak of. She would not discuss it, because in that moment it did not matter, could not have mattered less. All that mattered was the certain fact that she, Hazel, was Jasmin's mother, and she was free, and she must see her baby and make her well.

It was visiting time at last. Hazel turned away from Francine, towards the hospital and the narrow bed where her daughter lay waiting.

37

When Tom arrived at the office, Gerald was already on the telephone, scribbling as he spoke.

'Thomas, my man!' he said as he put the receiver down. He stood up and took his jacket from the coat-stand. 'Hello and goodbye.'

'Going out?'

'Interesting tip-off.' He tapped the side of his nose in an imitation of Crow. 'Need-to-know-basis.'

Tom smiled. He wouldn't put it past Gerald to have invented the tip-off; he had a mistress in Holland Park, and would often return from a hush-hush interview smelling of French scent.

'You'll be back this afternoon?'

'Doubtful. Off to the Home Counties.'

'Ah.'

'Everything A1? You're looking rather bewildered this morning, old chap.'

Tom shut his mouth and sat down at his desk. Gerald was in a hurry, and he needed time to explain about Hazel. He'd have to wait until this evening or tomorrow: whenever he could get Gerald on his own.

'Everything's fine, thanks. Just a bit weary. Wretched siren.'

All morning his thoughts crashed and collided. He tried to summon a fraction of Petra's calm from the previous night, her wisdom, but calm was impossible. Should he visit Jasmin? He was a stranger to her. What comfort could he offer, in the unlikely event they let him in to the hospital? The infection was serious, Hazel had said. If it killed her . . . no, he couldn't, couldn't begin to think.

He would write to the prison governor, at least. A letter might help Hazel's case in some small way. He wound a fresh sheet of paper into the typewriter but before he had struck the first key, the telephone on his desk rang.

The line was crackly but her voice was unmistakable. Surprising that the prison should let her use a telephone, thought Tom. But then he began to absorb what she was saying. She was ringing from Chichester. She had been released yesterday evening, just a few hours after he'd visited the prison. 'Thank you', she said. 'If you played a part – thank you.'

'I'm afraid there's nothing to thank me for.' He took a shallow breath. 'I was just writing a letter now. Nothing's been sent.'

'Oh.' There was a pause for a moment, and then she garbled something about a wardress. 'It must have been her. Must have.'

'You've seen Jasmin?' asked Tom.

Hazel began to cough. When she spoke, her voice was tight. 'The fever is still very high.'

'I want to visit. Can I see you, Hazel? See Jasmin?'

*

It was Friday, and the three o'clock train was crowded. Sunlight angled in through the compartment window. A young boy with a crooked fringe sat opposite, crunching noisily on a carrot as he stared at Tom's left hand. Tom tried to smile but the boy shrank away, cuddled closer to his mother's side. Tom tucked the hand in his trouser pocket, though the heat made his scars throb.

At Chichester he saw her before the train had come to a halt. She was standing on the platform in a yellow dress, her hair loose around her neck. Now he was opening the compartment door, and he was on the platform, and he saw that she was crying. As they clung together he could not stop his own tears. She kissed him then, and took his arm. They walked through the city, along the time-worn pavements, past the cathedral and on towards the hospital.

Tom took a sip from his pint. She'd agreed to join him in the Bell after the hospital visit. They were on to their second drink and their conversation, stilted and emotion-choked at first, had finally begun to soften. It was the right time, he decided, to explain to her about the letter; the reason he'd stopped writing to her from Spain.

'A letter came from home, you see, just after Christmas in Albacete. When I read the gossip about you – you and . . . other men – I suppose I just gave up. I was weak. Too proud.'

'I can never forgive her for telling those lies,' said Hazel. She circled a finger around the rim of her port glass. 'I can see it clearly now. She's twisted, jealous.'

Tom drew in a sharp breath. Hazel couldn't be blamed for her reaction – yes, the letter had been wrong, it had been hurtful and destructive – yet it pained him to hear his mother described in such terms when she had simply been over-protective. She wasn't twisted or malicious. She *was* jealous, that was true, but jealous only of his well-being and his happiness.

'There were reasons behind it –' he began to say, but Hazel wasn't listening. She was talking about Lucia, how possessive she could be, sulky if she didn't get her own way.

'Lucia must have been desperate to separate us,' said Hazel. 'And you fighting for the communists, too. Did she sign with a false name? Or anonymously?'

The realization hit. Tom opened his mouth to speak and then took a gulp of beer. Hazel thought that Lucia had sent the letter to Albacete. She'd taken 'home' to mean London, England, not Boone Street, Lewisham.

He should interrupt now, set the record straight.

Yet what did he owe to Lucia? Lucia, who had ratted on her supposed friend when the police came calling. Lucia, who had claimed credit when Hazel saved the drowning boy. Lucia, whom Hazel already hated. Why bring his mother into it, when Hazel had satisfied herself with a perfectly feasible explanation?

Tom reached out and took Hazel's hand across the table. 'We needn't ever speak of it again. I should have been more trusting. It's my fault. I should have believed in you, not some daft letter.'

She sighed and raised the port glass to her mouth. Tom watched as she swallowed. When she set the glass back on the table her lips glistened deep red.

'It doesn't matter anyway,' said Hazel. 'All that matters is Jasmin.'

'Of course.' His mind returned to the darkened ward, the still body in the hospital bed. 'Jasmin.'

Hazel's fingers tightened around his, and he closed his eyes, wishing with all his being that there might be a God to hear his prayer.

38

On the day of the wedding they drive into Soho, to Baudin's where the wine cellar is still stocked with champagne and the kitchen serves an excellent steak tartare. They park on Romilly Street. A working girl stares from a high window as they step from the Brough onto the pavement: Charles in his white tails and Francine in a black Schiaparelli embroidered with large white lilies.

Inside the club, no heads turn. To be overdressed on a Saturday afternoon? There are stranger sights in this louche basement: a stocky man in a sequinned leotard, a woman with one breast spilling from a too-tight bustier.

The champagne is poured by the sommelier himself, his small hand firm against the ice-wet bottle. Charles raises his glass, meets Francine's mid-air.

'To the Uninvited,' he says.

'The Uninvited.'

Their glasses chink. The band strikes up a rhumba.

They dance and they dance, fuelled by the champagne and the perfect steak and the lines of white powder that Charles has secured in the velvet-draped side room. As the afternoon slips into evening, Francine thinks she has never been happier. She was made to choose and she has chosen correctly.

Oh, it would have been nice to see Jasmin in her flower-girl frock, but what does Jasmin care for her, Francine, now that the Smart woman has appeared on the scene? 'Nanny,' Jasmin calls the woman, tugging at her skirt and smothering her drab face in kisses, while the blackshirt boy smiles on, his ugly hand around Hazel's waist.

They can all go to hell.

At ten the warning comes but nobody cares. They are in the right place, aren't they, safe below stairs? When the ceiling plaster begins to crack and crumble, they dance on.

'Just like confetti!' giggles Francine, and she lifts her face to the ceiling, licking away the flakes of musty white paint.

Wall lights fizz and spark. Dancers falter, caught out of time. Dark shapes hurry across the floor.

Charles laughs, takes Francine's hand and leads her towards the wine cellar. But the wine cellar is already full, painted faces smiling up, glasses held aloft, cocktail cherries trembling.

They stumble towards the cloakroom, but rubble has blocked the stairway to the street. In the darkness they kiss. Strings from an abandoned violin vibrate as a high-explosive bomb slams through the Soho sky.

'I've always loved you,' Charles says. 'Only you,' and Francine smiles as a white light screams through the black.

39

The sweet peas in the garden had almost gone to seed, but on this sunlit evening the perfume of the last few blooms hung heavy in the warm air. Bea picked the flowers and held them to her nose. She closed her eyes against the sun and opened her mind to the Inward Light.

Allow the light to shine into all the dark corners of the mind.

There was a time when shadows were stubborn, but now the light came easily. She had only to think of her granddaughter and her mind became a dazzle of possibility and hope. When Jasmin smiled it was almost like having Jack back: the light in those amber eyes, the tilt of her dimpled chin. She pictured Jasmin's face as they'd leafed through the photograph album that morning. *Yes, that's right, love. It's your daddy when he was five years old. And there's your grand-dad Harold. You never met him but he was a very good man.*

Bea walked down the steps into the Anderson and pulled open the door. She blinked into the darkness until her eyes grew accustomed and she could see the enamel jug on top of the narrow cabinet. She arranged the sweet peas in the jug; they wouldn't last more than a day or two, but how

318

pretty they looked, such delicate colours. If there was a raid tonight, Jasmin would be cheered to see fresh flowers in the shelter. She noticed little things like that. You might even say she was a touch too curious – it was one question after another! After elevenses today, Jasmin had somehow spotted the torn-up letter in the kitchen bin, though Bea had covered it with a flattened box of Lux flakes. 'Why's this letter all ripped, Nanny?' she'd asked, clutching a shilling-sized scrap of notepaper that was scrawled with black ink. Bea looked up from her ironing and of course it had to be the fragment where the Knight girl had signed her name.

'Put that back in the bin and go and wash your hands,' Bea had said, unable to keep the sharpness from her voice.

'But—'

'No buts. Curiosity killed the cat.'

Jasmin had looked alarmed at that, and she spent the next hour in the garden fussing over next door's puss.

It was odd about the letters, though. Why Lucia persisted in writing when no one ever replied, Bea couldn't say. Anyone would think she was lovesick.

This summer heat was so tiring. As Bea sat down on the chair in the corner of the shelter she heard the distant swish of the bead curtain at the back door, the heavy tread of brogues down the path.

'So this is where you're hiding,' said Tom. He came in and sat on the wooden bunk that ran along one side of the shelter.

'Where's Jasmin?' he asked.

'They've gone for an ice. Mr Boyne let Hazel off early. Should be back shortly.'

Tom nodded and reached out to rest a hand on her shoulder. They sat for a while longer as the setting sun beamed a shaft of gold through the open shelter door. Bea wondered whether to tell Tom about today's letter. No; that would only cast a shadow. Hazel had made it clear – ignore any post from Lucia. Put the letters, unopened, into the bin. Lucia would give up eventually, of that Bea had no doubt.

From the house came the sound of the front door banging, the clank of faltering piano keys, 'London Bridge' again. Tom chuckled to himself.

'Jasmin's determined, I'll give her that,' he said, standing up from the bunk. 'Better go and say hello.'

Bea watched him stroll down the path as Hazel appeared on the patch of lawn holding the small watering can in one hand and a cigarette in the other. She kissed Tom's cheek and he put an arm around her waist, said something that Bea couldn't hear. Hazel smiled and stretched up to kiss him again. Wisps of smoke curled above their heads, and the hem of Hazel's dress shifted in the breeze.

'They're home, Harold,' Bea murmured. 'All of them. Home.'

The sweet peas glowed in the sunlight, and it seemed to Bea for that brief silent moment as if the whole world was at peace.

Author's Note

Many books and sources helped to inspire *The Faithful*. The following were especially useful:

Booker, J. A., *Blackshirts-on-Sea: A pictorial history of the Mosley Summer Camps 1933–1938* (Brockingday Publications, 1999).

de Courcy, Anne, *Diana Mosley* (Chatto & Windus, 2003).

Durham, Martin, *Women and Fascism* (Routledge, 1998).

Gottlieb, Julie V., *Feminine Fascism: Women in Britain's Fascist Movement* (I. B. Taurus, 2000).

Griffin, Frank, *October Day* (Secker and Warburg, 1939).

Harris, Carol, *Blitz Diary: Life Under Fire in World War II* (The History Press, 2010).

Jump, Jim ed., *Poems from Spain: British and Irish International Brigaders on the Spanish Civil War* (Lawrence & Wishart, 2006).

MacDougall, Philip, *If War Should Come: Defence Preparations on the South Coast 1935–1939* (The History Press, 2011).

Pugh, Martin, *Hurrah for the Blackshirts: Fascists and Fascism in Britain Between the Wars* (Jonathan Cape, 2005).

Rosenberg, David, *Battle for the East End: Jewish responses to fascism in the 1930s* (Five Leaves Publications, 2011).

Sweet, Matthew, *The West End Front: The Wartime Secrets of London's Grand Hotels* (Faber and Faber, 2011).

Wheeler, George, *To Make the People Smile Again: A memoir of the Spanish Civil War* (Zymurgy Publishing, 2003).

While some of the events described in *The Faithful* are factual – such as the blackshirts' seaside camps and the wartime detention of Mosley's fascists – this novel is a work of fiction. The lead characters – Hazel, Tom, Lucia, Francine and Bea – are entirely imagined.

Acknowledgements

Heartfelt thanks to Sophie Orme for helping to shape this novel, and to Sam Humphreys, Associate Publisher at Mantle. It's been a privilege to work with two such wonderful editors. I am indebted also to Maria Rejt, Mantle Publisher, and the excellent team at Pan Macmillan including Josie Humber, Laura Carr and Jess Duffy.

Thanks to my agent Hellie Ogden for her advice and positivity, and to all at Janklow & Nesbit including Jessie Botterill, Kirsty Gordon, Rebecca Folland and Rachel Balcombe.

For valued comments on various drafts, I'm hugely grateful to Isabel Ashdown, Torben and Victoria Betts, Alex Bristow, Alison Laurie, Jane Osis, Angela West and Steve Wilson.

Many people have helped with research queries, but particular thanks are due to staff at the Imperial War Museum, the Screen Archive South East at Brighton University, the British Library and Bognor Regis library, as well as Dr Julie Gottlieb of the University of Sheffield and Val Bentley at the Sussex Ornithological Society. Any inaccuracies are my own.

Thanks to Joan Barker, Stuart Coupe, Elayne DeLaurian, Louise Gilchrist, Joan Goddard, Sam Kendall, Mary Laven, Ron MacKenzie, Sandra Walsh, Roger West, Gill and Jim Wilson, friends at The Prime Writers and Horsham Writers' Circle.

Most of all, my thanks and love to Steve, Izzy, Jessie and James.

Reading Group Guide

1. Why do you think Hazel was drawn to Tom, and Tom to Hazel?

2. *'Political cranks,'* Francine had said, hurrying past with a look of distaste. *'Don't flatter them with your attention.'* What do you think initially attracted Hazel to the blackshirts?

3. Francine and Bea are two women with very different attitudes towards motherhood. Which family would you rather have grown up in? Who was the 'best' mother?

4. Blackshirt seaside camps were held regularly on the south coast during the 1930s. Do you feel this real-life setting worked well as a backdrop for the novel?

5. Did your attitude towards Hazel change after she joined the blackshirts?

6. Charles is based on a real-life character. Do you think that Charles's line of work was immoral, or was he simply offering a service?

7. Was Hazel right to keep her secrets from Tom for such a long time?

8. Were you surprised to learn that women, including former suffragettes, supported British fascism in the 1930s? What do you think motivated 'ordinary' women like Bea to join?

9. *'I've been useful, that's all.'* Was Lucia right to accuse Hazel of using her? How do you view their relationship?

10. Discuss the ending of the novel.